PRAISE FOR BETHENY LYNN REID

"Under the Autumn Moon delves into a relationship between a rock star and an author, showing us how two people with different backgrounds...can discover safety, love, and confidence together."

— ALEX TEMBLADOR, AUTHOR OF *WRITING AN IDENTITY NOT YOUR OWN*

"A fierce, heady plunge into love and longing."

— LORI ANN STEPHENS, AUTHOR OF *BLUE RUNNING*

"Finally...an adult romance!"

— CINDY KING, FOUNDER OF GET LIT ROMANCE READERS

UNDER THE AUTUMN MOON

BETHENY LYNN REID

Hardcover: 979-8-9926505-6-3

Paperback: 979-8-9926505-4-9

Ebook: 979-8-9926505-5-6

First paperback edition 2025

Breakthrough Books

We all look up and see the same moon.
May she inspire us to be true to ourselves and never be shy to love.

DISCLAIMER

No one in this book is real. (Really.)

CHAPTER 1

It started, appropriately, at a north London bookstore. Lexi was on tour to promote her latest bestseller. The publisher had given her a choice of B&Bs, and she chose this location, knowing the rock star she'd had a crush on most of her life had a home in the area. She didn't actually expect to see him but thought she might "happen" to walk by his famous house just to feel his vibe.

Her family, including her late husband, and friends always teased her about her obsession with that hard-charging rock group, and especially the founder and lead guitarist. She knew her fans would be shocked if they knew, because of his bad-boy reputation, but it was what it was. Obsessing over him fueled a low-burning rebel deep inside, which surprised her. Scared her a little. And made her want him even more.

It was a chilly, sunny morning and she decided to pop in the nearby bookstore to sneak a peek at the display for her books before taking a walk past his house. It was an affluent neighborhood of historic houses, hilly streets lined with shops as well as local restaurants.

Her habit of visiting bookstores to look for her books began when she first was published. In the early days, she would slip into a bookstore and find her books—usually there were only one or two copies available. She'd take her special pen out of her purse and sign them: *Thank you for buying my book. Love, Lexi.* Then she'd arrange the books so the covers were facing out and, therefore, more noticeable. She even started carrying stickers that said *Author Signed Copy* to place on the front of the book. Then she'd post on social media: "Find my signed books @" and name the store.

It wasn't long before her books sold better, much better. She'd introduce herself to the store staff, take selfies with them, sign copies and post. She'd also help the staff move her books to more prominent displays, "now that they're signed by the author."

This morning, she wanted to see what they were doing with her books, but also gin up her courage to walk past Patrick "Paddy" May's house.

Several posh-looking customers milled about, even though the bookstore had only been open fifteen minutes.

North London for sure, she thought.

At the front entrance stood a large display of books by another author she knew. *Good for you, Colleen.* The two Texans were friends and sometimes made appearances together.

For a panicked second, Lexi thought her books weren't featured anywhere. Then she saw a large display of all her books along with a poster featuring her photo and announcing her appearance at the Royal Charity event the next night.

Then she froze.

There he was.

Standing at her display, holding her current release.

He glanced up, looking straight at her, seemingly as stunned as she was.

He mouthed, "Oh my god, it's you."

They stood for a few noticeable minutes just looking at each other. Then he smiled his trademark sweet smile and walked toward her, lifting his right hand at first to shake, then switching to his left hand when he remembered his favorite author had only one hand, her left hand. Her right arm ended just below the elbow.

Lexi loved Paddy even more because he was thoughtful enough to "shake left." The warmth of his palm pressing against hers melted her nervousness.

"You are my favorite author." Paddy's voice was soft and gentle like his smile. "I have everything you've ever written, including your essays, and even your poetry books. Like everyone else, I also watch your *Cally* series on the BBC."

Lexi was flushed and stumbled for words. "Well, you're my favorite rock star, guitarist, producer, song writer...everything."

They laughed and held hands much longer than a typical handshake. Finally, they both looked at their hands and let go.

"You're even more beautiful in person and your hair is much redder than I thought."

"Oh." Lexi put her hand to her head.

"I'm sorry. Of all the things I want to say to you about how much your writing has meant to me, and I say that. I'm such a huge fan, I'm just gushing."

"At least you can gush. I'm so thrilled to see you. I can't think of a thing to say, and I'm the writer."

They stood like school kids waiting for one to ask the other for a date.

He squared his shoulders, took a deep breath, and made the move. "Would you like to get some coffee? There's a place just around the corner."

"Yes. That would be lovely."

They walked toward the door when Paddy said, "Wait. I need to buy your book first." He held up the latest in her series *Cally's Summer Adventures* and walked to the register, where he greeted the young woman at the counter like an old friend.

"Scarlett, I almost stole my first book from you this morning."

She laughed. "Oh no, Paddy, I was watching you. I know where to find you. Besides you'll be back in a couple of days, and I could charge you then, with interest added."

Lexi took the opportunity to study her crush. He was clearly a creative person, with near shoulder-length curly hair, jeans and a colorful paisley shirt, but he was also an English gentleman. The shirt was collared, his shoes were expensive trainers and he had on a jacket that coordinated everything.

Paddy knew she was studying him. Fans had done that his whole life. This was different somehow. He liked it.

She watched his hands. Long, slim fingers that she'd studied many times on videos of his performances. Fingers she'd imagined pleasuring her—she wondered now if that could become a reality. After all, they both were single. At least, according to the tabloids, he was single.

She felt a warm wet flush between her legs. Something she'd not felt in a long time.

At that moment he glanced at her, smiling.

She blushed. *He read my thoughts. I know he did.*

The tea shoppe was the neighborhood bakery with six tables inside and four smaller ones sitting on the front sidewalk. Everything inside was white. The walls. The marble countertop. Everything except one entire wall that displayed the colorful teas. The Twinings yellow, blue and green tins with gold lids. Yorkshire round cannisters with red lettering. Tetley vintage porcelain pots.

"Don't worry," Paddy assured her with a wink. "They can make you a very good cup of coffee."

She noticed how he held the door for her, gently placing his hand on her back as she entered.

"Morning, Paddy."

"Morning. Barbara, I'm sure you'll want to make my new friend here the best coffee in the world."

The shop owner was looking down, organizing glasses and cups. She wiped her hands on her cloth rag, finally looked up, then shouted, "Oh my god, it's Lexi Maxwell! Paddy, how did you find our favorite writer of all-time?"

"At the bookstore. Where else?"

All three laughed. A couple of customers looked up from their tables.

Lexi thought, *He definitely wasn't faking that I'm his favorite writer. I'm in a dream. If so, please let me sleep a little longer.*

There was a window seat available, but Paddy guided her to a table in the corner.

"We might have more privacy here," he said. She noticed he held her chair as she was seated. He had his back to the front entrance of the shop.

I wonder, does he do that so fans won't bother him?

Barbara brought over coffee, tea and a sampling of scones and pastries.

"I brought some of Paddy's favorites, hoping you might like them as well. Let me know when you'd like a refresh on your coffee. And thank you for your books and the TV series. Paddy and I have a Lexi Maxwell book club that meets here every year when you publish a new one, and I see he's carrying your new book for our meeting next week. So, Cally's in Istanbul this time?"

Paddy turned red and looked inside his tea pot, as if to check if it was brewed enough. He clearly was embarrassed.

Barbara continued, "I know this ruins his reputation as a wild rock star, but he really is quite the reader. I'm being rude now, but if you are here for a while, and if your schedule allows, our little group—"

Paddy interrupted, "Barb, maybe..."

"Yes. You're right, Paddy. Oh god, I should know better. Let me leave you alone and let you two just be normal people."

Barbara turned and spoke to a young couple who just entered. She stood between them and Paddy and diverted their attention to the display of tea and scones.

Paddy poured his tea and said, "That's the first time I've seen her go all fan-girl on someone. I know you really rate with her, but still..."

"I like how she's protective of you. She's keeping this young couple from coming over to our table right now."

"She's good at that. It's partly why I come here. Mostly though, it's just neighborhood families here, but the internet has made it easy for fans to find the houses of famous people who live around here."

"Like you."

"Like me."

"I'm going to confess. My publisher gave me a few choices of where I could stay, and I asked her to find a place near Patrick May's North London house."

Paddy's eyes narrowed, and he leaned over the table toward her.

Lexi was scared she might have just ruined her chance at a friendship.

"Then it was fate because you couldn't have known how much I've wanted to meet you."

Lexi lifted her coffee mug.

"Here's to the mutual admiration society."

Paddy lifted his teacup.

"And here's to the start of a lasting friendship."

They held one another's eyes a long time then glanced away, breaking the spell.

Lexi was no longer feeling like a fan. She was feeling like she'd found an old friend. Not one who you just chatter with about the day-to-day, but the one with whom you explore the deep wonderings of your soul. She was ready to dive past small talk with Paddy and was curious to see how he responded.

"What do you think happened between us just now?" she asked.

Paddy looked at her without moving his eyes. "You're referring to that moment right before. When our eyes looked somewhere deeper? When something stirred inside us?"

"Yes."

Still holding eye contact, he said, "Recognition. Recognizing an old, long-lost friend and a desire to connect...and hold on."

"You really aren't just a wild, heavy drinking, drugging, women-chasing rocker, are you?"

His smile was slight and sad.

"I have been those things. Though the women chase me. I'm not saying that to avoid my part in it but—it's just that women, and some men, really throw themselves at me. The whole band, really." He sipped his tea. "But, yes, there has been a lot of booze and drugs. And yes, I haven't shied away from women, especially in the early years."

"Young women."

"Hmmm." He grimaced and asked, "How old were you when you first had sex? If I may ask. Since we are being so candid."

"Sixteen. On my sixteenth birthday, actually."

Paddy raised his eyebrows as if to say, *See my point about having sex at a young age?* "Remember, I was only nineteen when our first record made the top of the charts, and we were on tour in America and Europe. Owen was the oldest, and he wasn't quite twenty-one. We behaved no differently than typical American fraternity boys."

"You're right. I never thought of it that way. Only your life was splashed over media far and wide."

Lexi wanted to ask about how much sex, drugs and boozing he was doing now, but decided against it. "Let's go back to talking about love."

"A much better topic."

"Yes. What do you think love and spirit are?"

"Hmm. That's heavy, and I've only had one cup of tea."

"Sorry. I know I dive too deep too fast. I'm just not interested in chit-chat."

Despite Barbara's efforts, the young German couple sat at the table next to Paddy and Lexi and were clearly listening to their conversation. Paddy's back was to them and Lexi motioned.

"We have listeners."

Paddy didn't turn around, but the couple took it as a cue to engage.

"We're so sorry to bother you, Mr. May, but we are huge fans of yours and came to this area to see your home."

Barbara hurried over. "Please let my friends have their breakfast in peace."

Paddy finally turned around.

"Thank you, Barbara. It's okay."

Paddy turned all the way around, facing the couple.

"I'm glad to hear you like the band. How can I help you?"

Lexi noticed how Paddy had taken a deep breath just before he turned to face the couple. A breath that said, *This is part of the price I pay.*

The young man said, "Can we have a selfie?"

"How about over here."

Paddy stood in front of the wall with the tea display. Lexi noticed he pointed for his fans to stand on either side of him, but he didn't put his arms around them as if friends. He did smile his trademark, adorable smile.

"Thank you. Thank you so much, Paddy. We will always remember this day."

"You're welcome. Enjoy your visit to London."

Paddy sat back down with his back to the couple again. Lexi watched the couple each get on their cell phones, clearly posting their picture.

"We should probably finish our drinks and leave," Paddy said. "I'm sure they're posting."

"Yes, they are."

"That means Barbara's store will have a surge of fans here in about ten minutes or less. Would you like to go for a walk?"

"Yes. The morning looks glorious."

Paddy stood, nodded to the German couple and held the chair for Lexi.

"Barbara, I'm sorry, for you know what's about to happen."

"It's okay, Paddy. I'm sorry you and Ms. Maxwell have to leave sooner than planned."

Paddy kissed Barbara on both cheeks. Lexi started to put on her daypack when Paddy said, "Would you like me to carry this for a while?"

"Sure. Thanks."

"Can I put your book inside?"

"Sure." Lexi suppressed a laugh.

"Did I do something odd?"

"No, no, not at all. I was remembering when I started high school, my dad said, 'Lexi, there will be boys who will want to carry your books and you need to understand they are doing so because they like you, not because you have one hand and need help.'"

"Well, your father was right." Paddy leaned down to look her in the eye and winked.

It was very subtle, but Lexi noticed Paddy was careful not to touch her now. Before, he would gently touch her back or arm or elbow to guide her through the doorway or into the chair, but now that they were outside, he was physically close, but definitely not touching.

He slung her pack over his shoulder and in one continuous motion reached inside his blazer, pulled out a cigarette, lit it and inhaled the smoke deep into his lungs. He held it a few minutes, then exhaled, as if clearing years of frustration at not being left alone in public.

Lexi immediately started coughing uncontrollably. She'd always had a severe reaction to cigarette smoke and hadn't been around it in a long time. She doubled over and almost gagged.

Paddy quickly tossed his cigarette on the ground and stomped it out.

"I'm so sorry, Lexi. I'm so sorry."

"No, it's me. I can't handle smoke. Never could."

She was still coughing, but not as severely. She noticed how Paddy picked up the snuffed cigarette and looked for a trash can. Finding none, he brushed off the tip and slipped it in his pants pocket.

CHAPTER 2

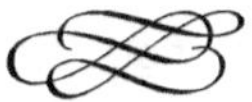

Patrick (Paddy) Edward May III was born into a family where both his father and grandfather were Sirs. His mother was Irish, which caused quite a scandal when his father married her, because, even though she had a university education, the Irish were still seen as "less than" to English "pedigree."

Additionally, while officially Catholic, his mother was more connected with her Celtic and Druid spiritual history and raised Paddy to develop that part of himself privately while publicly he attended Catholic Church. He was a choir boy in his very early years. His father was Anglican and sent Paddy to a prestigious school where he was an "exceedingly gifted child who excels in his studies without much effort" as his reports said year after year.

His mother's brother had given him an acoustic guitar when he was barely six years old. He'd been named Patrick after his uncle and the two shared an extra close bond. Uncle Pat was in a band that played cover songs in clubs, small venues, local festivals, and sometimes as the warm-up band for more successful (but not hugely successful) bands. They played "a little bit of everything so we can keep working."

Paddy carried his guitar with him everywhere and even slept with it in case he thought of a tune in the night, which he often did.

He started performing with Uncle Pat's band at local festivals and small events. The BBC featured him on a talent show when he was only eight years old. His mother dressed him in a suit and tie and cut his hair shorter than the usual chin length he wore it. He had to fight his parents, teachers and priests to keep his hair longer, and cutting it before the BBC show made him furious.

"Mam, no rocker wears a suit and tie and has short hair."

"Well, the Beatles wore suits and ties in their early days and had hair the length I've given you."

His appearance on the BBC talent show made him a household name. Photographs of the young boy in his suit wearing one of his father's ties while holding an acoustic guitar almost as big as him and tapping his foot to the beat while he sang seemed to be on the cover of all the London's papers.

Finally, his father made a deal with his strong-willed, talented only-child: "You keep your grades and your attendance at school, and we'll let you continue to play your guitar, dress the way you like—as long as the school allows it—and you can go play with your Uncle Pat now and then."

Paddy was thrilled.

What his parents didn't know was that the young schoolboy prodigy had terrible performance anxiety and threw up before every appearance. He did let his mother know he was sick before church choir, but he only told her that so she would let him quit before he was ten years old.

By the time he was twelve, he was regularly sipping booze from his Uncle Pat's bottle before performances. He smoked cigarettes, lying that the smell of smoke on his hair and clothes was the result of being around his uncle and the band.

His mother tried to stop his performing when he was fourteen after she found him doubled over in the bathroom, coughing blood.

He overheard his parents talking in the kitchen while he was supposed to be sleeping in his room.

"Edward, I can't believe we didn't see this coming. What were we thinking?"

"Cara, we did what we thought best. And he's been with his uncle. I'm disappointed Pat didn't keep a better eye on Paddy."

"Don't blame my brother."

There was a long silence. Paddy slipped out of bed and opened his bedroom door wider to hear better.

"Cara, we have to find another way to support Paddy's love for music…"

"Edward, he's so gifted…"

"I know. I don't want to hinder his progress."

"He loves it so much."

"Yes, he does, but it's already killing him. I think we have been deceiving ourselves that he's not already smoking and drinking. Maybe drugs too."

"He's done his part of the agreement, you know. He's stayed at school. His marks are excellent."

More silence.

Paddy stepped outside his bedroom.

His mother continued, "I love listening to him play in his room late at night. His music is beautiful. It's different when he's on stage because that music is electric and rock. But when he's just playing alone on his acoustic guitar, I feel like he's expressing his soul. It's so tender, you know."

There was a pause.

"Yes, I know. He really is…gifted. He's extraordinary. I'm so proud of him. We have to find a way to help him navigate this rock and roll world we don't understand."

"Let's talk with Pat tomorrow. We need a better plan for Paddy."

"Okay."

Paddy returned to his bed. He'd never heard his parents,

especially his father, talk about him like that before. He vowed he would stop his smoking and drinking. A promise to himself he struggled, unsuccessfully, to keep.

CHAPTER 3

After they left the bake shop, Paddy led Lexi through a back ally. He didn't say anything, but she noticed he would glance over his shoulder now and then.

"I assume this is a secret get-away path you've taken before."

"That obvious, huh?"

"Yes. That must be miserable."

"I don't have much difficulty with fans in London, especially in my own neighborhood."

"Yeah, I guess I'm surprised you don't have a bodyguard."

"Well, you don't see them. Surprisingly, I really am not harassed in London very often. Sometimes the paparazzi, but not too badly by fans. I must have at least two guards on me at all times, though, when I'm in the States. You Americans..."

He leaned down to look her in the eyes. He was grinning.

"We love fame," Lexi conceded.

"Indeed." Paddy was smiling in delight at being with his crush.

"But the States made The Crashers huge."

"Oh, absolutely. The band—me—we love the fans and are forever grateful. No doubt, we'd probably still be playing clubs without the

States catapulting our success. Don't misunderstand. We even like visiting the States. But we never have privacy there. Ever."

They were back walking through another leafy green, affluent neighborhood. People passing them on the sidewalk rarely noticed them. Now and then she'd see someone give Paddy a double-take. Occasionally someone would nod at Paddy, and he'd nod back. Lexi could tell these were just fans being respectful of his privacy, but it made her realize that, while people may not always approach Paddy, he was on display at all times.

"Sometimes I think I'd like to be better recognized in public," Lexi shared, "but then I realize that there would probably be a level of privacy that I'd lose. And I need that ability to sit alone, in a public place, and observe. I used to joke with my husband that I don't really write fiction, I just report on reality!"

"I imagine your readers recognize you easily. After all, how many beautiful redheads with one hand are there in the world?"

Paddy worried if he shouldn't have said anything about her arm but quickly realized she didn't even notice his remark.

They smiled and laughed like old friends sharing a secret. Lexi started to lean over to nudge him with her shoulder, then stopped, remembering Paddy wasn't touching her in public now.

"Your *Cally Adventures* series is so clever. You know The Crashers played at that Glastonbury festival where your second book in the *Cally* series was set."

"I know. I was there."

There was a quiet hum to the neighborhood. Even though buses were passing by, and more people were on the sidewalks, it wasn't noisy like in the States. People spoke in almost hushed voices. There was something nice about the traditional English reserve.

"I've noticed you haven't touched me since that couple in the bake shop spotted you."

"True." Paddy flashed her a sheepish smile. "Sorry. While people may not always approach me, I have learned—the hard way—that they are probably sneaking a photo with their phones and posting it.

That's why I zig-zag through the streets and alleys, so those who follow the posts can't find me too easily."

"Oh. So, you're always having to throw them off your tracks."

"Exactly."

"Do you have to be anywhere today? I don't want to keep you."

"No. I was just going to ask you the same."

"No. This is one of my unscheduled days. A day planned to have no plans. A bit ironic, huh?"

"But we have to do that, don't we, or our days can consume us."

Lexi never understood how most people were unaware of energy that exists between people. There is a rhythm that can be awkward, soothing, thrilling, sexual or fiercely negative.

She and Paddy had an energy that started as a spark of excitement at the bookstore, moved into "hand in glove" comfort at the bake shop and now was weaving into a union of, what was it? Old friends? Buddies? Soul mates? It felt like long-time lovers, which made Lexi blush to think about.

The backs of their hands would gently brush as they walked along. They wanted to hold hands. It felt like the most natural thing to do. It reminded Lexi of long walks with her late husband.

"Our hands want to hold one another." Lexi couldn't believe she said such a flirty thing.

Paddy smiled. "I've noticed. They'll have to wait, though, won't they? I know what the onslaught of social media would do with a photo of us holding hands, and we don't need that. Not yet, at least."

He looked at her. *Is he saying he believes we will one day hold hands in public?* she wondered.

The quiet neighborhoods gave way to the busier part of London with restaurants and shops, and many more people. In some ways, Paddy gained more anonymity being among a crowd of Londoners and tourists.

Lexi remembered an interview with a hugely popular actor once saying how he would take the tube when in London because, he suspected, no one expected him to be in such a public space. Maybe that's how it was for Paddy as well.

"Do you wear your signature outfits on stage during concerts so you can wear more regular clothes, like now, and not be recognized?"

"I call them my stage clothes, not outfits."

They laughed.

"What made you think of that?"

"I was noticing that you seem to be almost invisible now that we are walking through a much more crowded area. I thought it would be the opposite."

"People don't expect to see me. And, besides, everyone is in their own little world and not really looking around."

Lexi was definitely not in her own little world. She was becoming exhausted on their walk because she not only noticed all the people hustling by them, but she noted details about them. She noticed schoolgirls in uniforms who expressed their personalities with brightly multi-colored nails and different styles of dark shoes. She was especially interested in the young men wearing tight-fitting suits and shiny leather shoes and ties with geometric drawings. *That must be a new trend.*

Paddy noticed she closely watched everything around them.

"You don't miss a thing, do you?"

"Hmm?" His question broke her reverie.

"You're like a sweeper collecting every detail from what's around us."

"Well, I am a writer."

"And that's why you're the best one."

"Paddy, I'm hungry. I don't know why, but I'm starved."

Paddy looked at his phone.

"It's almost half past one."

"What?"

"Yeah. I can't believe it either. We are a long way from where we started walking."

"Oh god, I better text Jarius. My phone's in my backpack. Can you turn around?"

They stepped to the side of the busy sidewalk. Paddy turned around so Lexi could reach into the small pocket of her pack. It took her a few extra moments with the zipper. She pressed the fabric flat with her right arm and pulled the tab, but it kept sticking because she couldn't keep the fabric flat enough to move the zipper.

"You need help?"

"No. I'm good. I just need a minute."

"Who's Jarius?"

"Oh dear. He's texted and called so many times."

She started texting.

J- so sorry. Just saw all these. You're not going to believe it. I met Paddy May at the bookstore and we're walking around London together. I CANNOT BELIEVE IT. He's so sweet. We're near Hyde Park now. CAN YOU BELIEVE THIS?!?!

What?!? You must be in groupie heaven.

I'm not a groupie.

Yeah, right. Be careful.

What?

You know. Just keep your wits.

I always do.

True. But this is Paddy May. Are you going to hang with him today?

I think so.

Don't go to bed with him

Jesus.

Just sayin.'

When have you known me to do something like that?

Haven't, but still, Paddy May.

Ok. Bye.

Here if you need me.

Lexi handed the phone to Paddy, who had removed the backpack to put her phone back in the pocket so she wouldn't have to struggle with it again.

"Thanks."

"Who's Jarius?"

"Oh. A family friend who lived with Steve and me while he was in grad school. He travels with me now and keeps me organized. He works—wants to work—in managing artists, so he manages my schedule and things."

"Doesn't your publisher handle that?"

"They schedule, but publishers don't manage as much as you'd think. Jarius has been a godsend. He's laidback, but thorough. He's creative as well, a graphic artist, a writer, but seems to enjoy taking care of me."

"Don't you have an agent or a manager? You know, someone to handle the business side of your career."

"Well, yes and no. I have a literary agent who's good. I mean, she gets my books published, reviews the contracts. But I also have my own attorney who looks at contracts."

"Forgive me for being intrusive, but that doesn't really sound like management."

"True, but Jarius, my agent and attorney have taken good care of me so far. After all, my *Cally* series seems to being doing fine."

Paddy was already thinking about who he knew who would know someone in entertainment management who would better represent her.

"While you're contemplating how to improve my management, can we find a place to eat? I'm really starving."

Paddy shook his head and laughed.

"Yes. Well, a good manager makes all the difference, in any business. That was the first thing I did when putting a band together. I had Nigel before I even had a drummer or bass player."

"Well, I think I'm doing okay."

"Yes, you are. Let's get you some food and we can talk about it. Or not."

Paddy saw that Lexi was shutting down. She was looking down as they walked, not meeting his eyes. Paddy had obviously hit a nerve. He tried to reroute the conversation.

"I know a place over there, on the other side of the park. We can sit on the patio if you'd like."

"That sounds nice, if there's a table available. It's such a gorgeous day—it may be packed."

They walked into the crowded, upscale bistro and the host immediately approached them.

"Mr. May. So good to see you. I believe your table is available."

Lexi noticed a few guests took at second look at Paddy, but it was the type of place where people wanted to act as if lunching with well-known celebrities was an everyday occurrence.

An amber-colored drink in a cocktail glass was placed in front of Paddy's seat before Lexi was even settled in her chair.

"And what can I serve you today, Miss?"

Clearly, Paddy was a regular and drank enough that he didn't even need to order his beverage of choice.

"Water is good for me," Lexi said.

"Still or sparkling?"

"Still."

Paddy handed the waiter his untouched glass of alcohol.

"Kent, I'll have ginger ale today, please."

Had she not been watching closely, Lexi wouldn't have noticed Kent's stunned look that lasted only a fraction of a second. But it told Lexi that Paddy was still drinking heavily enough that the wait staff just assumed he'd want his drink.

A little chink in the armor of my shining knight, thought Lexi.

"So, this must be a favorite place of yours," she said.

"Yes. Great food. Great service. And look at this view!" Paddy waved his hand towards the colorful well-kept gardens in front of the restaurant and the lush park across the street.

Lexi watched his hands holding his menu more than she was reading her own menu. She was drifting into her "space cadet world" as Steve used to call it. She observed everything around her, wondering how she would describe it in a book.

She obsessed over his hands. His long, thin fingers. His nails were well manicured, but not buffed shiny, thank god. She wondered about the callouses on his fingertips from a lifetime of playing guitar.

Paddy folded the menu closed, resting it on his placemat, and looked up at her. He laced his fingers together, setting them on top of his menu, and watched Lexi watch his hands.

Kent appeared next to the table so quietly that it startled Lexi.

"Oh," she said as she jumped.

"I'm so sorry, Miss."

"No, it's okay. It's me. I was in a trance."

"Shall I return?"

Lexi looked at Paddy who said, "I don't think we're in a rush."

Kent said, "I'll return."

"No!" Lexi said too loudly.

More quietly, she added, "No. No. I'm starving. I'll have the ginger soy salmon and vegetables. No rice."

"How do you like your salmon?"

"Done medium well, please."

Kent hesitated.

"I know that's not correct," she said, attempting to recover. "Somewhere between medium and done, but not done too much."

"I understand." Kent tipped his head a little and turned to Paddy.

"Surprise me, Kent. This is my no-decision day. I'm just enjoying the day and letting it be whatever it is."

"That's perfect, Mr. May. I won't disappoint you."

"I know you won't. You never do."

He's such a wealthy, English gentlemen, thought Lexi. *How does he toggle back and forth from this life to that of a wild rocker?*

Paddy's eyebrows creased as he looked at her. "Lexi, did I offend you earlier talking about managers and such? You've drifted away since that conversation."

"Oh no. No." She paused, wondering, again, how truthful to be with him. "No. I drifted into your hands. Specifically, your fingers. I'm mesmerized by them."

Paddy immediately dropped his hands into his lap. He blushed. "I didn't expect that."

Lexi decided to go all in. "Okay. I may regret this, but this is a magical day for me, being with you."

"Me too."

"And I'm not going to waste it. I'm just going to dive in and be me, really me. I hope you like it."

"I do so far."

"I have always obsessed over your hands, particularly your long thin fingers. I replay videos showing you fingering your guitar and, yes, I fanaticize about them exploring me. All of me."

Paddy put his hands back on the table and started lacing his fingers in and out.

"You're teasing me now, Paddy May."

"Yes, I am."

"Do you have callouses on your fingertips?"

Paddy opened his hands and spread his fingers like a fan across the tabletop. His hands were bigger, his fingers longer than she expected. Lexi reached out to touch them.

"I wouldn't recommend doing that. Two women at a table over there are recording us on their phones."

Lexi diverted her hand to her water glass, as if that was what she was reaching for all along.

"Maybe later, somewhere, I could study your hands. If that's not too weird."

"It's a bit weird, but I like it." Paddy placed his hands on either side of his place setting.

Lexi took a breath. "But here's the thing. I'm not a slut or a fast woman or a groupie. And we're not having sex, at least not today."

Paddy was very still, listening.

"I am a huge fan, but I've already spent the morning with you and now I want to know you, for you. Not the image, the star, the expectations. Let's be real with each other. And part of me being real is that I will observe you, closely. It's what I do. I'll watch how you walk, sit, talk. I've noticed how much of a gentleman you are in all your interactions with people. I'm desperate to touch your curls as the wind blows your hair. But I won't because well, for one thing, that's too forward even for me and, two, you've shown me that we are probably being watched by every cell phone everywhere we go."

Lexi spoke as if a one-hundred-year flood just burst over the dam. Paddy watched her face with a mixture of interest, caution and amusement.

Lexi continued, "I want to talk about you. What you think. What you want in your life now. Your children. Your likes and dislikes. I just want to know *you*. And yes, I want to touch you, Paddy, but that will have to wait."

Lexi stopped talking as Kent served their food. He brought Paddy some kind of oriental fish dish that complemented, but was different than, Lexi's.

"Lovely, Kent."

"More ginger ale?"

"No. Just still water now, please."

They each lifted their forks and said, "Bon appetit" at the same time. They took their first few bites in a comfortable silence.

Paddy shifted in his seat, his shoes briefly tapping hers. "Sorry."

Lexi clamped her feet around one of his, holding it. "It's okay."

They looked at one another.

Lexi looked away, embarrassed, and released his foot.

"Lexi, I'm not going to lie, I'm incredible sexually attracted to you, and it's increasing as the day goes on. Usually by now I'd say something like 'one of my houses is close by, would you like to come over, and I'll play guitar for you.' You know, pick-up lines like that."

"Watching you play guitar sounds good."

They laughed.

"In due time, but I—you are really special to me. Your books are my favorites, and your poetry and essays have touched me in ways I never expected. And I've read about your life, watched all your interviews. I've been as obsessed with you as you seem to have been with me. There is something very special, very different about how I feel being with you today. I don't want to ruin my chance to be, I don't know, more real with you than I usually am with others."

"This energy between us feels sacred, Paddy."

A bolt of fear surged through Paddy, and he thought of that amber-colored drink Kent had sat before him when they arrived. He sipped his water.

"That scared you, didn't it?"

"Oh yeah. Very much."

"Is true intimacy a challenge for you, Paddy?"

"You really have no filters."

"Sorry. No, I told you earlier I don't do chit-chat well."

"I do have filters. Maybe it's actually barriers. You know, my success started when I was super young. I don't think I've ever—well, my relationships are—well, the women I'm with are usually just temporary. You know, other than Sofia, I don't think I ever have had what you would call a truly 'wholesome' relationship. I don't think I've had what you and Steve had. I thought Sofia and I were going to be forever, especially after we had our children, but then..." He drifted off.

"But then you took a bad turn with drugs, didn't you."

"I took a very bad turn, which I'm finally out of now."

"And Sofia?"

"She's moved on. Married. Good man. I like him. He loves the children, and they seem to love him too."

"Are the children involved with you?"

"Yes. Sofia is a saint about that. I agreed to let them live with her and visit me, which required her supervision when they were very young. I have been—well, I've been living the full rock and roll life most of their lives. I'm forever grateful to Sofia for not giving up and creating a family, of sorts, for us. I'm able to be a father to my children because of how she handles it. She never gave up on me, but I also knew she'd never be with me again."

They talked more about what his two children were doing and family holidays. Lexi talked about her son. Their children were roughly that same age and sounded as if they had similar interests. They all enjoyed traveling the most.

They finished eating. Their plates were removed, and Kent sat a dessert menu in front of them.

Lexi said, "Do you have raspberry sorbet?"

"Yes."

"Make that two please, Kent."

"Tea or coffee?"

"Tea please."

"Two please."

Paddy looked at Lexi with surprise. "Have I made you a tea drinker already?"

"I imagine they do a good job with it here."

Afterwards, they stood out front on the sidewalk, neither wanting to leave the other.

"Shall we walk in the park over there, it's quite lovely."

"Perfect."

Lexi started to step into the crosswalk when Paddy grabbed her by the back of her shirt and jerked back onto the sidewalk, just as a car sped by.

"Shit. I keep forgetting to look left."

Paddy was rubbing her back, instinctively knowing how to calm her down. Lexi took three huge clearing breaths.

"God, that scared me."

"Me too."

The park was busy with people strolling arm-in-arm, nannies pushing prams, children running, a young couple flying a kite, and others sitting on benches or stretched out on the grass soaking in the sunshine.

"I didn't expect so many people in the park on a weekday. Is it a holiday?"

"No. It's a sunny autumn day, and we know it might be a while before we have one of these days again."

"Oh, I don't know. I'm convinced you Londoners are like people in Seattle. You say your weather is cloudy and wet just to try and keep us tourists away."

"Ah, you figured it out. But it's not working very well. We're always crowded with visitors."

"Yeah. Speaking of visiting. This is my sixth or seventh time to come here for a book tour, and maybe more with the BBC series. How come I've never seen you at my appearances before? I mean, you're clearly a fan."

"Believe me, I've kept an eye on your tour dates. But I have been on tour, out of the country, every single time you're here. And when you've made appearances in the States, I've been in either Japan or Australia, *every single time*."

"Do you like touring?"

"Yes and no."

"Tell me more."

They walked over to a spot on the grass that was near trees, but still in the sun. They sat down on the grass. Paddy set her backpack beside them.

"You know what, Paddy, hold that thought. I really need to do some writing. Do you mind?"

She pulled her notebook from her backpack.

"I don't mind at all, but can you spare an extra pen and some paper? I have notes playing in my head and I want to write them down."

"I think it's so impressive that you read and write music."

"Essential from my session musician days."

"I have questions about those days too, but later. I've got to write."

They sat in a very comfortable quiet for a long time while they each wrote the symphonies they heard in their heads. Once, without being asked, Lexi tore off more blank pages from her notebook to hand to Paddy, who was still composing.

They didn't speak when she handed him the paper, but he gently patted her leg. It reminded her of how Steve would rest his hand on her leg every time they stopped at a light while driving. It was his way of connecting. Paddy seemed to be doing the same.

The park grew busier. Around them, young couples in love sat or lay back in the grass. Some were wrapped in each other's arms.

After a while, Paddy stretched out on his back, one hand curled under his head for a pillow. In just minutes, Lexi heard the very soft rumble of a deep and peaceful snore.

She smiled and returned to her journal. Eventually, she too, put away her writing and laid beside Paddy. Not touching, but close enough to feel the warmth of his body.

The raindrops tickled and woke Paddy first. He looked at Lexi, who was curled up close to him and looked so deeply content.

God how I want to just kiss you and keep you, he thought.

The wind blew a burst of rain that woke Lexi.

"It's starting to rain, Lexi." Paddy stood up and put his hand out to help her up. She pulled her umbrella from her backpack.

Most people in the park had noticed the darkening skies and had already left, but a few were now running for the tube station, taxis or elsewhere.

"Over there." Paddy pointed to a bench that was nestled in a cove of thick hedges that curved to make a canopy. The bench provided a mostly dry shelter, but the splash from the sidewalk made their pants wet. They both pulled their legs up on the bench.

Lexi held the umbrella in front of them to block the splash.

So, there they were, huddled tightly on a bench, hidden by a thick cove of hedges with an umbrella blocking anyone's view of them.

"It's like we're in our own secret Hobbit hole." Lexi grinned in joy.

The space was small and so, of course, they were touching, but he didn't put an arm around her. When they turned toward one another, their faces were close enough to feel each other's breath. But Paddy turned away.

They sat quietly, listening to the rain. Their bodies relaxed into breathing in unison. Lexi thought this was the perfect moment for a first kiss, but when she turned to him, he was just looking out over the top of the umbrella at the now-vacant park.

She decided to take a risk.

"Paddy, tomorrow night I'm presenting at the Royal Charity Gala, and I wondered if you'd like to be—"

"I know. I have VIP tickets. I purchased a sponsorship to be certain I would meet you."

Lexi's face flushed with emotions she was trying to control.

"I guess you already have a date, then?"

Paddy turned toward her with a very sad face.

"Yes."

They sat quietly for a long time then Lexi asked, "Why do you have a date if you bought a sponsorship so you could meet me at the VIP reception?"

Paddy shook his head, bewildered.

"I don't know. Penny saw I was a sponsor, and she just assumed I'd take her and I didn't... Lexi, I can try and get out of going tomorrow night, but Penny is looking forward to the occasion and probably has bought a new expensive outfit."

"Penny. Penny *Alexa?*"

Paddy nodded.

"The world's top model. Gee. Of course you have a date. I don't know why I thought—I mean, it makes sense. I should have thought of that before being so dumb to ask." Is she just a date or a girlfriend?"

"Lexi."

"No. You're right. That's rude of me to ask." She paused, then continued, "You know, it's been three years since Steve died. I really had no interest in dating. Friends have set me up a few times in the last year or so. Nice men."

"Successful men."

"Oh, so you've read."

"Yes."

"Yeah, well, that surprised me because I'm not a celebrity or anything. Anyway, nice men, interesting men, successful men, but there was zero energy with them. I didn't think that part of me would ever wake up again and I'd kind of decided that was okay. And then, I meet you this morning. Has it really only been since this morning?"

Lexi didn't want to, but she started crying. She couldn't stop it. She rarely cried, but when she did, it was sloppy, wet and ugly. Her face puffed out and red splotches whelped everywhere.

"Jesus, I'm such an ugly crier."

"No. Paddy put his arm around her for a quick comfort hug. "Lexi, don't worry about Penny. She's just a friend."

"A friend with benefits I bet."

Paddy pulled his arm away from Lexi.

"I'm sorry, Paddy. That was rude of me. I'm really sorry."

Lexi wiped the snot from her nose on her t-shirt. She didn't care how she looked.

The rain was letting up, but still steady. Lexi lowered the umbrella so that she too could look out over the top. She'd stopped crying, but her nose was still running. She dug through the backpack for tissues and blew her nose without regard to how loud it was.

Paddy smiled at how genuine she was. *No pretense with her*, he thought.

Lexi's voice was reflective. "You know, my son said he never knew that rain could be gentle and steady until he moved out of Texas for prep school. Where we live, rain comes out of nowhere with lightning and thunder, horrible winds, and attacks the area for about twenty minutes. Like an apocalypse. Limbs ripped from trees, scattered everywhere. Then it's over, and the sun shines."

At that moment, the rain stopped, and the sun shone.

Lexi closed the umbrella that had been their shield against the rain—and any prying eyes. Paddy watched how she closed the umbrella by pushing the base of her right arm on the handle and pushing the lever with her left hand. He realized he didn't think of her having one hand, but every now and then, like now, he enjoyed watching how she did things. It made him adore her more.

"Paddy, you and Penny come tomorrow and enjoy the evening. I'll have my shit together by then. Really."

They stood up.

"I'm starving again. What time is it?"

Paddy looked at his watch.

"Can you believe it's after seven?"

"What?"

"I know another place not too far from here, and it's on the way back toward your place. Have you noticed we've almost walked halfway around central London today?"

CHAPTER 4

The first time Lexi and Steve made love was during a rainstorm.

They grew up together and had always been friends. In high school, they became "running buddies" with three others they'd known their entire lives. The group was two guys and three girls who hung out together all the time. They were each other's study mates, personal advisors and first loves. Each young woman, at one time or another, was with one of the guys. It seemed to work easily. Sometimes, some members of the group were paired off; other times, no one was paired off with another one; and now and then, someone in the group was dating someone outside the group. Very fluid. Very supportive.

They liked to rent cabins in the woods of east Texas on weekends to hike and cook out. One afternoon Lexi and Steve were alone while the others drove into town for more groceries. Clouds darkened and the distance rumble of thunder became louder, bringing soft rain then a strong and steady shower. The air cooled quickly. Lexi and Steve ran into the cabin, jumping underneath the covers in one of the beds to warm-up.

Their laughter and playful tumbling slowed to soft caresses and slow kisses. Without speaking, they removed their clothes and made love. It was gentle and caring. Something only long-time friends who discovered more in their relationship could experience.

After graduating high school, the five friends left for three different universities. Only Lexi and Steve stayed together, going to University of Texas at Austin. Again, it was fluid and easy.

Then Lexi got pregnant the fall semester of their sophomore year.

They used condoms, but Steve insisted an organic condom was less restrictive. It was. It failed. They shared the news with their parents. They were, after all, only twenty and twenty-one, and totally financially dependent on their parents.

Her parents offered—insisted—on paying for an abortion.

Steve and Lexi were surprised by her parents' reaction. They didn't even ask the couple if they wanted the child. Lexi and Steve had not decided what they wanted to do, but the fact that her parents just assumed, "You'll get an abortion, we'll pay, no problem, you're too young to ruin your lives," was too flippant for the expecting pair.

"Lexi, I'll do whatever you want to do. It will be hardest on you because you're the one carrying the baby," Steve said as they sat in her childhood bedroom during winter break.

"*Our* baby."

"Yes. Our baby."

"I'm stunned at how cavalier my parents are about an abortion. It's usually the other way around, isn't it?"

"Yeah. That kind of surprises me too."

"Steve, I've not thought much about our future, with or without a child, but, as I think about it now, I don't see us not being together."

"I feel the same."

"People do it, you know. Have good lives with surprise babies."

"Yep."

They sat quietly for a long time. Then Steve kneeled on one leg on the floor.

"Alexandra Victoria Maxwell, will you marry me and have our baby?"

Lexi slid off the bed onto the floor beside Steve. "Yes, Estevan Andres Jenson, yes I will."

They made love on her childhood bed with posters of the Rolling Stones and an iconic poster of The Crashers, Paddy May, looking down on the couple.

Her parents weren't happy. They were furious. "He's a nice guy, Lexi, but.. ."

Lexi stopped her parents before they finished that sentence.

"Stop there. He's in my life to stay, don't say things that you'll regret later."

Steve's parents were thrilled. They adored Lexi and already considered her their fifth child. Bringing the first grandchild into the close family only made things happier for them.

Lexi's parents offered very little support. She had a full scholarship, but they had been paying her room and board. They stopped their support her spring semester, and so she found a work-study job in the English department.

Steve also had a full scholarship and a paid internship at an engineering firm; not much changed for him school-wise.

They married January 2, just before returning to the university. That allowed them to move into married student housing, which was located in the old army reserve barracks way off campus. The university bus to and from campus stopped at married housing three times a day.

They only had what had been in their dorm rooms. Friends brought them hand-me-downs for the kitchen. No dining table or chairs. Not much room for it, anyway. The couple who had moved out over the break, and the only reason Lexi and Steve could get a place, had left a futon which served as the couch. The futon wasn't bad.

"No stains either!" exclaimed Lexi on move-in day.

Lexi's due date was the last day of the semester, so their focus was on completing their studies and finding a way to finish their undergraduate degrees and then pay for graduate school, he in engineering and she in English. The firm where Steve worked gave him a raise when they heard his situation and confirmed he could continue with them during grad school.

Lexi had published some short stories and poems in various literary magazine and journals. Total payment for all was less than $2,000. Prestigious publications, good feedback and one great review, but not enough money for anything other than kindling hope.

None of the challenges bothered the couple. They knew they had made the right decision the moment Steve cut the umbilical cord and handed their son to Lexi in the delivery room. He was a big boy with a head full of hair. He instinctively knew to find one of Lexi's breasts to nurse. Steve wrapped his arms around his wife and child, happier than he'd ever been.

The other couples in married housing took turns caring for each other's children. Weekly schedules were coordinated among the residents. It was a strong communal atmosphere sharing food, child sitting, clothes, books and anything else.

Lexi and Steve made it work and were happy, even proud at the life they had created. His firm gave him a plum job in Dallas when they completed grad school. They settled in a less gentrified, more culturally diverse, artsy part just south of downtown.

"That's so impressive you're moving to Kessler Park," said her parents.

"It's not Kessler Park. That's the rich part. It's more Bishop Arts."

"Well, we're proud of you. You didn't fail."

Fail at what? wondered Lexi.

Lexi's son, Jack, was starting kindergarten, freeing up her mornings to write. And write she did. She was disciplined and determined. She was still publishing, making a little more money, but felt guilty about not doing her part in supporting the family.

"We're fine, Lexi. You keep writing and let me know if we need to find a sitter for Jack after school."

"We can't afford that."

"Doesn't matter. We will find a way. We always do."

And they did.

Less than a year after moving to Dallas, Lexi's first book, *One Texas Farm*, was published with success—albeit success that was mostly out of state and out of the region. An indie bookstore owner had a podcast with her counterpart in London. He loved Lexi's book and made it a popular seller in the U.K. It sold okay in the Texas five-state region, some in the Midwest, and one indie bookstore in DC where she made friends with the owner when she went there on Steve's business trips.

It was when her college friend, Rob, published his first travel guide that Lexi's writing life became focused in a different way and became hugely successful. Rob had published *Don't Be a Tourist in Austin* as a way to counter the onslaught of visitors to their beloved university town that had been known for proudly "being weird," but that was rapidly becoming commercial. It was the first book in a series of travel *Don't Be a Tourist* books. The *DBAT* travel books became popular in part due to Lexi's idea that she would create a crime-solving series to cross-promote Rob's *DBAT* books.

Their pattern was established. Rob would travel to a city, then write a *DBAT* book about it. The following year, Lexi would publish *Cally's Summers Adventures In* and name the city of Rob's *DBAT* book from the previous year.

Lexi's Cally character was an elementary school teacher in her twenties who would travel to a featured *DBAT* city on summer vacation, only to find herself accidentally solving a local murder mystery.

The second book by Rob and Lexi featured Glastonbury. While Rob's book was focused only on the travel aspects, Lexi's book featured Cally trying to solve the disappearance of a major rock star from the Glastonbury Festival. The "disappearance" was total fiction in Lexi's book, but the details were so vivid that fans to this day thought Lexi's imaginary rock star was real and still missing.

Lexi's strategy to cross-promote with Rob's books opened a new market of readers for each of them, boosting sales, and setting a dependable pattern that was now in its tenth year. The *Cally* series was developed by the BBC into a top-rated show, making the lead actress a global star.

Lexi loved the routine of traveling in the summers with Jack and Steve to research the next *Cally* book.

Then Steve died.

Steve was in DC seeing a client when he was killed by a drunk driver. The driver of the large black SUV ran a red light at full speed, hitting Steve's car, leaving it and Steve unrecognizable. The driver of the SUV was barely bruised. He was someone in some foreign embassy, though Lexi's attorneys purposely never made clear to her who he was.

Diplomats have immunity, but the embassy representatives still insisted on compensating Lexi and Jack for the horrific accident. It was the payoff for her to not make it a "media sensation" that this man had killed the love of her life, the father of her child, her best friend, lover, and husband. More money than could ever be spent was moved into her account. Lexi just wanted to walk away from it all, but her attorney said, "No way in hell, Lexi. You have lost Steve, but you are not going to lose your financial stability."

Before the accident, Steve had been looking at prep schools for Jack to play hockey. Jack was considered a top AAA youth hockey player, and while the youth team in Dallas was consistently ranked in the top, it would not give him the necessary exposure to eventually be recruited by a major university.

Lexi hated the thought of Jack moving away from home at such an early age. "I didn't have Jack to not be with him!" she said frequently to Steve.

"I agree, Lexi, but look at him—he's a born hockey player. He's known what he's wanted since birth. And we'll just fly up and see him often."

Jack told Lexi just after the funeral that he had selected The Millbrook School in the Hudson River Valley, New York as his school of choice.

"Mom, you can get a place in New York City with Dad's money and come see me on the weekends."

Jack labelled the settlement as "Dad's money." It did somehow make it feel like Steve was still caring for them.

Everything happened fast. Steve's younger brother helped her move Jack into his prep school. The hockey coach had clearly briefed the team about Steve's death. All the boys came out to the car when Jack arrived, and without asking, they started carrying his equipment and luggage to his room. They gathered around the tall Texan who hovered over them by almost a foot in some cases.

The Millbrook tradition on move-in day was to have a picnic on the beautifully manicured grounds.

Steve's brother whispered, "This is pretty hoity-toity."

"Yeah. Except the dorm rooms. I was surprised at how, hmm, let's just say *modest* they are."

Lexi and her brother-in-law laughed.

"You're paying a ton of money for that modesty."

"True, but look at Jack. This is the first time I've seen him smile like that in ages."

The hockey team had insisted Jack sit at their table and the camaraderie was obvious.

Lexi managed not to cry when hugging Jack goodbye, but she didn't speak during the ninety-minute drive to "the City."

Steve's sisters had helped Lexi find a co-op on the upper west side, 83rd street, just off Central Park West. They were receiving the furniture deliveries while Lexi was settling Jack in at school.

She had the top floor of her building. Windows all around with a view of Central Park on one side.

Steve's siblings stayed a few days to run errands, grocery shop and create Lexi's New York home. She was keeping the home in Dallas and her plan was to travel back and forth.

Finally, it was time to be alone.

Steve's siblings returned to Dallas. Jack was happy with his new routine. He was good about texting "hello" in the morning which became their daily touchstone.

Still, loneliness crept in. The apartment was lovely, but lacked the lingering air of family. She had some family photos on the walls, but the furniture had no nicks from Steve and Jack roughhousing. There were no stains on the carpet or couch from a sippy cup when Jack was a child.

Lexi walked Central Park every morning, sometimes ending up at the Met for a coffee or down near the zoo to sit on the benches and watch locals and tourists walk by.

Eventually she could write about her grief. The loss of Steve, but also the loss of Jack being a child in her home. The loss of her life with both of them in Dallas.

Sorrow was a small book written as if in a trance. It was a series of prose poems in chapters that read like a mystical journey from one land far away into a new world.

The book was an immediate critical and popular success. It seemed every venue wanted her to speak and sign books.

Her popularity in UK exploded after *The Guardian* and *Financial Times* each carried glowing reviews.

"The *Financial Times*?" Lexi said to her agent.

"Can you believe it? It seems that even business people grieve."

CHAPTER 5

It was the end of the day in London. The streets were busy with people stopping at pubs on their way home from work and children in uniforms walking home or taking the tube.

A large group of school children walked past Paddy and Lexi. The children were in matching red and blue uniforms, carrying heavy backpacks and jostling one another as they paraded down the sidewalk.

"Look, look!" a child about five or six years old exclaimed loudly, elbowing his schoolmates and pointing at Lexi. "She only has one hand."

An older girl, maybe his sister, angrily jerked his hand down, shushing him as the group continued to walk as if nothing had happened.

Paddy whispered, "I'm sorry, Lexi, does that..."

"Happen? Yes, fairly regularly."

Lexi stopped walking and looked at the young boy. "Hi. Did you have a question about my arm? It's okay to ask."

The students stopped walking. Some mumbled to each other,

some couldn't look at Lexi, but the young boy who had noticed her stepped forward.

"What happened to you?" He pointed at her arm.

"Well, I was born with one hand." Lexi pointed at his hands. "Just like you were born with two, I was born with one. My right arm is just like yours, only it stopped growing here past my elbow."

Paddy smiled gently as he watched Lexi hold her right arm so the young boy could look at it carefully. *She's so sweet to that boy.*

"Does it hurt?"

"No. It's really exactly like your arm, only it just didn't grow as much."

"Can I touch it?"

"Gavin!" The older girl who seemed to be the boy's sister yanked him away.

"No. It's okay," Lexi said to the girl. She turned back to Gavin. "Yes, Gavin, you can touch my arm. And it's not an 'it,' it's my arm."

The other students huddled around Gavin and Lexi, carefully listening and watching.

Lexi continued, "See my right elbow here?"

"Yes." Gavin touched her elbow.

"Now touch your right elbow." Gavin touched his elbow. "It kind of feels the same, doesn't it?"

"Yes."

An older female student asked, "How does it happen, having one hand? Is it a disease? Or hereditary?"

"No. I don't think anyone knows for sure why. It may be the position in the womb."

"It makes you special in a way," someone said.

"Yes, I think so. Gavin, may I give you a suggestion? It's really for all your friends here too."

"Okay."

"When you see someone with a physical difference, don't point and yell at them. Imagine how that would feel if I did that to you."

Lexi grimaced and pointed at Gavin, mimicking what he had done to her.

"How did that feel?"

"Awful."

"Yeah."

"I didn't mean to. It just came out when I saw you." The little boy was starting to cry.

Lexi touched his shoulder.

"It's okay, Gavin. Next time you see someone with a physical difference, look them in the eye just as you would anyone. If they respond with a nod or a smile, that might mean they are open to talking. Just like any other person. If you really need to know, you might say, 'Can I ask you a question?' If the person says yes, then say, 'May I ask about your physical difference? I would like to better understand.'

"Now, Gavin, not everyone with a physical difference wants strangers coming up to them and asking them questions. I'm okay with it because I'd rather you understand, but many people are not that way."

"Do you ever get pissed that people stare at you?" one of the older boys asked.

"Yes. I do. Some days I'm just not in the mood to deal with you two-handed people. You can be so annoying."

Everyone laughed.

Gavin hugged Lexi. The students started to walk away when one shouted, "Oh my god, you're with Paddy May!"

Suddenly the students were a jumble of excitement, pulling out their cell phones.

Paddy said, "Okay. All of you, let's gather together for one photo."

"I'll take it," Lexi said as she accepted one of the phones.

"No, we need you in it too," someone said.

A young woman walking nearby heard and offered to take the picture.

The school children surrounded Paddy and Lexi, smiling and happy. Some hugged Lexi and some hugged Paddy as they left.

Paddy looked at Lexi as they walked away. He was impressed by her kindness.

Lexi wondered if conversations about her arm were going to become more frequent if she was with the famous Paddy May. She decided to return to asking Paddy about his life.

"Did you wear a uniform as a child?"

Paddy laughed.

"Oh yes. I wore gray trousers, a blue jacket with light-blue piping around the collar, the school crest of two lions and something that looked like a mountain on the pocket, and a tie. I wore a tie every school day from the age of eight until when I left school at fifteen."

"And look at you now. Mr. Fashion."

Paddy looked down at his clothes.

"I'm quite understated today."

"True. But still with a bit of flair."

"Well, you're not so bad yourself, Miss 'always has a scarf of some kind' tossed around your shoulders."

"We do have scarves in common, don't we?" Lexi tugged at Paddy's long, thin scarf that served as a sort of tie. "So, you stopped school at fifteen?"

"Yes, but I passed my O levels, with perfect results I'll add. I actually took my O levels when I was thirteen. I wanted to prove to the Head of School I'd already learned everything they could teach. I was born to be a guitarist and needed to go play."

"Your parents were okay with this?"

"Mammy was a schoolteacher and she—both my parents—knew I was smart, but my love was art and music. From a very early age I was drawing and playing piano, sneaking my uncle's guitar."

"Why do you call your mother mammy? I thought it was mummy here."

"She's Irish. It's mam or mammy there."

"What a blessing to have parents who let you be who you are, especially at such a young age."

"I love my parents. I think you'll really like them, too." Paddy looked at Lexi, waiting for some response.

She swallowed, her heart in her chest. "I'm sure I'll like them." One more tiny confirmation that they each wanted to be with the other, without openly admitting it.

They were approaching Buckingham Palace, and Lexi recognized where they were.

"Oh, I love St. James' Park just over there!" she said. "Our first trip as a family here was when Jack was six, and we went to the playground in the park every afternoon for him. Let's just buy from a vendor and sit in the park, okay?"

Lexi and Paddy sat close to one another on a bench, eating fish and chips wrapped in newspaper and watching the few children who were still playing late in the day. Mostly, they watched young couples strolling arm-in-arm or laying on the lawn, undoubtedly dreaming of lasting love with each other.

"They look so carefree, don't they, Lexi?"

"Maybe that's what they're saying about us too, huh?"

"Hmmm. I didn't think of that. Probably. We are carefree at the moment, aren't we?"

"This has been a magical day."

Paddy squeezed her hand and quickly released it.

"It's been a perfect day."

It was dark and streetlights were turning on. They sat in comfortable silence for a long time.

"Paddy, how are we going to handle tomorrow night?"

"What do you mean?"

"At the gala. Specifically, the VIP reception when you come with Penny. I mean, you told her you are a patron of the event just so you could meet me, right? Your favorite author."

"Oh. That. Yes. Hmmm."

"Yeah. You've met me now. I don't think we can pretend otherwise."

"No, and I wouldn't want to do that. That wouldn't be honest, and I want our relationship to be completely honest, in all ways."

"Relationship?"

Paddy blushed.

"Friendship. For now. But let's also be honest with each other, Lexi; we both are thinking this friendship could become more."

"Yes."

"I have some things I need to take care of first, before I feel like I can officially ask you out."

Lexi smiled, a little perplexed. "Are you always this formal with women?"

Paddy looked at her intently. "Never. That's why I know this is so special."

Lexi let herself drift into the cocoon surrounding her and Paddy, their energy pulling them together. She stared at his hands and imagined them holding her, caressing her, playing guitar just for her. It felt as if they had always been together.

"I think your phone is ringing," Paddy said, breaking the spell.

Paddy had been carrying Lexi's backpack all day. He handed it to her, and she dug it out. It was Jarius texting.

Are you still with Paddy May? WHAT ARE YOU DOING??????

Paddy asked, "Everything okay?"

"Well, J is pretending to be worried about me, but I think he really wants to know if I'm having sex with you."

"What?"

"Yeah. When I told him this morning that I was walking around with you, he said not go to bed with you."

They laughed.

You'd be proud of my self-restraint. We are sitting in St. James Park. Just finished fish and chips. mmm good.

Plans?

Probably walk around some more then come home.

Make him walk you home. It's dark.

OK

"Jarius wants to be sure you'll walk me home because it's dark now."

"He's protective of you."

"Very."

"That's good. Unless he's overly protective."

"No. He's perfect. We get along great."

Paddy looked down at his hands, as if wanting to ask something.

"No, Paddy, J and I aren't romantic."

"Was I that transparent?"

"Flashing lights transparent." She sighed. "I probably should head back to my place. I have a huge day tomorrow."

"Of course."

They took the tube back to Paddy's neighborhood. The streets were very quiet, since it was close to midnight. The amber-tinted lights and cobblestone streets made everything seem mysterious. Lexi was hoping for fog to roll in to make it a classic London foggy night where people and ghosts appeared out of the mists.

No mist, just the quiet click of their heels as they peeked into the windows of antique shops and posh boutiques. They were trying to delay the end of the evening, though neither said so.

Lexi started singing, "I Only Have Eyes for You."

"My love must be a kind of blind love..."

Lexi danced on the sidewalk in front of Paddy, who joined in singing.

"I can't see anyone but you..."

The two carried on until Lexi stopped in front of an elegant two-story Queen Anne style estate with an iron gate and cultivated garden in front.

"This is lovely," said Paddy.

"Yes, but we're around back. I think we have what was once the carriage house. Still quaint and lovely, though."

Lexi led them around the side of the large house through a

narrow passage that was lit just enough to see it was lined with flowers, shrubs and trees. In the back was a two-story carriage house renovated as a complete separate home. The couple stood just off the porch, avoiding brightness of the nightlight.

The passageway had been narrow, causing them to touch shoulders, and now they were reluctant to stand apart.

Paddy touched her hand briefly. "This may have been the best day I've ever had."

"Magical. A gift."

"Yes."

They stood, their bodies weaving back and forth so slightly, as if strands of energy were trying to untangle from being woven together all day. But Lexi and Paddy didn't want to be untangled.

Paddy leaned close to Lexi's face. She thought he was going to kiss her. He stopped himself by putting his hands on her shoulders and letting them slide down her arms.

He laced his fingers in and out of her left hand and cupped her right arm in his hand. He was absorbed in touching her hand and arm, just lost in the feeling.

Steve had been the only one who had ever held her arm like that before. And no one had ever caressed her arm the way Paddy was. He wasn't thinking about how he was touching her; he was lost in feeling.

Paddy stood very still. Looking down at Lexi, trying not to kiss her and ask to spend the night. Lexi felt his struggle.

"Look up, Paddy."

Still holding Lexi, Paddy leaned back just enough to see the full autumn moon.

"Lexi, let's remember this night every time we see a full moon, okay?"

"You are such a romantic, Paddy May. I didn't expect that."

They stood silently looking up at the moon shining down on them.

Lexi decided to take the first step toward coming back to reality after their fantasy day. "So, we never decided. How do we act tomorrow at the VIP reception since Penny knows you're going there to meet me?"

Paddy's eyes cleared and he shook his head to think.

"Umm." He released her arms. "I think I'll tell Penny that I met you at a bookstore today. Which is true. And that we visited. That way we can greet each other like we know each other, which we do now."

"Yeah. I call that making an honest statement, but not telling the truth."

"What?"

"Well, it's honest that we met, but the truth is, maybe more than just a casual conversation."

Paddy shrugged. "What do you recommend?"

Suddenly the door to Lexi's place flew open and a twenty-something, tall lanky man said, "Did you forget the door code again?"

Everyone stiffened.

"Oh wow, sorry, Lexi. I saw on the tracker you've been standing here a while and assumed you forgot the door code again."

"Jarius, this is Paddy May. Paddy, meet Jarius Harjo."

The men shook hands, both smiling, but clearly scrutinizing the other.

Jarius said, "I'm sorry for interrupting, you two. Nice to meet you, Paddy. Love your music beyond what you could imagine. I'm going back inside now. Lexi, you know the code, and you know it's almost tomorrow? And tomorrow's a huge day."

"Yes."

"Great. Bye now."

After the door closed, Paddy and Lexi looked at each other. The quiet between them was different now—still comfortable, but real life intruded at the edges.

Paddy raised his eyebrows. "He said he saw you on the tracker."

"Yes. He tracks my phone. My son tracks me too."

"You're okay with that?"

"Yeah. They do it more for their comfort, I think. You know, kind of like a 'Where's Waldo.' I think it's cute. And it does give me comfort knowing someone knows where I am. I have no secrets, you know."

They stood still. The energy between them still strong, but less entangled now as they knew they had to part.

"Lexi, I've never felt this way about someone. It's very different for me. I need some time to sort a few things out, but I don't want to lose our connection while I do that."

"I probably shouldn't say this, but I feel like we've made love all day."

Paddy grabbed her and hugged her wholly against his body. He held her while he touched her hair and put his cheek against her forehead, breathing in as much of her scent as he could.

Then he pulled himself away, abruptly stopping their connection. He stood up taller as if to strengthen his will power.

"Can we exchange numbers?"

"Gosh, yes." Lexi started to fumble through her backpack, but Paddy had pulled out his cell and was putting in her name. "Just give me yours." She did and he texted her his number.

"Okay."

"Okay."

"Tomorrow night."

"Tomorrow night."

Paddy waited while she punched in the door code. She glanced back at him as she stepped inside. The tears in his eyes glistened from the light.

CHAPTER 6

Paddy waited until he was on the sidewalk in front of the large manor before he pulled out his cigarettes. He lit one and watched the red tip flame and burn down almost halfway. He was making up for an entire day of not smoking. By now he would normally have been through a pack. He didn't always smoke the cigarettes completely. He often lit one and set it aside while he composed on the piano or guitar, but there was always one lit.

He remembered how Lexi had a coughing fit early in the morning when he lit one. *She didn't exaggerate that. She really is allergic.*

He lit another one off the first and wondered how he was going to quit these.

Worse, how was he going to stop drinking so much. He was surprised that he hadn't had anything to drink and didn't miss it much. Still, she said she rarely drinks, if at all.

The streets were totally quiet, only the sound of his shoes on the pavement. The smoke from his cigarette was mixing with the fog beginning to blanket the neighborhood.

The music he had composed earlier in the day was playing in his head. His place was only a fifteen-minute walk from Lexi's. *She really did find a place near me.* He smiled. He liked that she wanted to be near him and that she had admitted it to him.

His cats, Panda and Vesty, were waiting at the door, meowing furiously.

"I know, I know. I'm sorry."

They all went to the kitchen, where he fed the cats and, without thinking, poured himself a bourbon straight. He downed it in one gulp and was pouring a second before he'd barely swallowed the first. Then he stopped.

Bourbon bottle in one hand, he pulled his cell out of his pocket and cued up Woody Taylor's number. Woody had been one of the elite rockers from London who, along with Paddy, exploded worldwide and still sat at the top of the charts.

Tonight, though, Paddy thought of how Woody had also been one of the first to get sober, stay sober and be public about it.

The bourbon didn't taste as smooth tonight. In fact, it burned. *And I haven't had a drink all day until now. Maybe I can do it. Maybe it's time.*

Paddy poured the bourbon out in the sink then looked at his liquor stock and thought about how much liquor he had at this house and his other properties. Was he really going to dump thousands of dollars down the drain? Maybe someone else could use it all.

Paddy started rationalizing about why it didn't make sense to dump dozens of bottles. Then he remembered the time after a charity event when he and Woody were on stage together. Woody had to subtly show Paddy the chords to one of The Crashers' biggest hits. Chords Paddy had composed himself. Paddy was so drunk he'd lost track of his own music.

Later that week, when they saw one another in the neighborhood, Woody had just said, "Hey, if you ever want to change your drinking habit, let me know. Call me anytime. And I mean *anytime.*"

It was almost 2:00 a.m., but Paddy decided he wouldn't call Woody—he was going to Woody's house instead. Paddy knew he needed to get away from the bottles who were calling his name like sirens.

Woody's house was literally around the block. Another palatial Queen Anne Manor with a wrought iron fence surrounding the property.

Paddy stood in front of the main gate and called his long-time buddy.

No answer.

For several minutes, Paddy stood looking at the house. Finally, he turned to walk away when his phone buzzed. It was Woody.

"Hey man, where are you? You know it's two in the morning in London."

"I know. I'm standing in front of your house."

"You don't sound drunk."

"I'm not. And I want to stay that way, Woody."

Paddy heard the rustling of sheets.

"Stay there, Paddy. I'm on my way to the door now."

Two minutes later, Woody stepped out of his house in his pajamas and bare feet. He hadn't bothered wasting time with a robe or slippers.

He waved at Paddy as the front gate swung open electronically.

The men hugged. Paddy held Woody longer than usual, which Woody noticed.

Inside, Woody's longtime wife, Ann, was in the kitchen starting the kettle and setting out tea. She gave Paddy a hug and kiss on the cheek.

"There are snacks in the fridge. Help yourselves, boys. Call me for anything." She pulled her robe closer, kissed Woody, then went back upstairs.

Paddy looked at Woody, who was brewing the tea. "You've done this before. Having a late night, what is it? Intervention?"

Woody laughed. "I don't think this is technically an intervention. You came here on your own. That's great, Paddy."

Paddy reached in his pocket for a smoke, remembered Woody also no longer smoked, and put it back.

"You can smoke if you need to, Paddy."

"No. No, I smoked hardly at all today, and I only had one drink, and that was just before I called you."

The men were sitting around the kitchen island with teacups in hand.

Woody knew to move very slowly, letting Paddy take the lead on what he wanted to say and when.

Paddy kept stirring his tea even though he'd not put any milk or sugar in it.

Finally, he looked at Woody. "I had the strangest—no, most magical day today, and something changed in me."

Woody smiled at him, curiosity sparkling in his eyes. "Do you want to tell me about it?"

Paddy told him about his day with Lexi. Woody listened carefully, nodding, smiling when Paddy did, and secretly sending thoughts of support.

The sun was rising when Paddy finished. "Woody, I don't think this is a schoolboy crush. And I don't think I want to get sober just because I want to be with Lexi—though that wouldn't be a bad thing, would it?"

"Paddy, we've known each other since we were schoolboys, and this does seem different from how you've talked about women before. Very different. There's also something different in *you*. Whatever has you wanting to get sober is a good thing."

Paddy wiped a hand down his face. "I came over here to get away from all my liquor bottles. I have booze everywhere, in all my houses. I didn't trust myself to dump them alone. I thought I'd talk myself out of it, which is why I called you."

Woody's cook came in the side door and paused, not expecting the men to be there.

"Good morning, Natalya. This is Paddy."

Natayla nodded and smiled. "Would you like breakfast, Mr. Woody?"

"Yes. Please. We will take it in the conservatory."

The men walked to Woody's favorite room. The place where he cultivated exotic plants and show-winning flowers.

"This really is something, Woody."

"This is what you can do when you're sober."

Paddy laughed. "I'm not the gardening type."

"No, but you are an artist. I remember our school days, mate. Beautiful drawings. And then there's your music. Beautiful."

Natalya created a full breakfast with scrambled eggs, baked beans, and fresh-baked bread in what seemed like just minutes.

"So how do I do it, Woody? I don't have to attend those group meetings, do I? Please say no."

Woody was still, then said, "Paddy, you and I live and work in a world where almost everyone has a severe drug or drinking habit, or both. I'm lucky because my whole band is sober now. But your band. Oh mate, honestly, I've been worried you guys are about to self-destruct."

"I'm off drugs now. Weed now and then, but less and less and nothing else."

"That's good. Really good. The thing is, though—your mates aren't, are they?"

"No. Well, not Eric at all. Owen and Paul are very controlled in their use."

"And your manager, Nigel?"

"No. He's a mess."

"You need a support group, a system, a way to have what you need in a second to make the decision to not drink. Just like this morning. You knew I'd be here for you. You knew I would say yes to whatever you needed, and you called. If I hadn't been home in London, I would have stayed on the phone with you as long as you needed."

"I know. Thank you."

"Paddy, the truth is the AA program works, and you can find a group anywhere in the world, which blokes like you and I need when we're on the road. In fact, I have three or four mates coming over in about an hour. It's my own neighborhood group. You'll know a couple of the men I think."

Paddy shifted in his chair. "I don't know."

"So, what are you going to do if you go home right now?"

Paddy laughed. "Probably wish I was right back here."

"Stay." Woody stood up. "I need to get dressed. Help yourself to my studio. You know where it is."

Paddy walked out the back and across the lawn to Woody's carriage house that had been converted into a recording studio.

He took down a Fender and started playing the song he'd composed with Lexi. It was a soft, lyrical acoustic piece. He was so absorbed in playing that he didn't notice Woody had been standing and listening in the doorway.

He let out a low whistle. "That's the most beautiful music I've heard you play. Mate, it's the most beautiful music I think I've ever heard."

"I wrote it when I was with Lexi yesterday."

"It's definitely a love song. Do you have lyrics?"

"No. I guess I'll ask Eric."

"Or maybe you can write some. The guys are here. Are you ready?"

"No. But I'll come anyway."

CHAPTER 7

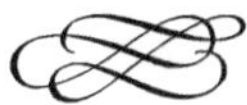

J arius Harjo was on the couch pretending to work on his laptop
when Lexi walked in after spending the day with Paddy.

"Well, you had quite the day, Ms. Maxwell."

Lexi was grinning, but her eyes showed concern. "Yes, but I'm
not sure where this is headed."

"Headed? Already?"

"I haven't felt this way in a long time."

"Yeah, well, he's had a lot of experience with women, a lot of
women..."

"I know, J."

J closed his laptop. "Big day tomorrow, today now actually. I'm
going to bed." He kissed her on the cheek and hugged her, holding
her longer than usual. "I want you to be happy. You have such a good
reputation. Paddy's reputation is mixed. Very mixed. He's so high-
profile, there's no way you can just test him out privately. It's gonna
be full-blown press, if it isn't already."

"What do you mean?"

"You just spent an entire day walking around London with

Paddy May. There's no way you weren't noticed, and I'm sure someone filmed you with their phone and posted it."

Lexi hadn't considered that *she* would be in any social media posts. She thought they were just looking at Paddy. Paddy wasn't as much a wild boy as he once was, but he was a global superstar and people loved following posts about him. Was Lexi ready to have people think she was dating someone? She'd never been the focus of popular media. Her media presence was with literary press and book review editors and bookstores and her fans.

She walked upstairs to her bedroom, passing J's room.

"Nite, J. I love you."

"Love you, too."

Lexi usually imagined washing away the day when she took her evening showers, but not this night. She let the suds flow down from her hair over her body and moved her hands slowly over her breasts, hips, thighs and between her legs, imagining it was Paddy.

Afterwards, in bed, she pleasured herself. It had been a long time since she'd imagined anyone other than Steve when she climaxed. It was intense and repeated several times. She finally collapsed, sweating, panting and smiling as she fell asleep.

CHAPTER 8

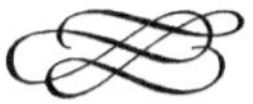

"Mornin', Paddy."

"Mornin', Barb."

"You're up early today."

It was another sunny day, and Barbara's coffee and tea shoppe was bustling with customers at the tables and chairs scattered on the sidewalk.

"Well, I..."

"You've been up all night? You look good for pulling an all-nighter, Paddy."

They laughed.

"It wasn't like that. It was, well, better. A night of good reflection, Barb. Good reflection."

Barbara was letting his tea brew. "Do you want take-away tea this morning? You might need to hide today, since you're on the cover of the news."

"What?"

Barbara motioned to copies of *The Sun*. A photograph of Paddy stretched out on the lawn in Hyde Park the day before with the headline *Even Rockers Enjoy A Sunny Day* in large type across the top half of the paper.

Paddy grabbed the copy. It showed Lexi sitting next to him writing in her journal, but the angle made it appear that she was just one of many people sitting around him, but not necessarily with him.

"Do you think she's ready for the media onslaught that comes with being your friend, Paddy?"

Paddy sighed. "Nobody is ready for that. Not even me." He tucked the paper under his arm. "I'll have a take-away, and the paper, please."

Outside, Paddy recognized a couple who lived near him. "They just won't leave you alone will they, Paddy?" asked one of them.

"I guess not."

"Did you know that was Lexi Maxwell, the writer, sitting next to you?"

Paddy's stomach tightened. *Do I tell the truth or not?* "Yes," he decided to say.

"Is she a friend?"

"Oh, I'd only just met her."

"Is she as wonderful as people say? She's supposed to be such a nice person."

"As best I could tell, she's as wonderful as we'd all hoped. Enjoy your day."

"You too."

Paddy wanted to talk about Lexi, to rekindle her presence—but he knew if he did, the rumors would start. He was aware that every other person sitting on that patio was eavesdropping on the conversation with his neighbors and that a few not-so-discreet photos were being taken of him.

When he entered the privacy of his home, Paddy opened the paper to look at the photographer credit, but Panda and Vesty distracted him by meowing and rubbing on his legs.

"Sorry boys, I've been a bad Dad again, haven't I?"

He looked again at the photo credit: *Samantha Peters*. His whole body seared in a hot flash as if someone had pierced him with a knife.

"Shit, Sammie."

He met her when she was just out of art school and trying to work as an artist, any kind of artist. She decided to be a photographer. She was smart and playful and sexy with long legs and a naturally beautiful face that needed very little makeup, if at all.

She'd been at one of the parties Paddy used to attend when he first started The Crashers. She had a camera, and no one seemed to be bothered by the invasion of their privacy. He knew she had identified him to be her prize for the night and took pleasure in watching her flirt with him. She didn't need to bother. The minute he saw her, he'd decided he was going to take her to the flat he kept just for sex.

He had so much fun with her that night, he invited her to go with the band on the European leg of their first tour. It was close enough to London that he could easily send her back if he got bored with her.

Her photos of The Crashers catapulted her from obscurity to fame the first week. She was a decent photographer, but the unfettered access to the band provided an unfiltered peek into the life of the world's rapidly ascending rock and roll group who everyone was trying to befriend.

Paddy was snorting massive amounts of cocaine during that tour, and combined with his usual heavy drinking, he was in a dazed, hedonistic state of self-absorption, sex all the time with Sammie, drinking, drugging and playing his beloved music with his favorite mates every night, and he loved it.

By the time the band reached Spain, rumors of their wild behavior were just that—unproven rumors. The band was touring on their own private train. Fans had started trying to follow the train; their manager tinted the windows so the band could see out, but the fans couldn't see in.

The privacy allowed for even more wild behavior, with women often naked in the passages, going from car to car. The women, some still teenagers, would blindfold each other and walk down the passages of the train, letting whomever do whatever to them. Booze and drugs littered most tables. It was Sodom and Gomorra. Paddy and Eric, the lead singer, were barely nineteen; Paul, the bass player, had just turned twenty; and the drummer, Owen, celebrated his twenty-first birthday at the start of the tour. Their manger, Nigel, was only twenty-eight.

Paddy frequently would hold up a bottle or a joint and exclaim, "Isn't this a great life!"

Then, it all changed.

When they arrived at the Atocha Train Station in Madrid, the platform was so crowded with fans and photographers that the policia had to send several units to control the crowd from blocking other train passengers and from jumping onto the tracks.

At first, the band thought it was simply the result of what was already being called the most successful rock tour ever. Then their manager came into the dining car where the guys were eating and tossed a copy of *El Pais* on the table. The cover photo was of Paddy, passed out on one of the train couches with his shirt open, his pants unzipped, partially exposing a post-coitus bulge, a bottle of bourbon almost slipping from his hand, and a woman's thong strewn across his thigh.

Putas del Rock and Roll was the headline.

Samantha Peters was the credited photographer.

Paddy looked at the picture a long time, threw it aside, and said to their manager, "Toss her out now."

Sammie went on to become *the* rock and roll photographer, but the photo of Paddy was always the iconic one shown to represent excess in the extreme.

Spain was the last time Paddy saw Sammie, but he knew she was always lingering around. Nigel put security on alert to keep her away from the band.

Now, years later, it looked like Sammie was going to intervene in his life again.

Paddy tossed the London paper on the couch and walked to his bar. He grabbed his favorite bottle of bourbon, then remembered the photo on the cover of *El Pais*. He walked back to his couch, bottle still in hand, and looked at the photo of him stretched out in the grass next to Lexi.

"Lexi, I want to be with you, and I can't do *this*," he said, looking at the bottle, "if I want to be with you."

He walked back to his bar and poured all the alcohol out, bottle by bottle.

He was still pouring out bottles when his long-time housekeeper arrived.

"Elga, it's time. I'll do the pouring out, but can you help dump the bottles in the trash? You might need to call Graham to help. In fact, yes—please call him. We'll need the car to go out to the Thames House after this and start dumping as much as we can today."

Elga and Graham had both been with Paddy for years. While she was technically the housekeeper/cook and Graham was the head of security and Paddy's personal driver, they were the two people who kept Paddy from completely careening into harm when he was high. Though he had stopped doing drugs a couple of years before, his drinking had accelerated.

Both Elga and Graham had dreamed this day would come for Paddy, but had given up hope long ago.

CHAPTER 9

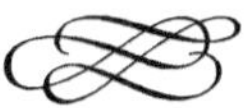

Lexi was drinking coffee and writing in her journal when Jarius returned from his morning run. He threw the morning paper on the table in front of her and stood glaring at her, waiting for her reaction.

Lexi looked up, perplexed.

"What?"

J just motioned to the paper.

"Oh shit."

"Yeah, oh shit."

Lexi studied the photograph of Paddy and her. "Well, it doesn't mention me. And I look just like another person in the park."

"For now. You're lucky that the photographer and the editor of the paper don't know who you are."

"He really has no privacy, does he?"

"No. And you won't, either, if you start seeing him."

Lexi touched the photo as if she were stroking Paddy's hair.

"I'm going to shower. The books will be here within the hour."

"Books?"

"Remember, you agreed to sign books to distribute to the VIPs at the gala tonight. You remember the gala, right?"

"Of course."

"I don't know, Lexi, you seem to be in a big fog with this Paddy thing."

"I am." She smiled. "But I'll burn it off, just enough, by tonight."

"Just enough?"

"I don't want it to go away, J."

Jarius sighed softly, then disappeared to the bathroom.

Left alone, Lexi imagined how the night would go. The Royal Charity Trust Gala was not only the largest, most high-profile event where she was the presenter, but now there would be someone in the audience who she was fantasizing about. It wasn't a fantasy, though. She, and he, were actually crushing on each other. Both thinking about what it would be like to have more days like yesterday. To hold hands openly. To have sex...

Was this going to lead to a real, sustained relationship?

J's right. Do I really want a life of no privacy? Right now, I can easily move about, being free to do what I want. With Paddy May, I lose that.

The boxes of books arrived, and she sat at the kitchen table, several pens set out to be certain no book was signed with faded ink. J brought her the wrist brace she wore at book signings. As the crowds grew at signings, her hand started hurting more and more, which was why she now signed books in advance and had them distributed at her appearances.

J turned on the radio and the song playing was the Crashers "She's A Whole Lotta Woman to Love."

"Of course." He looked at Lexi, who didn't pause signing.

"He's everywhere, J. He's everywhere."

CHAPTER 10

Paddy spent all day pouring booze out of the bars at both his London home and his home on the River Thames. Elga stuffed the empties into bags, boxes, whatever she could find, and Graham loaded Paddy's Range Rover and carried them to the landfill. This took most of the day.

Though he hadn't slept at all the night before, Paddy felt good. Each load that left the house lifted a weight off. No one spoke. Elga and Graham knew this was a process of cleansing for Paddy. Years earlier, they had attended Al Anon meetings to learn how to protect their own sanity while being the two people closest to a raging drug and alcohol addict. They loved Paddy, and he treated them as much like family as one could, given they were technically paid staff.

They also knew this would be the trickiest time in an addict's recovery process. Just because these two houses were now cleared of booze and weed, it didn't mean Paddy was in the clear. He could snap back into addiction in a second.

Elga made sandwiches after Graham's last run to the dump. The three sat on the dock of Paddy's Thames House.

"I spent the morning at Woody Taylor's house," Paddy said. "He was having an AA meeting. I can tell you that because he's been so public about his addictions and recovery. You know about AA, right?"

"Yes," they both replied at once.

They all laughed. "Something tells me you two have been waiting for this day. A long wait, huh?"

Elga spoke first. "Paddy, Graham and I have been going to Al Anon for a while now. We have done so to be able to continue being with you and..."

"And keep your sanity."

"Yes."

Graham chimed in, "But mostly we did so because we wanted to be ready to help you whenever you were ready to stop."

"You're not just our employer, Paddy."

Paddy reached out to hold Elga's hand.

"I know." His face flushed. "I have a lot of emotions right now, and I'm not used to feeling my emotions. I don't know how all of this is going to go. I met someone yesterday and realize if I want to see her, I can't be an addict. And I know I have to quit for me, not her—but, well, it's all a jumble."

Paddy told Elga and Graham about his day with Lexi.

Elga squeezed his hand.

"Are you and Penny still going to the gala tonight?"

Paddy sighed. "Yes."

Graham asked, "How are you going to handle seeing Lexi? You need to plan how to handle possible triggers for your drinking."

"Yeah. Woody and his group told me about that. And Lexi and I talked about it."

The three sat in comfortable silence.

Elga said, "How about you let me pick your clothes for tonight while you clean up?"

"Okay, but not too wild a look tonight, Elga."

CHAPTER 11

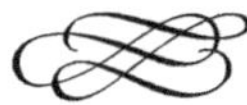

"Ugh, I never have anything to wear, J. Why? When am I going to finally find clothes I like?"

Lexi haphazardly threw clothes on the floor and bed. She'd spent the day signing books for the gala VIPs and writing in her journal, trying to process her emotions about Paddy.

J came in and took the clothes from her hand.

"Go outside and take a walk."

"What?"

"Now. Go outside and take a walk. You've been inside all day and that's not normal for you. You have the time. Go. Set your timer. Thirty minutes one way, thirty minutes back. I'll have the perfect outfit selected for you when you're back. Go."

J was right. It was typical for her to have taken several walks by midday. Her pattern, when writing, was to take a ten-to-fifteen-minute walk every two hours or so; otherwise, she'd become physically stiff, and her writing would lose its fresh clip and focus.

It was another sunny day. She thought about turning left at the end of the walkway, a direction that would take her by Barbara's coffee and tea shoppe and Paddy's city house.

But she decided to turn right. Paddy's date for the gala might be with him, and she didn't want it confirmed by seeing Penny leave his place.

What she didn't know was that Samantha Peters was hiding near Paddy's house, waiting to catch photos of him. Sammie was trying to reenergize her photography business and her candid shots of Paddy always brought her clients. Her picture of him napping in the park the day before reminded her of how the one where he was passed out on the train in Spain when he was barely nineteen years old had catapulted her onto the global scene for celebrity photographs.

Most of her subjects over the years hoped a photograph of them by Samantha Peters would result in as famous a shot as that iconic one of Paddy. However, her photographs of other rock stars, entertainers and celebrities were never as much a violation of privacy as the one of Paddy. That violation was why Paddy had avoided her all the years since. Sammie had made a fortune selling prints of the "Paddy Passed Out" photograph. That photo was always used in stories about the "sins of rock and roll."

Paddy never spoke of it publicly other than to say, "I was a teen. What were *you* doing when you were that age?"

Now, all these years later, Sammie knew candid shots of Paddy would sell and put her name and social media back on top. And it worked. Her first photo of Paddy in years resulted in her byline being on the cover of *The Sun*. Now, she wanted to see if there was a market for more of Paddy in London.

So Lexi was lucky that she chose not to walk by Paddy's house. Sammie was too observant and too smart and would have noticed that the woman she thought was just casually sitting next to Paddy in the park yesterday was also the woman walking near his house today.

Lexi's timer buzzed. Thirty minutes. Time to walk back to her place.

Lexi took big, deep breaths in and out, balancing her energy, which had been knocked off-rhythm ever since she'd met Paddy the morning before.

Has it really only been a day and a half? I feel like I just jumped into the deep end with him.

Back at the house, Jarius had three outfits for her: jeans to wear to and from the Royal Albert Hall, since they planned on walking instead of taking the car and driver the event had arranged; a dress for the VIP reception; and another outfit to wear during her stage presentation.

"Thanks, J." Lexi sighed. "I wish I could just wear jeans and a T-shirt the whole time."

J looked deflated.

"J, you know I like what you've chosen, but you also know me."

"I know."

"I'm not a fancy girl. And the outfit for the VIP reception is a bit sexier than usual, a bit more cleavage, huh, J?"

"Yes. I may have some hesitations about the publicity that comes with Paddy, but I want him to regret that he's with that fancy model tonight and not you!"

"Yikes."

The two laughed and carefully put the clothes, along with the notes for Lexi's reading and protein drinks for afterwards, in a daypack. They then scraped together a meal of cheeses, nuts and fruits for a light dinner, took the tube part of the way, and then walked to the *Royal Prince's Charity Trust Gala featuring Lexi Maxwell.*

CHAPTER 12

Lexi and J stood at the edge of Hyde Park, looking across the street at the Royal Albert Hall. The massive round structure built during Queen Victoria's reign represented everything Lexi loved about London—history, art, literature, music and her success with the *Cally's Summer Adventures* series on the BBC.

J took several pictures of Lexi and then they took selfies with both of them together.

"This is a big deal, Lex."

"I know." She teared up. "Oh God, where'd that come from? I miss Steve."

J put his arm around his friend and mentor. "I thought that might happen. Don't worry, I put your makeup bag in the pack."

Lexi wiped her face. "Am I all puffed up now?"

"Um, no. Not too much. Just...no more tears now."

They walked around the side entrance where the security guard had to call a supervisor to assure him that the woman in jeans was the featured presenter. Lexi and Jarius laughed when they heard a voice on the walkie talkie ask the guard, "Does she have red hair and one hand?"

The guard waved them in, lowered his head and whispered, "yes" back to his boss.

It was an hour before the VIP reception was to start and the hall was empty, except the caterers setting up and the ushers receiving their assignments.

Lexi went to the dressing room to change while J met with the house manager to discuss details.

Her publisher was setting up a table in the lobby with her books, and cards for the audience to write questions were scattered throughout. J and the house manager practiced how to connect J's playlist to their house sound system.

The director of the Royal Charity Trust knocked on the dressing room door.

"Ms. Maxwell? I don't mean to disturb you."

"No, I'm fine, thank you."

"I'd like to present you to a few of our patrons, if I may, before others arrive."

Lexi's stomach dropped and a flash of panic hit her. *Breathe in, breathe out,* she told herself.

She repeated her mantra and calmed down.

She almost started laughing when the director introduced her to the Prince and Princess, because she was more nervous that it was going to be Paddy and his date than she was meeting actual royalty.

J came into the dressing room and was introduced. He tidied up her things and gathered her notes and journal, which he would hold until it was time for her to go on stage. They looked at one another. J smiled, "Show time!" And they stepped out into the large VIP area.

Lexi hadn't been aware that the reception was already full of guests and that she was going to be introduced by the Prince.

J stood near Lexi, gauging when she needed a drink of water or if he needed to intervene with overly talkative fans.

She was radiant. The deep emerald cocktail length dress with shimmers showed off her trim body and there was just enough cleavage for elegance. She managed flats for the reception instead of her sneakers.

Then there he was.

He was walking in the far entrance. He was at least a head taller than most people there and Lexi watched him feeling the tingle of her crush.

Paddy looked sexy and confident in coattails with a very subtle design of Celtic circles and his signature long thin scarf instead of a tie.

J moved closer to Lexi to...alert her? Prepare her? Protect her? He wasn't sure, but knew it would be a critical emotional moment.

Paddy hadn't taken his eyes off Lexi and walked straight to her even though other guests were trying to catch the attention of the rock star. He and Lexi stood looking at one another without speaking, as if they were inhaling each other's presence.

"Paddy, thank you for being here and supporting this evening."

Lexi made the first move and hugged Paddy.

He kissed her on both cheeks. "You look radiant."

"Thank you."

"Lexi, this is Penny."

"Penny, thank you for being here. You're very kind to indulge Paddy's interest in my books."

"I'm sorry my schedule doesn't really allow me to read much, but I watch the show on the telly that's taken from your books. *Cally's Summer Adventures*, right?

Lexi nodded yes.

"And I know Paddy is over the moon being here. And he told me you two met at the bookstore yesterday. How lucky was that?"

"Very lucky. I'm as big a fan of his as he seems to be of me."

Penny gave a little nod, turned and walked toward Woody and his wife, Ann.

Paddy looked at Lexi, shrugged, and said, "Well, at least she knows your books from the BBC series."

More VIPs were surrounding Lexi, and Paddy was pulled away.

He and J shook hands and hugged, sharing a knowing look, and Paddy followed Penny as she worked the room. He barely took his eyes off Lexi, though.

She could sense his eyes on her, but stayed focused on whoever was in front of her.

Finally, J tugged at her elbow. "You need to get ready." He motioned to the President of the Trust, who announced it was time for everyone to take their seats.

J followed Lexi into the dressing room to help her change and to see how she was doing mentally and emotionally.

"I'm good, J. Feeling fine. I'm in the groove for the night. Feeling my power. Okay, it's showtime. We can do this."

J handed her the notes she'd prepared for the evening and watched her smile and mouth "thank you" to all the people working backstage.

The President of the Royal Charity was already feeling exuberant about the sold-out event, and now he was going to be the one to tell the crowd that Lexi's new book would be announced in the press the next day as the number one best-seller in the UK and that the BBC series modelled after her *Cally's Summer Adventures* books was being renewed for another season.

Lexi waited offstage in the dark as the President of the Royal Charity walked into the spotlight.

"Ladies and gentlemen, thank you for being here on—what we have just learned—is an even more special evening than we could have planned ourselves."

Paddy was on the third row from the stage with his date and friends. Woody leaned over to him and inquired, "What's up?"

Paddy just shrugged.

"Ladies and gentlemen, as you know, our special guest this evening is known for not only being the creator of the international sleuth, Cally Mowry, but she is also the author of many well-respected and endearing books of poetry and essays.

"Tonight, I have the special privilege to share with you that her most recent book has just been named the number one best-seller in the UK and that *Cally's Summer Adventures* has been renewed for another season."

The audience burst into applause.

"Please help me welcome the charming and delightful and number one best-seller author, Lexi Maxwell."

Lexi wondered what had happened to the typical British reserve. The audience leapt to their feet, and some hooted and hollered as she walked onto the stage.

Lexi spotted Paddy without even trying.

Their eyes locked. Paddy mouthed, "Wow."

Lexi lifted an eyebrow as if to say, "Who knew?"

She put her notes on the podium. She glanced up at the Royal box and did a slight dip. *Am I supposed to curtesy?*

This was one of the few times in life where she thought having two hands would be helpful because she wanted to press palms together in the Namaste greeting. Instead, she placed her lefthand on her chest and bowed slightly to each section of the Hall, saying *thank you, thank you, thank you.*

After several minutes she quieted the audience, and they sat back down.

She arranged her notes and took a few deep breaths. J was in the wings, watching every movement and softly muttering, "You've got this, Lexi. You've got this."

And she did. She was a woman who responded well under pressure and excelled as the pressure increased. Steve used to tell people, "If there's ever an emergency, just do what Lexi says to do. It'll be the right thing."

Lexi breathed in this moment. "People ask me why I spend so much time in London. I used to say it's because I enjoy the people, and they buy my books more than anywhere else."

The audience laughed.

"But now," she looked right at Paddy, "you will always be a part of this very special moment in my life with both my books and the television series being so embraced by all of you. Thank you."

The energy between Lexi and Paddy was electric. No one noticed other than Woody and his wife. Paddy's date was busy taking a selfie and posting to social media.

"Okay. I thought I'd read some to you tonight, and I see that only a few of you have turned in questions for me to answer."

Lexi held up a huge sack of cards that had been scattered throughout the lobby for fans to write questions. The audience laughed when she held up the enormous stack.

She started sorting the stack into smaller piles on the podium.

"I used to take questions from the floor and really prefer doing it that way, but, one event became very unpleasant after someone decided that, rather than just asking a question, he would pitch his book idea to me and the entire audience. I didn't know how to handle it, and it altered that evening as a result. Since then, I've figured out that I can take your questions with these cards and still keep the good vibe of the evening. Thank you for understanding."

She paused for a moment.

"I'm not going to be able to answer every question, but they do seem to be falling naturally into a few categories, so we'll cover the gist of it."

The audience was settled in, listening to every word, smiling and laughing at her jokes. Paddy was mesmerized. *She's adorable,* he thought.

Woody leaned over his wife to say to Paddy, "I had no idea she was so charming and entertaining. No wonder..." Woody's wife elbowed him into silence.

Even Penny said, "She's kind of funny. I didn't expect that."

Lexi read passages from her short stories, the iconic scene from her first novel that was made into a movie, and poems from her collections that only her most faithful fans, like Paddy, had read.

The audience was captured, silently listening, gasping at the intense moments in a story and reaching out to hold hands with their loved ones during the sweet poems.

When she finished her readings, she turned to the questions. She read the first one that almost everybody always asked.

"You write in so many genres. How do you get your ideas?"

Lexi looked at the row where Paddy was seated with his friends.

"Actually, ideas scream at me all the time. In fact, right this moment there is a story talking to me, and I need to jot down some key words so I can write it up later."

She pulled out a pen and wrote in her journal resting on the podium.

"Just think, in some future book of short fiction, a story that captured me here tonight will appear."

Lexi answered more questions about her writing habits, why certain characters did certain things, and many of the same questions writers attending author talks ask. There were several questions about the *Cally Summer Adventures* series, including, "Where is Cally going next year?"

"Cally always follows Rob Curry's *Don't Be a Tourist In* guidebooks. So just follow Rob, because Cally does." Lexi grinned playfully. She had charmed the entire crowd of 5,000 in the Royal Albert Hall.

Then she read a question out loud that caught her off-guard.

"How have you been doing since your husband died? Are you dating anyone? If not, can I take you out?"

The audience laughed with some caution, as it was clear Lexi was struck with emotion.

Her face puffed up red and eyes filled with tears. She cleared her throat.

"Oh boy. I didn't expect that. This has been such an emotional night with everything going on..." Her voice trailed off. She sipped water from the glass on the podium.

Someone shouted, "We love you Lexi!" The audience applauded encouragement.

Lexi stood at the podium, tears falling, while she shuffled the cards.

Jarius stepped out of the shadows of the side stage, just enough so Lexi could see him if she wanted.

Paddy wanted to jump on the stage and hug her. He wanted to protect her, a feeling he only remembered having when he saw his first child fall out of a swing, hurting herself.

Lexi shook off her vulnerability.

"I really need to look at these cards better before I read them out loud." She laughed gently.

"Well, first, thank you for asking about my husband, Steve. It's been three years since he died. I'm not dating any one person, yet."

She paused and glanced at Paddy.

Panic struck J. *Oh god, no Lexi—don't go there.*

She didn't.

"And thanks for the offer to take me out." She held the card up. "I notice you have given me your contact information."

The mood lifted in the hall. Everything was back to being a pleasant evening.

"This is the time in the evening when my closest friend, business manager and sometimes caretaker, Jarius Harjo, comes out and helps me select the song we play at the conclusion of the evening."

There were more than a few in the audience who applauded while the tall, lanky Indigenous American with long black hair walked on the stage and stood with Lexi at the podium.

"I see some of you know about this tradition. For those of you who don't know, we play a song after I leave the stage. The song specifically refers to someone in the audience, and you are to try and figure out who. The song can be as obvious as one performed by an artist who is in attendance, but usually I try and make it much, much more obscure. For example, I might be referring to the adult child of the lyricist of a song that was in the closing credits of a popular film. I won't make it easy for you."

Lexi was back to being her playful self.

"So, J, what are you thinking tonight?"

J playfully scrolled back and forth on his iPhone pointing out different songs to Lexi who pretended disgust and shock at certain songs. The audience roared appreciation. J's long black hair shimmered in the lights. He was grinning at his best friend.

They hugged.

"I love this guy."

J whispered, "This is always so embarrassing."

Lexi continued, "J, this is the song I'm thinking about for tonight."

J knew why she selected the song, smiled and shook his head at her moxie.

"And you know why I've selected it."

"Yes, I do."

"Okay?"

"Okay."

J waved and walked back offstage to applause.

"I'm probably not supposedly to tell you this." Lexi paused and looked around teasingly. "But I'm going to anyway. J and I are writing a book together."

More applause.

"J is a terrific writer, and we spend much of our lives together on planes and in hotels, so it came about naturally to start talking about characters and then stories. Maybe next year, we will return and do an appearance together."

The crowd was giddy with excitement and continued to be far louder and expressive than she expected from Brits, especially ones at a black-tie event with Royalty.

"Well, as much as I don't want the evening to end, it must."

The audience groaned.

Lexi became very still, and the room quieted.

"We will always have this very special night together. It wasn't just the announcement about the success of my book and the TV series that has made this night unique—it was you. I could feel your warmth, and, yes, love." She glanced at Paddy.

"I want to read one more poem for you. Then, remember to stay and try and figure out who I'm thinking about from the song we will play for you."

> *Created from*
> *the ethers of my*
> *dreams*
> *re-arranged*
> *molecules-*
> *the star dust*
> *of the universe-*
>
> *you here*
> *now*
> *with me*
>
> *afraid to touch*
> *and make you*
> *mortal.*

"Thank you. Goodnight."

Everyone was on their feet wilding applauding, shouting, "We love you, Lexi!"

Lexi stood centerstage, absorbing the energy. She took her time and deliberately looked at as many people as possible, bowing slightly in thanks. She looked directly at Paddy. Paddy put his hands together in Namaste and bowed to her without even thinking about it.

His date, Penny, chatted with other celebrities sitting nearby. Woody and Ann whispered to each other, but Paddy was waiting for the song.

Lexi walked offstage. The house lights flickered the signal that the song was beginning.

Several people were "shushing" others in the audience to hear the music.

Paddy stepped into the aisle, away from his mates, to hear better.

The music started. Paddy knew at the first chord what it was. Tears filled his eyes and his body flushed with heat.

Woody looked at Paddy, "The Flamingos."

Paddy nodded yes.

Woody chuckled, his voice raspy from too many previous years of smoking, "'I Only Have Eyes for You,' huh?"

The longtime friends smiled.

Woody put his arm around Paddy, "You lucky bastard."

Backstage, Lexi and J changed back into their jeans and T-shirts. They stayed in the dressing room long enough for much of the audience to disburse. When they emerged back into the hall, a few dedicated fans lingered around the side door. Lexi signed autographs and posed for photos. J kept close by and nudged her through the crowd by holding her elbow.

Outside, Lexi pulled on her hoodie. It wasn't that chilly, but she wanted to calm down. She was over-stimulated by everything and had learned wrapping herself in a blanket or pulling a hoodie over her head would calm her.

They were able to walk the London streets unrecognized since they were both in jeans and carrying small backpacks. They looked like tourists, which they were, in a way.

"Lexi! Lexi Maxwell, over here!"

A woman at an outdoor restaurant patio was standing and waving and yelling loudly, seemingly more for others at the restaurant to notice her rather than to attract Lexi.

Lexi noticed Paddy immediately. The woman was his date, Penny, calling Lexi over to sit with them and Woody and his wife.

Lexi and J walked over to the patio, but stayed outside the iron fence.

"Come join us." Penny was still standing and now everyone on the patio was watching. Someone said, "Thank you, Ms. Maxwell, for a lovely evening."

"Thank you." Lexi nodded.

Paddy stood up from the table, leaned over the patio fencing, kissed Lexi on the cheeks then hugged her, holding her for an extra second.

"Yes, Lexi, that was an amazing evening. I'm so—" Paddy stopped himself. He had almost said "I'm so proud of you," but that would mean he had some kind of attachment with her.

Paddy and J hugged like long-time mates.

Penny was motioning to the waiter to bring extra chairs.

"Oh no, no," Lexi protested. "That's very kind, but I'm exhausted."

J stepped in. "Lexi's had a long day. She autographed books all afternoon before going to the event."

Paddy said, "That's a lot of work before an intense night."

Woody spoke, "Lexi, you're going to need more handlers pretty soon."

"Well, J does a pretty good job." Lexi put her arm around him. "You're always my protector, J."

Paddy was still standing very close to Lexi, holding her arm like he would if it were her hand. Steve was the only other person in her life who ever held her arm as easily as Paddy was now. Neither man probably knew how much it meant to her.

Penny insisted, "You can at least stay for a drink. Let's get some champagne and toast." Again, Paddy's date was speaking more to the patrons on the patio so that they would notice that she was not only with two of the biggest rockers, Paddy May and Woody Taylor, but now with the famous author some had just seen at the Royal Albert Hall.

"No. Thank you, again. I have to go before I fall over."

Paddy leaned closer to her. "Are you walking home?"

Lexi nodded.

"I know you don't want me to get a car for you."

"No. I want to walk. After all..." Lexi looked up at the harvest moon—the same moon that, just the night before, had shone down while she danced and sang for him.

"Okay." Paddy hugged her, kissed her again on the cheek and whispered, "I'll call tomorrow, okay?"

Lexi nodded yes. "I'm sorry I can't stay with you all, but thank you anyway."

Woody gave Lexi a knowing wink, and his wife, Ann, said, "I look forward to spending time together soon."

Lexi noticed that only Penny and Ann had glasses of wine. Paddy and Woody had bottles of Pellegrino sitting on the table between them.J put his arm around Lexi as they walked off, giving her a loving squeeze.

As Paddy sat back down, Penny said, "Wow, did you see that squeeze her assistant gave her? I bet they're doing it."

Paddy sighed.

Ann said, "Oh, I don't think so," as she sipped her wine and smiled as a person does when they know a secret.

What Lexi didn't know was that her hugs and kisses with Paddy were all caught in the photographs Samantha Peters was taking from across the street.

Ever observant, Samantha realized that the woman standing at the patio was the same woman in her photos of Paddy May the day before. It couldn't be coincidence. The mystery woman and Paddy May knew each other. The woman was a mystery to Samantha because she hadn't attended the Royal gala and didn't read Lexi's books.

"Well, Paddy May, looks like you have someone new."

CHAPTER 13

Lexi and J walked back in silence. No one else recognized her, and they both knew they needed the quiet to re-charge after the extraordinary evening.

When they made it back to their place, she called her son. He was in New York, five hours behind London time, and she knew he would want to know about her biggest event to date in her literary career.

"We have to celebrate, Mom!"

"We will. I'm tired and need to go to bed soon. Let's make a plan to get together within a week."

She made it a point to ask him about his classes, his girlfriend, and the latest news that interested him. After a couple minutes, they hung up with promises to connect again soon.

Lexi and J showered in their own rooms, then rejoined in the den of their leased house, sitting in their pj's, drinking milk.

"Cheers." J lifted his glass.

"Cheers."

"Better than champagne."

"Much. Plus, I'll sleep much better with milk than alcohol."

"I noticed Paddy wasn't drinking."

"I noticed that, too."

"Woody's been very public for several years about his sobriety. I wonder if it's not an accident that Paddy's with him tonight."

"Paddy didn't drink yesterday even though the waiter brought him a drink." Lexi flopped back on the couch. "Was that just yesterday!"

"Yep."

"What happens now, J?"

"What, with you and Paddy? Or you and the success of this evening, or your number-one selling book or your TV series renewed for another season?"

"All of it."

"Our phones are on fire with texts from your publisher, media, friends. We're going to have to sort through it all, but not tonight."

J finished his milk, picked up her empty glass and went to the kitchen to rinse them in the sink.

"Not tonight."

A couple minutes later, J stood at the bottom of the stairs. "You staying up?" he asked.

"A little bit. I need to write."

He came back, kissed her on the forehead. "I love you, my friend."

"I love you."

CHAPTER 14

Penny had been in a party mood the rest of the evening on the patio. Woody and Ann clearly understood that Paddy wanted to be with Lexi. Woody had told his wife about Paddy's day with the author and how it was the trigger for him wanting to stop drinking.

"I don't understand why you're not drinking, Paddy," Penny complained. "It's a party night. I understand Woody not drinking, but you—you're always the biggest drinker wherever we go!"

Paddy winced. "My drinking days may be over, Penny."

Penny laughed and waved her hand dismissively. "What? No way. Not Paddy May."

Woody knew not to speak. This was Paddy's to learn to handle.

Ann said, "I can assure you, Penny, that sometimes a non-drinking man is more fun than a drunk. They can last all night in many ways." Ann winked and kissed Woody.

"Well, I can't imagine Paddy without a drink or a bottle in his hand."

Shortly after the meal, Paddy said, "I didn't sleep last night and am starting to feel it. Do you mind if I call it a night?"

Woody and Ann agreed, but Penny was obviously disappointed.

"But I'm all dressed up."

"It's almost midnight, Penny."

"That's early."

"I'm sorry."

The four sat in awkward silence, then Penny saw some friends inside at the bar. It was a famous actor and his entourage of models, press friends and hangers-on.

Penny waved, and the actor motioned them over.

"Come on, Paddy."

"Penny, would it be horrible of me to just let you go have your fun tonight without me?" Paddy pulled several bills out of his wallet to give her. "I know this isn't very gentlemanly of me, but..."

Penny took the money, kissed Paddy on the cheek, then looked at Ann and said, "I guess tonight's not one of those late nights with a sober man, huh?"

Paddy watched Penny prance to the bar, saying something that caused the group to turn and look at Paddy. He waved and lifted his bubbly water in salute.

"I like Penny, in many ways," he said to Woody and Ann. "I'm guessing, though, that she's not going to say 'yes' the next time I ask her out."

Woody stood up. "I don't think she's who you really want to ask out anyway."

The three longtime friends walked out of the restaurant, Samantha Peters clicking every frame of Paddy leaving Penny behind at the bar.

Paddy decided to walk home.

"You sure, mate? We can share a cab."

"No. I want to walk."

"Under this glorious moon where I'm guessing someone sang 'I Only Have Eyes for You' last night," said Ann.

"Oh, you figured that out."

Ann kissed Paddy goodnight. "Call or come by, Paddy. Any time. We are here for you."

"Thanks."

Paddy started singing the song as he walked. His security team discretely nearby.

My love must be some kind of blind love

I only have eyes for you

At home, Paddy and his cats went into his studio where he recorded several tracks and wrote lyrics to the beginning of a love song. It had been a long time since he wrote both the music and lyrics of a song. He usually just let the Crashers' lead singer, Eric, sort out the words while Paddy crafted the melody and arranged the music.

Not tonight. Tonight, Paddy May felt like the young boy who played full songs for his uncle for the first time when he was just eight years old. His uncle had immediately said, "Paddy May, you're a master musician, and the world needs to know it."

Paddy fell asleep on the couch in his home studio with his guitar and two cats beside him.

CHAPTER 15

Lexi woke up mid-orgasm. The sensation rolled deeper and deeper inside her, and she broke into a sweat. It had been a while since that had happened.

When over, she stroked herself to come again. It wasn't as intense as the first, but still satisfying.

She realized she'd been dreaming about Paddy. She'd never dreamed someone to orgasm since she'd been with Steve.

"I can't even be unfaithful to Steve in my dreams," she'd written in her journal once.

Yet now she'd had a dream orgasm that wasn't with Steve.

She wondered if it was Steve who had given her permission to dream and imagine how Paddy would feel inside her.

She rolled over and started writing in her journal as the sun lit her room with another beautiful day.

Lexi delayed looking at her texts. She knew there'd be dozens and she was going to have to go to work on the public side of her business.

Her reverie was broken when she wondered if Penny had spent the night with Paddy.

Ugh. It's like being in high school again. I don't need this.

She dressed and resisted texting Paddy.

The door to J's bedroom was open. His bed was made, which meant he was already awake and out on his morning run. She went downstairs, made coffee and eggs and popped open her laptop to check various websites while she ate.

She pretended she wasn't, but she was checking the London press to see if there were any reviews of her evening. There were several. She was a "simple joy," "a writer of precise words, and a speaker of great charm," and "our favorite Texan."

J walked in just as she was finishing the last review.

"How was your run?" she asked.

"Good. How are the reviews?"

"What reviews?"

"Yeah, right." J kissed her on the top of her head and looked at the computer screen. "The reviews are great. You've charmed them."

J sat in the chair across the table and put his feet on the chair beside him, trying to cool off. "What do you want to do today before your bookstore appearance?"

"I want to swim."

While Lexi's parents had their flaws, they raised Lexi to be "just like the other kids" rather than as "Lexi the one-handed." They enrolled their only child in swim lessons when the other neighbors enrolled their children. She took dance lessons with the girl next door and even made the varsity tennis team in high school.

The only downside to swimming and tennis was that the left side of her body became much more muscular than the right side. She tried working out with weights on her right side to "even out" her body. No one really noticed, but she could feel the difference. Her left side was slightly heavier, and the more developed muscles in her back made her slightly lopsided when leaning against a straight-back chair or laying on her back.

She never let it stop her, though.

The Camden Swiss Cottage Sports Center had the Olympic-sized pool she enjoyed most. The lanes were wide enough if you needed to share one, but Lexi arrived at a perfect time with few swimmers and open lanes.

For her, swimming was less about exercise and more about meditation. She'd always been a swimmer, but never competitively. After Steve's death, she started swimming four times a week and always carried her swimsuit, googles and swim cap when traveling.

The first few moments in the cool water took her breath away. She glanced at the clock—she swam for time, not speed—and started her laps. She focused on stretching out across the water and felt the rhythm of her hand and arm and feet moving in balance. She liked feeling how her hand sliced into the water and then the weight against her arms as she pulled them through.

Once the cadence of her kick and arm motion was established, she focused on the precision turn of her head to breathe. She turned her head right on the fourth stroke to breathe. Now and then, she'd take more strokes before breathing, but then realized it affected her cadence and therefore broke the Zen-like feeling. Finally, she noticed the very gentle roll of her body, side-to-side, now that her arms, her legs and her breathing were all in-sync.

A blissful swim was when the water seemed thicker and heavier, but not harder. The pores in her skin opened, and she imagined she was the water. The feeling of oneness would evaporate if she noticed it too much, so she would quickly note the feeling, then return to her "stroke-stroke-stroke-stroke-breathe" pattern.

She swam her usual hour. She rarely had to look at the clock to know when to stop. She was hoping there was a steam sauna, but had to settle for a hot tub in the spa area.

I need to schedule this every day. Too much is changing.

She was still in a quasi-meditative state on her walk back to "the servants' house" as she and J had started calling the place where they were staying. Clearly that was what their rental cottage behind the manor house once had been.

Lexi was absorbed in looking at the leaves in the trees and the changing fall colors. Now and then, she stopped to snap a photo of a tree trunk with beautifully gnarled bark and wondered out loud, "How old are you?" She greeted the squirrels and stopped to listen to the birds.

Lexi laughed to herself, remembering how Jack once said during one of their walks together, "Mom, you realize you talk to the animals all the time, right? People probably think you're a little crazy."

Jack didn't mind it about his mother. In fact, he was proud of her, and they texted every day about something or another and nothing in particular.

She realized she was walking up to Barbara's Coffee and Tea Shoppe and decided to stop for a coffee and something to eat and write in her journal.

Am I really hoping Paddy is here?

"You just missed him," Barbara greeted her as she entered.

"Am I that obvious?"

"You both are."

The women laughed.

Barbara continued, "And I hope it works out. This can be your secret rendezvous site. I'll even stay after hours for you two."

"We aren't quite there yet, Barb."

"I know, but Penny's not really his girlfriend as far as I can tell. She's his date-friend, probably with benefits truthfully."

"Okay. I don't want to know any more. Can I have a coffee and a yogurt parfait and write for a while?"

"Yes, please, on the house."

"No."

"I insist. It'll make me feel like I'm supporting the arts."

Lexi texted J who reminded her she needed to be ready to walk over to the bookstore by 4:30. It wasn't yet noon.

She texted: *I'll be back in an hour or so. Gonna take a nap today.*

Lexi had been working on a collection of short stories, but she felt a tug from a different thread now. She was feeling sexual and wanted to write about sexual love. She wanted to write about... Steve? Again? Or her imaginations about Paddy? She wasn't sure. What she did know was that this would be dramatically different from anything she'd ever written before. Also, very different from her wholesome, maybe even boring, image.

What's the different between romance, erotica and porn? she wondered.

She started writing but didn't know where it was heading.

She'd been buried in her journal for more than an hour when she glanced at her phone. Paddy had texted, *Is this a good time to talk?*

That was forty-five minutes ago.

So sorry, Paddy. I've been writing and didn't see your text. I can talk now.

The resulting pause felt like forever to Lexi. She stared at her phone, waiting for the telltale three bubbles that he was in the midst of a reply. Then the phone rang.

Her heart leapt as she answered. "Hey, sorry about that."

Paddy chuckled. "No need to apologize to me about being in the middle of creating and not paying attention to your phone. I saw you are appearing this evening at that indie bookstore. Would it be okay if I came? I'd slip in the back a few minutes after you start so no one sees me."

Lexi's heart raced. Once again, she felt like a teenager with her first crush.

"I'd like that, I think."

"I don't have to."

"No, I'd like to see you. This appearance tonight is going to be more intimate and having you there will make it more so. "

"Let's not then."

"No. Paddy, the answer is yes. Let's you, J, and I have dinner afterwards. I want you to know Jarius."

"And he needs to know me. Where are you, by the way?"

"I'm at Barbara's. She said I just missed you by minutes when I came here. I went swimming this morning."

"Really. Where?"

"Camden Swiss Cottage Center."

"That's a sports center."

"Have you been there?"

Paddy laughed. "No, no, I don't go to a gym. You'll be able to tell that when..." He trailed off.

They were silent. Each knowing what was not said: "When you see me naked."

Paddy cleared his throat. "Okay. What time will you start this evening, Lexi?"

"Um, let me check the schedule." She paused, checking her calendar. "Six-thirty."

"I'll be there just after six then, after the introductions and all. You sure it won't bother you?"

"Yes, I'm sure."

Neither wanted to end the call.

"Tonight."

"Tonight."

CHAPTER 16

Paddy's driver, Graham, drove him to the bookstore, dropping him off two blocks away so as to not attract attention in his Bentley.

"What time shall I return, Paddy?"

"Oh, I may be walking again tonight."

Graham grinned at Paddy in the rearview mirror. "Is this part of a new health plan, Paddy—all your walking lately?"

"It's more of a literary pursuit, Graham."

The men laughed as Paddy stepped on the sidewalk, pulled his jacket tighter and walked to a very public, well-attended, but small bookstore event with Lexi Maxwell.

As hoped, she was already at the dais speaking. The rows of chairs were filled with mostly women of all ages, and a good number of men, too.

A store clerk recognized Paddy and followed him in with a chair, since every other seat was already taken. Paddy nodded his thanks and sat behind the last row.

Lexi didn't miss a verbal beat when he arrived, but her heart did jump. She loved the feeling that he was there just for her. A second night when he came just for her.

Paddy hadn't taken his eyes off her since he walked in the room, so he wasn't aware that J was standing in the back corner watching Lexi—and now, also watching Paddy.

J noticed that Paddy May didn't appear drunk or high or anything other than a refined English gentleman interested in this writer.

Lexi thought Paddy was especially gorgeous tonight. He wore jeans with a striped shirt and blue jacket, along with his trademark thin scarf. His curls draped near his shoulders.

Paddy lifted his eyebrows in a brief "hello" when their eyes met.

The crowd adored Lexi, and she was having more and more fun as the ninety-minute session passed. Many university students in the audience wanted to talk about the craft of writing and how she chose her topics.

Paddy noticed that everyone seemed to have a copy of her current book.

"Well, the time has zoomed by, and I must end our time together."

"Noooooo," the entire room protested.

"Yes, it's true. I must. But I'm sure most of you know by now that my friend and assistant, Jarius Harjo and I have a tradition of playing a song when I leave that represents someone in this room, and you will want to stay and figure it out. So, thank you so much for supporting my writing, the TV series and being here tonight. It has been my delight."

Lexi gathered her notes and stepped off the stage, walking along the outer wall of the room. Paddy thought how lucky she was to be able to walk among her fans without someone lunging at her. She didn't even need to have security.

Paddy suddenly felt paralyzed as he realized the audience was turning their heads to watch Lexi, and some might recognize him. So he stood and quickly walked out before Lexi was halfway down the aisle. As he did, he heard the "mystery song" play. It was a new artist, the chorus a yearning "and I want you and I want you such it's an obsession."

Paddy wanted it to be about him.

The store manager was waiting for Lexi outside the room and recognized Paddy.

"Mr. May. What an honor to have you here."

"Thank you. And thank you for having my favorite author here. I've been trying to see her for years, but have always been on the road when she's in town."

Lexi and J came out, shook hands with the manager, hurried to leave the store, but not so fast as to be rude. Paddy walked with them, and it was clear to anyone that he was with Lexi and J.

Outside Paddy and Lexi hugged, but J said, "We need to get away from here unless you both want to sign autographs and pose for pics all night."

Paddy said, "I know a place around the corner."

It was a private club. A very private and very exclusive and very traditional English club with a stately Georgian architecture front. A doorman in a dark suit stood guard, assuring that only members approached the door.

The host inside gave the tiniest pause when Paddy entered with his two friends, all wearing jeans, but he immediately recognized Paddy and smoothed his face into a smile.

"Mr. May, so good to see you."

"Giles, good evening. I'm sorry I didn't make reservations, and we are underdressed."

"Oh, no worries, Mr. May, it's no trouble at all."

Lexi and J both noticed Giles seemed to lean in close to Paddy when shaking his hand, as if to sniff for alcohol. They both wondered if Paddy had ever made a drunken scene here. The reality of his alcoholism reminded Lexi of something she didn't want to admit.

"Giles, this is Ms. Lexi Maxwell, the acclaimed author, and her friend Mr. Jarius Harjo. Ms. Maxwell was..."

"The featured presenter at the Royal Charity Gala last night," finished Giles as he shook her hand and bowed slightly. "We are honored to have you join us this evening. And good that you can join as well, Mr. Harjo."

Giles led the trio into the dining room, where several club members in suits and fine dresses sat at tables covered in white linen tablecloths. Lexi noticed a handful of patrons turned and looked at the casually dressed trio. She could tell some recognized Paddy, and more than a few did a double-take at her arm. She knew it wasn't every day that people saw a one-handed person, but Lexi didn't feel patient about the stares tonight.

Paddy said, "Giles, I wonder if it would be possible for us to have dinner in a less formal area. It's a lovely setting in here, but it might be better if we sit where we are more appropriately dressed."

Giles nodded. "Mr. May, I believe I have the perfect table for you and your friends in the garden patio room."

"That sounds perfect." Paddy turned to Lexi and J. "Is that okay?"

Lexi said, "Much better, actually. Thank you, Mr. Giles, for understanding."

J whispered to Lexi as they walked down the hall, "Mr. Giles?"

"I didn't know what to say. Is it his first or last name?"

Just as on the day Lexi first met Paddy—was it only two days ago? —the waiter brought Paddy a cocktail without him needing to order. Again, Paddy declined, saying he wasn't drinking. He motioned to Lexi and J. "Please feel free to drink whatever you'd like."

Lexi said, "I'm fine with water."

"Still or sparkling, ma'am?"

"Still please."

J ordered sparkling water, and Paddy asked for the same.

"You two don't have to abstain just because I am."

"Lexi and I don't drink."

Paddy looked surprised. "Have you ever?"

"I did at college. Then I decided to do one of those 'dry Januarys' and really struggled to not drink for thirty-one days. I couldn't do it. So I tried to do a 'dry February.' It's the shortest month, and I thought, *I can do this month, surely*. Only, I couldn't. I didn't fail as many days as January, but I failed. It took months, but I finally did not drink in July."

"How'd you stop, if it's not too personal to share."

"No, it's fine. Lexi told me about AA. She kept it real low key, just told me she knew about it because she's gone to AL-ANON because of her parents. I was pissed at first. Afterall, I wasn't a falling-down, loser-old-man-drunk. I was excelling at my university. I was young. Good-looking."

Everyone laughed as J lifted his chin up as if posing for photos.

"But I kept thinking about drinking, and so I found a group I liked and have stayed involved ever since."

"Hmm." Paddy was listening closely, leaning in and watching J. Lexi was watching Paddy just as closely.

J continued, "I also turned to my native elder community back home in Tulsa. They surrounded me with attention and wisdom lessons."

"Wisdom lessons?"

"I won't—can't—go into too much detail because it is sacred to my people, but it involved traditional sweat lodges, vision quests, many of the things you think of stereotypically, but it is experienced with so much more intensity and meaning."

J paused a long time. Paddy knew to be quiet.

"It was forgiveness, compassion and love from my community, and Lexi and Steve, that helped me stay sober. They believed in me more than I believed in me and that carried me until I could hold myself."

Paddy nodded, then sat back in his chair.

"Maybe you can find your support group that's unique to you and really understands what you're facing in your life specifically."

"I think I have, Jarius. I've been going over to Woody Taylor's."

"That sounds perfect."

The waiter, who had been waiting and watching for a break in the closeness of the trio, came over.

"May I tell you about the chef's specials this evening?"

The communion of the group was lifted, but not broken. After ordering, Paddy glanced around the atrium to be sure no one was close.

"I haven't had a drink since I met you, Lexi. I know that's barely over forty-eight hours, but it's monumental for me. I went home after our first day together and, without thinking, took a gulp of bourbon, and it felt like fire and needles in my throat. It hurt so bad."

Paddy looked at Lexi with a mix of sadness and tenderness, hoping for acceptance.

"I stood there at my bar and knew, in that instant, there was an energy, a spirit, something, *something* telling me I was done with drinking. It was over."

Paddy folded his hands on the table. Lexi watched as he slowly laced his fingers in and out of each other. She had seen him do this when he was thinking deeply about something.

"I poured the alcohol out of all the bottles in my house and did that until dawn. There were literally hundreds of empty bottles when I was done."

Paddy let out a long, low sigh.

Salads were served.

J asked, "How did you feel after that?"

"Free, lightheaded, and then scared. I felt fear. About what, I'm not sure, but I went back to Woody's. He lives just around the corner. You know, Woody is very public about his sobriety. His whole band is sober now, in fact. He's told me for years that he'd be there for me. And he was. He and Ann. Wow, I'm sorry, I didn't mean to get so heavy. Let's talk about something light and easy."

"No, this is fine, Paddy. As you know by now, I usually dive right in on conversations and so does J."

"Well, this is new to me. And a lot this I'm still unsure of and it's embarrassing."

J spoke immediately: "Paddy, don't ever be embarrassed about anything with us."

Lexi watched Paddy and J hold eye contact and then each glanced away, as most men do who don't know what to do with genuine, emotional connection.

"One day at a time."

"One day at a time."

The three talked about how J and Lexi met through J's aunt, who was a recognized poet in the States. After J finished high school, he was accepted into a writing program at a university in Dallas, but was put on a waitlist for a dorm room and asked if he could live with Lexi and Steve. Then Steve died.

Lexi wanted to be physically close to her son who had just started his prep school in New York, so she moved to a New York apartment, and Jarius stayed in her house in Dallas for a while.

Lexi poured her grief into writing and driving to various hockey rinks to watch her son. Being in New York City put her closer to her publisher and the literary community.

Eventually, J enrolled in the MFA program at Columbia and moved into the second bedroom of Lexi's brownstone on West 83rd.

Lexi and J skipped the part where, the year just prior, there was one snowy evening after they had been walking through Central Park when the "good night buddy" hug on the second floor landing outside their bedrooms lingered.

They held each other. J hardened and Lexi let her hand follow its desire to caress his long, straight black hair. They kissed slowly and more gently than passionately.

They held each other again, breathing in unison.

Finally, Lexi said, "J, we clearly both want to make love, but do we want to change our relationship? Or are we okay with just acknowledging this moment and not being actual lovers?"

"We would be the best lovers the other could ever have, Lexi."

"I think that's true."

Still holding each other, they stepped back to look at one another.

"Can we have one night?"

J said it first, but Lexi was thinking it.

"I think we can."

And they did. They had one night that lasted until mid-morning and then they fell asleep until the afternoon. We they woke, they hugged and said, "Thank you." J went to his room to shower, and Lexi did the same in her room. They met downstairs, made dinner together and continued living together as closer, deeper spiritual friends, but not lovers.

Paddy could tell by how J and Lexi glanced at each other when they reached the part about living in New York City that there was something extra between them.

Paddy asked, "Do you still have the place in New York?"

"Yes." J and Lexi answered at the same time. J motioned to Lexi to continue.

"Yes. I still stay close enough to my son's school to go to his hockey games and special occasions. In fact, we're going back at the end of next week."

"What?" Paddy said so loudly that other club members briefly looked over at their table.

Paddy lowered his voice. "What? Why?"

J said, "Well, for one thing, our lease is up at our place here."

"I'll pay for it." Paddy had stopped eating and was leaning forward with a panicked look.

Lexi stepped in. "No, Paddy, thank you. It's not the money."

"Please."

"It's just that it's time for me to see my son. I've been away about a month now on this book tour, and my rule is that I don't let five weeks pass without seeing him."

J could feel Paddy's fear, and it reminded him of his own fear when he'd stopped drinking.

"Paddy, I think I understand your concern. You've started this new path and may feel like you're flying naked."

Lexi put her hand on top of Paddy's and rubbed her thumb back and forth across the back of his hand to soothe him.

"No. Yeah, yeah, I'm being slammed with emotions. Well, this is a bit much." Paddy returned to being more composed and less raw in his feelings. His "public persona" was creeping back in.

J said, "You know, I don't have to be back in New York any time soon. I've been writing short fiction set here in London and could stay here longer to soak in the details I need for my story. I'm not the same as Lexi staying here, but I know what the early days of sobriety are like."

The trio was silent.

"Thank you. I'd like that very much, J. I have a place on the Thames where you can stay."

"No. I can find a place."

"Please. I'd feel better knowing you're out there. And it's beautiful. I find it very inspiring."

"Why aren't you out there then?"

"Well, the acoustics aren't as good at my little studio there. I've been inspired lately and have been laying down several tracks, and I have a complete studio in town."

"Excuse me, Mr. May." Giles, the Club Director was at their table. "I regret to inform you, sir, that your fans seemed to have discovered you are here. Would you like us to call your team to help you and your guests leave discreetly?"

Paddy collapsed back in his chair and let out a huge sigh of resignation.

"I'm sorry to report this, sir."

"Giles, it's not your fault. How many?"

"There's probably two, three dozen. Maybe more."

"How did they find me?"

"It's hard to be a star, sir." Giles was trying to lighten the mood.

"Yes, it is sometimes. Thank you, Giles. Yes. Do you mind contacting Graham? You have his number, right?"

"Yes."

"Yes. Of course you do."

Giles and Paddy looked at one another, each recalling the many times when Paddy was stumbling drunk, and Giles would arrange for him to exit through the kitchen door to minimize his exposure and embarrassment.

Paddy stopped Giles from leaving the table.

"Giles, I want to thank you."

"Of course, Mr. May, my pleasure."

"No, Giles, I mean for all the times, and all the ways, you have had to help me. I've not always been on my best behavior, and I— well, I'm sorry for how that's been for you all these years."

Lexi and G both recognized that Paddy's apology to Giles was one of the steps in recovery from addiction. J was encouraged at Paddy's action, but wondered if Paddy knew this step instinctively or if Woody had explained it to him. Either way, J was more and more impressed with how different Paddy was than he expected.

"Mr. May, it is always my pleasure to see you. *Truly.*"

"Giles, I changed my mind. I'll go out the front."

"As you wish."

Paddy turned to Lexi and J.

"What would you like to do? Going out the front means I'll at least have to stop and wave, and sign and pose. It also means you'll be all over social media. Are you ready for that kind of attention?"

Lexi responded quickly, "I think we will just wait until you're gone and then we'll leave as if we were here on our own or something. I hate doing it this way, but I'd like our friendship..."

Paddy nodded understandingly. "To brew a little more. Like tea."

"Like tea."

"We can talk tomorrow."

Lexi observed that Paddy was taking multiple deep breaths. He seemed unsettled.

He looked at Lexi and J. "I just realized I've never left this club sober. And I've rarely faced my fans that way, either."

They knew he was scared.

"Do you want to go out back?" Lexi asked.

"No. That doesn't feel right to the people who, frankly, are why I'm successful."

J said, "You need to take care of yourself right now, Paddy. Do you want me to go out with you?"

"We can both go with you, Paddy." Lexi didn't really want the attention, knowing it meant she'd become sucked into the Paddy May publicity vortex, but she could see her new friend—her new love— was struggling.

J had an idea.

"Paddy, give me your phone. Let me take a photo of you and Lexi. That way you have something nice to look at when you get in your car."

"I'd like that."

Paddy and Lexi put their arms around one another and snuggled close. J took several pics, then jumped in for a couple of selfies of the three of them.

"There you go, Paddy. Remember, you can call me any time." J put his number in Paddy's contacts.

Paddy tried to say thank you, but his voice was caught with such emotion that he couldn't speak.

After hugs, Paddy stepped outside the club. The members inside could hear the loud shout as fans pushed to try and touch their idol. The club had been through this before and had set out stanchions with red velvet ropes and security guards to hold back the nearly forty fans gathered.

Paddy turned on his signature smile, posed for photos and signed autographs for about ten minutes, then got inside his Bentley and Graham drove him home.

Lexi and J watched the spectacle from the upper floor front windows. Giles brought them waters and let them know when the crowd left.

"Are you sure I can't have our private car take you home?" he offered.

"No Giles. Thank you. We are a little obsessed with walking as much as possible. And it's another gorgeous night."

Lexi and J stepped outside, relieved to see the crowd of fans had dispersed.

They didn't know that Samantha Peters was hiding in the shadows, waiting to take photos of them.

"Gotcha," she said to herself. "Now I know you're Paddy's new girl. Or is it the guy?"

Inside the Bentley, Paddy apologized to Graham for ruining his night. "I hate taking you away from your family, Graham."

"It's okay, Paddy. It's part of my job."

"Yes, but, still, I've pulled you away from them so many times, and you have..." Paddy's voiced cracked with emotion again. He continued, "Well, thank you, Graham."

"Paddy, I—my family and I—are grateful to be part of your life." Graham smiled at him in the rear-view mirror. "And it's never boring!"

The two men laughed.

Paddy's home was less than ten minutes away, but Graham drove for more than twenty minutes in the direction that would make any fans following them think they were going to the Thames House.

Paddy was looking at the photos of him and Lexi. Then him, Lexi and J. He enlarged the photo of J and thought, *What a kind, gentle man.*

"Graham, can we go to the Thames House tomorrow and get it ready for guests?"

"Certainly. Shall I ask Elga to join us?"

"Only if it's not her day off. "

"I'll talk with her. What time would you like me to pick you up?"

Paddy paused, thinking. "Graham, you pick the time and I'll be ready."

Graham glanced at Paddy in the rear-view mirror. He hadn't seen this kind of thoughtfulness since the early days with his employer. Graham was hired by Paddy's manager when The

Crashers started, when Paddy was only nineteen. Ten years older than Paddy, Graham was always "like a brother I never knew I wanted," according to Paddy.

Deep down, Paddy was a kind and thoughtful person, which was why Graham stayed with him even as the drinking, drugs and parade of women made it challenging at times to be with him. Paddy was extremely kind to Graham when he married and even more so when they had children. Even in his worse days of addiction, he remembered the birthdays of Graham's family members.

Tonight, Graham caught another glimpse of the Paddy May before the turn, and he was excited—but worried that it wouldn't last.

CHAPTER 17

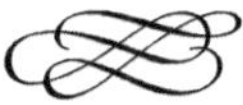

Back at the carriage house, J asked Lexi, "Are you okay if I stay here in London while you go back to New York?"

Lexi shrugged slightly. "I think so. It's funny, I realize you and I are together all the time, so the thought of not being together is weird. And then I think it's weird that I think it's weird."

"I don't have to stay in London."

"You should. The book you're writing is set here, after all. But, hey, what about our book and you being my manager?"

"Well, I'm still writing my parts on our book. And I'll still take care of you." J squeezed Lexi's hand.

"Okay. And what an offer, to stay at the Thames House. I've seen pictures of it."

"Yes. And there's the risk Paddy doesn't stay sober."

"Are you staying partly to be here for him?"

"That's tricky. Part of my sobriety, as you know, is to help others, but they have to help themselves first."

"Do you think Paddy's on the right track?"

"I have no idea. We don't know him, not really, Lexi."

"That's true."

"He seems to have been deeply impacted by meeting you, reaching out to Woody was huge for him, but he's been in an artificial world the last couple of days, right? He's not been in the studio with his band where apparently his lead singer is as bad an addict as he is. He's not been on tour. He's not been on press tours. His world is not conducive to sobriety, you know."

"Well, almost no part of the world, at least our western world, is conducive to sobriety."

"True, but his profession almost takes pride in excess."

"But Woody and his band have managed."

"That's what makes me hopeful for him."

J changed the subject. "Lexi, what about you? Suddenly everything has become about Paddy. What's that all about?"

"Good question." She sighed a long low breath. "Am I in a crush? Am I in love? Am I just wanting a fling? I feel knocked off my mooring, J. My steady, predictable and respectful writer and mom life feels tossed about. And I like it."

"But how far do you take it?"

"Indeed. And I worry about fame. You know, people have noticed me my entire life because I have red hair and one hand, so I'm kind of used to that. Then, having some people, not a lot, notice me because I'm a writer has been different. But my fans are readers. They are polite and give me my space.

"But fame like Paddy's? Yikes, I don't know about that. Like Paddy, I have a distinct reputation. His is the wild rocker, mine is the new-book-a-year-thoughtful-widow-mom-writer. We each are changing, but will we lose our fans in the process? Will I lose any ability to have privacy?"

J squinted at her. "Or your true self?"

"My true self? Maybe. Or maybe it's just my next self. Part of the evolution of living."

CHAPTER 18

Samantha Peters respected the ban from the Crashers mostly because she knew the manager would physically harm her if she tried to approach them.

Truth was, she adored Paddy when he was barely nineteen, and even now, all these years later. She was five years older than him, but even at his young age, he was so much older in many ways. His years as a teenage session musician working with men and women much older than him had made him worldly and educated about life in ways far beyond other men her age.

Plus, he was sensual. Paddy was an artist through and through. He read and wrote poetry, drew and painted, shopped vintage clothing, sometimes buying women's blouses long before it was acceptable for male artists to do so, and he was an attentive lover. He once told her that lovemaking was like playing his guitar, "Sometimes it's soft and gentle, and other times it's hard and a desperate hunger."

Just remembering when Paddy told her that made her long for him.

The most memorable lovemaking she'd ever experienced was with Paddy. It was just before his band's first tour. He was at his

Thames House sitting on the porch, playing acoustic guitar, when she arrived unexpectedly. They'd already had sex in his London flat a few days earlier after they'd met at a party, and he'd joked that he'd take her with him on tour. It was clear they were still attracted to one another, and she was going to make sure she was on tour with The Crashers. She took a chance, brought some wine and a picnic basket dinner, and showed up at his large property just outside central London.

He kept playing as she set up the picnic on the porch and opened the wine. The sun was setting, and it was a beautiful night. She purposely didn't wear a bra and made sure that a tease of her bare breasts could be seen when she leaned over.

Paddy kept playing, but was clearly aroused. She fed him a grape now and then as she finished setting up the plates and food. When she sat down on the blanket she spread her legs just enough so that Paddy could see she had nothing on under her skirt.

That triggered him.

He carefully set his guitar on the table and his fingers stroked her to wetness as he slowly, very slowly, started kissing her. He worked her to multiple orgasms without taking off his clothes. His fingers did things she'd never felt, and his lips were soft as they absorbed her mouth and breasts.

She was completely naked, and he was still dressed.

Finally, after it was clear she was spent, he stood over her and stripped naked. Everything about him was long and lean and hard. He was throbbing and seemed to enjoy delaying his personal satisfaction.

When he finally laid down and entered her, it was at first soft and gentle and then hard and hungry, just the way he had described playing guitar. She had another orgasm.

He stayed inside her and let their physical separation happen naturally.

He did not let her stay the night because he never let women stay there, but he asked her to travel with him the next day, much to the confusion of the band and his manager. The other bandmates were the ones with the steady girls. Paddy enjoyed flings, but never wanted any distractions from his true love: music.

The sex with Samantha at the Thames House was the last time he allowed a fling there. He felt so burned and abused by her after the photos in Spain. The Thames House was his sacred space. It was only after they had their daughter that Paddy let Sofia live with him there.

Now, years later, Sammie was back at her London home, looking through the photos she'd taken of Paddy, Lexi, and J during the last forty-eight hours. She wondered if Paddy would have stayed with her if she hadn't published that photo of him. Part of her knew it was a horrible violation of intimacy. The other part of her knew that's why she was successful, famous, and wealthy.

She pulled up the photos from outside the private club on her large computer screen and enlarged various parts of the trio to study their facial expressions and body language.

"Who are you, one-armed lady? And how in the world is Paddy May with you? You look so...regular. Pretty, but a regular person." For some reason, Sammie hadn't thought to use facial recognition to determine the identity of Paddy's new lady.

"And who are you?" she said as she enlarged photos of J's face.

"You are an indigenous American, that's for sure."

She returned to the photos she took of Paddy leaving the Club and looked carefully at his eyes.

"Paddy May, are you sober? Or at least not stumbling drunk as I'd expected. That's two nights in a row of socializing, and you're not drunk. What is going on here?"

CHAPTER 19

Paddy walked Lexi to Paddington Station so she could catch the express train to Heathrow Airport. The weather was much cooler now, and the day overcast. They were both bundled in coats and hats. Paddy tucked his hair up and had started a beard.

"Lexi, I think a beard might disguise me some now that you're making me walk all over London," he said to her a few days ago. He could grow a full beard in two days if he wanted, but he kept it trimmed, for now.

J had moved into the Thames House, and the three of them had spent Lexi's remaining days in England out there talking, cooking and wondering where this friendship was leading.

Paddy didn't spend the nights there, though. "It's your place now, J, until later, whenever that is." Lexi and Jarius still couldn't understand why Paddy wanted—insisted—that J stay at the Thames House.

Lexi had to pick up the last of her things from the rental in London, and Paddy met her to start the long walk to the train. They stopped at Barbara's shoppe so Lexi could say goodbye. Barbara had noticed that Paddy was no longer hungover in the mornings, and he was also very happy.

No, it's not happy, she thought. *Paddy's deeply satisfied, content, at peace. Oh dear, what happens with Lexi leaving?* Barbara was worried about Paddy's ability to stay sober.

"I'll take care of J," Paddy said as they walked away from Barbara's shoppe. Paddy pulled her carry-on suitcase and wore her backpack.

"He's very resourceful," Lexi said. "But this will be different for him. I don't think he's been out of the States without me. Remember, he's much younger than he seems."

"I remember."

"And let him take care of you, Paddy. This is a careful time for you."

"I know. I will."

"How have you been doing? It's been a while now."

"Yes. Exactly." He brushed the back of her hand with his. "Can you believe this, us?"

"Not long, is it?"

"No, but we've put a lot into it."

They walked in silence and then Paddy said, "The drinking doesn't feel like an issue. I'm still sneaking a puff of cigarettes, though."

"I know."

"The smell still that bad?"

"A little, but I know you're trying and succeeding. You're trying to stop two addictions at once. That's huge, and you're doing it."

"Day by day."

"Day by day."

"Lexi, I don't want to lose this," he motioned to the two of them. "We are off to a strong friendship, but I want the door to be open to something more."

"I do, too."

Paddy looked at her. "You sure?"

"I am. And we need to let it brew."

"Like tea."

"Like tea."

"But not too long, because then the pot gets cold."

Lexi laced her arm in his, leaned in and said, "Well, let's find ways to keep the fire burning at just the right level until we're ready to turn it all the way up."

"I don't really know how to do that, you know. I don't have a lot of experience in normal dating."

"Sofia?"

"We were hot and hotter. Had our two children, then flamed out badly."

They were at Paddington Station. Arched glass ceilings over multiple train tracks. The hushed business of hundreds of commuters, tourists and school children making their way, weaving in and out of one another.

"Paddy, we do this relationship by being crazy honest with each other, just as we've been so far. Call, text when we want, but also allow space or not. Right now, I feel like you are part of my daily life, but we're both about to return to our normal lives—you to the studio, me to my son and to writing daily."

"Let's have a promise like you and your son have. A promise we won't let five weeks pass without seeing each other." Paddy sighed. "And that feels way too long, five weeks."

"Let's start with no more than five and make it sooner if we know we need it."

Paddy had gone as far as he could without clearing security at the track. He put Lexi's backpack on her shoulders and slid the roller to her.

They stood close, their bodies swaying toward one another, that invisible energy pulling them together again.

Paddy leaned down and kissed her slowly, and for a long time. They had never kissed like that before.

Their eyes were full of tears.

"I'm going to write about loving you the whole flight home, Paddy May."

"I have a song that will be ready for you when I see you next."

Lexi had to run to board the Heathrow Express before the doors closed. Paddy watched her the entire way.

So did Sammie Peters.

Paddy wiped his tears as he turned to the exit.

"Damn it." Sammie missed the shot of him crying.

It was raining hard. Passengers were opening umbrellas and pulling coats closer as they left the station. Paddy pulled out his phone to call Graham, then bought an umbrella instead.

He took a selfie of himself as he stepped into the torrential rain and texted it to Lexi. "You'd made me into a walker. Miss you already, Red."

He'd only called her "Red" a couple of times, but she liked it. He loved her long red hair.

Paddy thought about walking through Hyde Park where he and Lexi walked their first day, but decided to take a more direct route home. He glanced over his shoulder, feeling like he was being followed. He wondered if a fan had spotted him. Out of the corner of his eye, he caught the tip of a camera being yanked behind a shrub to avoid detection.

His gut punched him. *It's Sammie.* He knew.

He walked slowly, thinking about whether or not to confront her. Then he realized she probably took photos of him and Lexi at the train station. The kiss. The tears.

"Fuck."

He stepped under the awning of a corner building and lit a cigarette. He tried breathing slowly and deeply to relax, but felt— what? Panic? Anger?

Sammie hadn't seen him duck around the corner, and she walked past, trying to spot him down the sidewalk.

Paddy stepped out, surprising himself. "Here I am."

Sammie stopped but didn't turn around at first. They hadn't

spoken since she was kicked off the tour train when Paddy was just nineteen. Now here he was, a grown man. A wildly accomplished grown man she still dreamed about.

She turned to him, tucking her camera under her trench coat.

"Oh, Paddy. Nice to see—"

"Cut the shit, Sammie."

Paddy was shielded from the hard rain by the awning and wasn't about to make room for Sammie, who was getting wet under her umbrella. Paddy put out his cigarette and looked around for a trash can. Finding none, he rolled out some of the tobacco, then put the stub in his pocket.

Sammie noticed the care he took not to litter.

"Okay," she said. "I'll shoot straight. Who's the girl? You've been with her a lot this past week."

Paddy's anger flashed back to the first time he saw Sammie's photo of him on the train.

"You haven't changed, have you, Sammie? It's been a long, long time and you're still trying to make money by violating my privacy."

"You're a big star, Paddy. You don't have privacy. You know that by now."

Paddy remembered J telling him he needed to have compassion and forgiveness for himself. But now, he realized it also applied to others.

"Hate only bounces back to you," a character in one of Lexi's books said.

Which book was it? he wondered. He'd almost forgotten Sammie was standing there in front of him. He studied the photographer. She was a pretty blond, but he could tell from her slightly muddled skin that she was drinking heavily, and he could smell the cigarette smoke on her clothes. *That's how I've been most of my life too,* thought Paddy as he studied her carefully, causing her to shift uncomfortably in his gaze.

"Good day, Sammie Peters. I wish you a good and decent life."

Paddy walked away, leaving the photographer stunned and disappointed.

Paddy smiled. He, too, was stunned at his remarks and very happy about it.

Several school children wearing their uniforms passed him. They looked about twelve or thirteen. The boys weren't carrying umbrellas and were acting like they weren't trying to walk under the girls' umbrellas to stay dry.

Paddy remembered when he was that age. He carried his umbrella, but it was to protect his ever-present guitar, not his clothes. Some days Paddy forgot his books, but never his guitar.

The Crashers' lead singer, Eric, lived around the corner from his childhood home, and the two would sing songs they were writing. They'd been doing that since Eric's family moved into the neighborhood when the boys were seven.

The headmistress would confiscate Paddy's guitar at the school entrance, but his mother had negotiated—pleaded, really—an agreement for the school to let Paddy play his guitar at lunch, on breaks, and during the exercise period, but only after he ran one lap around the futbol pitch first.

Paddy's agreement with his parents was to keep his grades at top levels.

By the time they were fourteen, Eric and Paddy were regularly playing weekends with Paddy's uncle in area clubs and community events. Playing in clubs was illegal, but the boys were so obviously gifted, and had a steady following, that club owners let them slip in and play.

Seeing the school children made Paddy's stomach tighten, and he wondered why. He'd learned from Woody, J, and Lexi the past few days to "feel the feelings and breathe into them."

He lit another cigarette and started thinking about his childhood school years.

What is this feeling? he wondered. *It's triggered by seeing those children.*

Paddy was trying to take deep breaths between puffs on his Dunhills. He laughed at the irony, started coughing so strongly that he doubled over, his umbrella falling forward, and a bucket of rain falling on his back.

"Good lord." He straightened up, coughed some more, looked at his cigarette, and said, "Well, my dear, it may be time we part, too." He snuffed out the smoke and pulled out the pack from his jacket to throw it in the bin. "Ah, not yet." And put the pack back in his jacket.

He kept walking, labeling his feeling. *Anxiety? Fear? Nervousness?* The feelings were associated with going on stage with Uncle Pat's band. He would throw up before every performance. Eric knew but was sworn to secrecy. "I've told Mam and Father I don't get sick anymore. If they knew, they'd stop me from coming."

Somehow Paddy had walked around a few blocks and ended up in front of Paddington Station again.

He looked up at the dark, still-raining skies and said, "Okay, I get it."

He went inside to buy a ride back to his parents' house in Epsom.

It was a route he'd taken dozens of times while a schoolboy to reach his London gigs with his uncle.

He called his childhood home just before boarding the train.

"Hi, Mam."

"Paddy." His mam knew something was up. She just knew.

"You and Father home today?"

"Yes."

"Great. I'm about to hop on the train. I'll see you in an hour or so, okay?"

"That's wonderful, son. We'll be here."

Cara May set down the receiver on her landline phone and looked at her husband.

Sir Edward May III had entered the room when he heard his wife say Paddy's name.

"Is he okay?"

"I'm not sure. Something's up."

"Could you tell if he was drunk or hungover?"

"He didn't sound that way, but he sounds...different."

The couple stood, looking at one another, remembering the last several years watching their only child reach the heights of global fame and success, and suffer through extreme addiction. They never gave up on Paddy and were grateful he kept them in his life, calling regularly when on tour, even if it was in the middle of the night for them.

Sofia kept the Mays involved with the children she and Paddy shared. She never had other children, though she was happily married and living in London.

Now, Paddy May was on the train for the first time in years, riding the same route from London to Epsom he'd taken so many times with his Uncle Pat after playing in London clubs on Friday and Saturday nights. Pat's band would sleep on couches at various friends' houses, Paddy usually relegated to the floor. Then, on Sunday afternoons, they'd take the train from London back to Epsom. The bandmates frequently slept because they were severely hungover, but Paddy—at least in the early days—was not as badly hungover, and he would look out the train window during the hour or so trip home.

Looking out the window now at the leafy green suburbs, he thought of the first time he and Uncle Pat met Rita and Kate. The sisters boarded the train just as it was pulling out of Paddington station, and Pat went into immediate action, flirting with the two redheads.

He had convinced them to let him and his nephew get off at their stop "for a cuppa."

It was so fast that Paddy wasn't sure what was happening. He grabbed his guitar case and followed his uncle and two women they'd just met off the train, his uncle motioning to a bandmate who seemed to understand the signal and gave a thumbs up.

By the time they were off the platform, Pat had convinced the women to take them to their flat which was a short walk away. Uncle

Pat wasn't too much older than Paddy and, therefore, was more like an older brother than an uncle. Still, Pat was near thirty and Paddy only fourteen. Paddy had only kissed and fondled the breasts of one girl.

Seeing and feeling the sexual energy between his uncle and one of the sisters stirred unsettling feelings in the boy. Within minutes of arriving at the girls' flat, Rita was showing Pat her room, leaving Kate and Paddy sitting in the kitchen with the kettle warming up.

This became the Sunday afternoon pattern, Pat and Paddy getting off the train to visit the sisters. Kate suggested she and Paddy walk around the town while their siblings were "getting to know one another." She was nine years older than Paddy, but it wasn't too many Sundays later that, rather than walk or sit in the kitchen brewing tea, she decided to show Paddy her room.

The bathroom separated the sister's bedrooms and helped muffle the sounds. Kate had a twin bed pushed to one side. There was a desk under the one window, an armoire in the corner and books stacked high in a corner. The bed was the only place to sit in the small room.

She had a small sound system in her room and Paddy would put on music, mostly because he always wanted to listen to music, but also because it helped block the sounds coming from the adjacent bedroom.

Kate took the lead, but didn't rush Paddy. Women at the clubs had flirted with Paddy before, but his uncle had always told them to stay away. "He's just a boy, ladies; besides, my sister will kill me if I don't protect him from you."

Paddy didn't feel like a boy with Kate. She lingered over his kisses but could feel his urgency. She was surprised when he said, "Show me what to do. What you like. I haven't done this before."

They stood beside the bed, kissing gently, tasting one another while her hands removed his jacket, the long scarf that one day would become his trademark along with his long curls. She took off his shirt and rubbed her hands over his slim chest, noticing the peach fuzz that would grow into a dark tuff that would one day peak out of his open shirt during concerts.

Paddy was much taller than Kate. Actually, he was, at fourteen, on his way to being taller than most people. The front of his pants pressed against her stomach, and she knew then that he would be the largest lover she had ever had. It was confirmed as she unzipped his tight jeans. She let her mouth linger next to him as she lowered his pants. So close to him that her warm breath tickled him into an even stronger and larger erection.

Paddy rested his hands on her shoulders as he stepped out of his jeans. She briefly licked him as she stood. He gasped, closed his eyes and leaned his head back. She remembered that same look years later, standing in the crowds at his concerts. Fans talked about how Paddy seemed to make love to his guitar and Kate knew it was true because she knew what he looked like when he was making love.

They were still standing. Paddy completely naked, and Kate fully dressed.

"Now you undress me, Paddy."

He followed her example and, starting with her sweater, slowly took off all her clothes. He lingered down below and instinctively knew to separate the hair between her legs, his fingers stroking the moist skin and then he took a "little taste" as he came to call it.

Kate pushed him on the bed, straddling him. She guided him inside her by lifting and lowering her body over him, so he went deeper and deeper inside her.

Paddy didn't take his eyes off her, his hands roaming around her hips, her waist, her breasts, and then he exploded. The suddenness, the intensity and the length of time his orgasm lasted surprised them both. He was quivering afterwards. Kate laid on top of him, their arms around one another.

Paddy's heart was pounding. Kate nuzzled the nape of his moist neck, her face nestled in his curls. She felt absorbed in his body.

They stayed connected a long time, letting Paddy naturally slip from her.

"I'm so sorry, Kate."

"What?" Kate rolled over beside him.

"I didn't expect to just come like that. I wanted to please you, too."

"Paddy May. There are many ways to please a lady. That felt good for me."

"But you didn't come."

"We're not done yet, young man."

They giggled and spent the rest of the afternoon exploring more ways have sex.

At the end of their first Sunday together, Kate told Paddy, "You may not have done this before, but you are already the best lover I've had."

"Why?"

"Because you are looking at me and touching me with total focus. You seem fascinated by my body."

"I am."

Paddy's uncle Pat feigned concern when he realized what his nephew was doing in Kate's bedroom, but just said, "Be careful not to get her preggers."

That scared Paddy, but Kate assured him she was on the pill.

The entire relationship was in her bedroom, each exploring all the ways they could make their bodies feel good, separately and together. Kate once said, "You're my teacher, Paddy. You've taught me how to be totally in the true moment of lovemaking, not performing."

She started asking Paddy to play his guitar, usually after, but sometimes before they made love. He played his guitar completely absorbed in the moment, closing his eyes and eventually tilting his head back, letting the sound wash over his entire body.

One Sunday, Paddy found several books by the famous Irish writer W.B. Yeats in Kate's stack of books. He held one up and said, "You know, I'm related to him."

"Really? No."

"Yes. My mam is full Irish from County Sligo."

"That's Yeats' country."

"I don't know exactly what he is in our family. He's a great something or other, but, honestly, I can't remember."

"I love Yeats."

"I can tell." Paddy motioned to all her Yeats books.

Kate continued, "I like that he believed in the magical, the fairies, the unseen."

"It runs in the family." Paddy didn't elaborate, and Kate never asked, something she regretted years later when rumors circulated that the Crashers were so successful in part because of Paddy's mystical Irish beliefs and practices.

Sunday afternoons with Rita and Kate lasted about six months, then stopped with a jolt.

Paddy grabbed his guitar case that Sunday and stood to leave the train at the sisters stop when his uncle pulled him back down into the seat.

"We're not getting off here, Paddy. Not anymore."

"What?"

"Paddy, please. Sit down, mate."

"No. What are you doing?"

Pat held Paddy back from leaving, and the train left the station.

Pat put his arm around Paddy's shoulder and pulled him close, whispering, "Paddy, listen to me. You can't see Kate anymore. It's dangerous for her."

"What?"

"Paddy, it's illegal for an adult to have sex with someone your age. A neighbor has reported our visits to the police, and we just can't go there anymore. Kate could be arrested. I should have never let this happen. I'm sorry. I know you really like her. And I know she really cares about you, Paddy."

Paddy couldn't see outside the train because he was crying.

"Paddy, what I'm not sorry about, though, is you got to have a wonderful woman who cared about you for your first time. I don't even remember my first time I was so drunk. I know this hurts, but really, mate, this is extremely dangerous. Extremely dangerous for Kate."

"What about you and Rita?"

"We're good. We enjoyed what we had, but we knew it was always just temporary."

"Wow. How do you do that? Just turn it off?"

"You'll learn." Pat looked at his nephew. "Or maybe you'll be lucky and never learn that. Maybe you'll always keep the magic about love and sex, Paddy. I can see that in you." He patted Paddy's knee.

Now, all these years later sitting on the train to his childhood home, Paddy thought about the letter he mailed Kate thanking her for "friendship I will always remember." He was careful not to reference their lovemaking in the letter, in case someone else saw it. He never heard back from her. He also never knew she kept a sweater he had left behind, bought all his music, and never missed a concert of his in England.

The walk to his parents' house from the station was about a mile. No one had recognized him on the train. Or, at least, no one let on that the leader of the number-one band in the world was riding the trains like everyone else.

Paddy mentally thanked Lexi for the gift of encouraging him to walk and take the train again instead of being chauffeured. He pulled out his phone to text her, but realized her plane was somewhere over the Atlantic. He texted anyway so she'd have it when she landed. *Thank you for teaching me to walk and take the train again. Took a trip down memory lane going to my parents' house after you left. Can hardly wait for them to meet you.*

His parents clearly had been watching out the window for him because they opened the door before he had walked up the steps of his childhood home.

CHAPTER 20

Usually on the flight from Heathrow back to JFK, Lexi indulged herself binge-watching free movies on the plane. Not this flight, though.

Paddy's kiss at Paddington Station ignited something in her—a swell of emotions, including fear.

Fear. What is that about? she asked of her journal. She'd kept a journal since she was given a pink diary with a key lock on her sixth birthday. For years, she had started her writing with "Dear Olivia" as if there was a person on the other side of her entries. She didn't remember where she heard the name Olivia, but it was an exotic name at that time in Dallas, Texas.

Once in a while, she still started her entries that way, but Olivia was rarely summoned anymore.

Lexi was seated in the emergency exit row in deluxe coach. She only flew business class when event producers insisted on booking her that way. She didn't have long legs and was able to sleep sitting straight up, which was more important to her than an expensive upgrade. Money wasn't the issue; it was the principle of staying as regular a person as possible.

Her presence in coach was often a surprise to her readers on the plane. Eventually, it became part of her mystique. "No matter how successful her books, Lexi Maxwell is still one of us."

A couple of people had asked for her autograph early in the flight, but then she was left alone with her thoughts and writing. Flying was where she did some of her best writing.

Today, her writing was all about the feelings the kiss from Paddy had stirred in her. She was thinking about Steve and love and loss. He wasn't her first or only love, but they first made love when she was barely seventeen, and they never separated until he was killed.

The crash was horrific, but the hours it took for Lexi to fly from Dallas to DC to reach her husband were unbearable. She knew he was already dead, but she felt his spirit lingering. He wanted to say goodbye to her and Jack.

She realized now, on this flight from Heathrow to JFK, that she had never fully grieved for Steve. She had never grieved for her own loss. She had moved immediately into "Mom mode," taking care of Jack while dealing with the funeral and then all the legal issues when the representatives from some embassy of a rich nation contacted her to "give you a gift to help you and your son." The gift was millions of dollars transferred into her bank account.

The accident happened just before Jack's first year at the Millbrook Prep School where he was recruited to play hockey. Steve had traveled with Jack for tryouts during the recruiting sessions. Lexi didn't know anyone there. *How can I not know anyone there but the coach?* She refused to let herself lose it. She was a single parent now and had to think about what would be best for her son.

The roads to the expensive prep schools in the Hudson River Valley were narrow, hilly and winding. The beauty of the area was breathtaking, and Steve and Lexi had stayed a couple of extra days after touring the school. Never would they have imagined that they would let their son move away from home at age fourteen, but he was a phenomenal hockey player and determined beyond his years.

Millbrook was obscenely expensive, but the scholarship offered for both hockey and Jack's academics made it possible.

"Ravioli or chicken, Ms. Maxwell?"

Though she was looking straight at the flight attendant, her eyes were seeing her life three years prior.

Shaking her head, she said, "Oh gosh. I'm so sorry. I was off in la-la land. Um, ravioli please."

Lexi picked at her food. She was aware that the man sitting next to her wanted to talk and had wanted to the entire flight. Lexi didn't want to, though. She put on ear buds, but didn't play anything.

Instead, she closed her eyes and let herself go back to feeling the loss of her husband. She knew what she needed to write. She had written about Steve's death and grief right after the accident. The book became a best seller, but Lexi was feeling a very different kind of loss now.

She needed to feel the grief, the loss of love, the loss of the touch of the man who had been her lover and best friend for so many years. She realized she needed to heal, and the only way to do so was to let herself turn back around and go fully into the past. And write about it.

There was something else about the feelings Paddy's kiss awoke in her. A sexual, deeply erotic, feeling that she really hadn't felt since before Jack was born. Maybe she had never really let herself feel her sexuality quite this way before.

Memories of her early years with Steve flooded her thoughts, and she knew to pull her laptop out of her backpack and start writing.

The first memory was when she and Steve went to her grandparents' home on historic Swiss Avenue in Dallas. They were not home, and so Steve and Lexi decided to take a bubble bath and have sex in the clawfoot iron bathtub.

Lexi loved that bathroom.

It was an old house with wood floors and high ceilings. The towels in the bathroom were black and jade, which made the black-

and-white tile floor pop. The window was high enough to not require curtains and so the sun would stream in the warm afternoon light.

Lexi and Steve had been having sex for most of their senior year in high school. They were not each other's first, but they were each other's first steady lovers.

Steve had his father's tall Nordic athletic build and his mother's Mexican honey-colored skin. That afternoon, at her grandparents' home, she started the hot bath water. Steve was hungry for her in a way he'd never expressed before. He wanted her, and wanted her badly. He came up behind her as she turned on the taps. He was already hard, and she could feel his heart racing as he pulled her against him. He rubbed on her through their jeans, and she was convinced he was going to come.

Before she could catch her balance, he'd pulled off her shirt and bra and was cupping her breasts with one hand and unzipping her jeans with the other.

She was excited now. She turned to face him, and they took off their clothes as fast as they could. Again, Steve surprised her and lifted her up on the sink ledge, spreading her legs so he could stand between them and thrust inside her.

He was breathless as he plunged in and out of her. He was so large and throbbing that it was impossible for Lexi to not start to tingle inside, but she needed a different position to come. She wasn't going to get it that time, though, because Steve was exploding. He was sweating, his heart pounding, his breath uneven. His body hunched over as he held her bottom pulled up under him.

The ledge of the sink was hard against her back, but she wasn't going to change the moment. He was spent. Totally.

"Oh God, the water!" Lexi noticed the floor was about to be flooded. She pushed Steve off and pulled the tub plug out. The bathroom had steamed up, and she stood, just looking at the way the light hung on the steam in the air. She was less aware that Steve was leaning up behind and stroking her for more pleasure.

She plugged the tub and turned off the water. Stepping into the hot water, she invited Steve to join her. He slid in behind her, and she leaned against him, the top of her full breasts bobbing on the bubbly water. The rest of their bodies hidden underneath the suds.

Lexi sat with her eyes closed, remembering how they stayed in that tub until the water was cold. They both drifted somewhere, some magical place where there was no time and no reality. At least until they heard her grandparents come home.

Lexi was grateful that her grandparents never came upstairs that afternoon and acted as if it was nothing when Lexi and Steve came down several minutes later with their hair barely towel dried.

Her grandmother simply said, "Hungry?"

Lexi jumped when the plane landed. She still had about three hours ahead of her to rent a car and drive to see her son at his prep school. She had learned over time that it was easier to rent a car from the airport and drive straight to the Hudson River Valley, stay in a hotel or B&B near her son's school for a few days, and then return the car to the airport and, finally, return to her upper west side co-op.

This trip was the first time in a long time that she'd made this journey without Jarius, and it felt different. It made her wonder what her relationship with J was really.

"I wish you a good and decent life" is what he had said to Sammie Peters after she had followed him out of Paddington Station.

"A good and decent life."

His remark, and his behavior, were unexpected, but stalking Paddy the past several days revealed the young Paddy May that Sammie Peters had once known.

She walked, direction-less, in the rain for more than an hour after Paddy left her that morning at Paddington Station.

She was thinking about how Paddy wasn't drunk or hungover. He was walking—in the rain, no less—instead of being driven in his fancy car by Graham. And he had kissed the woman she'd seen him with for the last few weeks. A loving, *you-are-my-world* kiss, not a *I-know-cameras-are-watching-and-it'll-be-on-social-media* kiss.

Paddy is very different now, Samantha thought, and she was determined to be the first to break the story. She still hadn't sorted out who the woman was, but she had enough pictures from Paddington Station that she could run through her facial recognition software and maybe have a chance of finding out who the lucky lady was.

The Crashers' manager, Nigel Auchincloss, had been able to keep Sammie away from the band for all the years after he threw her off the train in Spain. His team would even find her at their concerts, where she had bought a ticket like a regular fan. Within minutes of pulling out her camera at those shows, two large men would somehow appear and stand in front of her, blocking her view. She wondered how they found her. It didn't matter how close or how far she was from the stage or the arena garages where the band's cars arrived. Huge men appeared and would block any chance she had of snapping pictures.

A few years prior, she had decided Nigel had some kind of facial recognition system and so she disguised herself for the Glastonbury Festival. It was a huge night for the Crashers. They had the number one, two, three, four and five top-selling songs in the world. They were the headliners at the five-day festival. People camped out for *weeks*, not days, to be there. It was a frenzy, and the band had to be flown in by helicopter.

It took ten minutes for Nigel's men to find her, but they did, even though she had cut her long blond hair, died it black and wore clothes she would never wear regularly. Ten minutes.

The men didn't just block her view this time. They walked her backstage, making sure she was nowhere near the band, and put her in a black SUV that quickly drove her away from the festival grounds and to the train station.

It was certainly illegal what they had done, but she could tell by the looks on the faces of the security, roadies, and all the people behind the stage that she passed while being escorted away, that no one was going to come to her defense.

People in the music industry knew that if you were a friend of Sammie Peters, you were not going to have access to The Crashers. Nigel had one focus in life: protecting the band Paddy May had asked him to manage. Nigel was fierce in his job.

Sammie's popularity as the "go-to photographer" was beginning to dim, but The Crashers' fame was as big as ever. She knew if she could break the story about "the new Paddy May," she had a chance of being the "go-to" again.

She didn't care about the impact her photos had on Paddy's personal life. Or was it that she was really jealous of what others had with Paddy, and she wanted it for herself?

CHAPTER 22

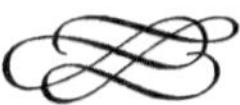

J had never been in anything like the Thames House.

Graham drove him out to the historic, eccentric house located on the pastoral outskirts of London to help him move in. Less than an hour from bustling London, J found himself in a small English village with narrow lanes. The cozy houses were neatly manicured and fresh, with window-boxed flowers that brightened things up in the fading fall light.

Tall hedges blocked the view of the house from the road. "Wow," was all J could say when Graham turned into the drive that curved around casually maintained lawns and led to the large rambling house that was to be his "for as long as you'd like."

"Wait until you see the inside and the dock side." Graham grinned. "And that's not even the most interesting part."

"I'm not sure about this, Graham. Do you really think it's a good idea for me to be here?"

"Honestly. I was surprised Paddy insisted. He never, and I mean *never*, lets anyone stay here. Not even his parents, and he's very close to them."

"Now I'm really not certain about this."

The gravel driveway crinkled as the Bentley pulled up to the front door.

"Your biggest challenge here, J, will be the fans."

"Yeah. I was surprised there's no gates or fencing."

"There is security, though. Quite a bit of it. Look there." Graham pointed to the cameras on the eves of the house. "We have cameras everywhere outside the house and all around the property that are being monitored around the clock. At night, you'll activate an alarm system when in the house."

"Oh. Suddenly, this place doesn't feel so quaint."

"Well, someone attacked Paddy here once long ago. I was brought in after that. I still don't know how he escaped harm. Security is now Paddy's largest expense."

"But he doesn't have bodyguards."

"Not that you see. Paddy May is never alone. We just try and create the illusion for him that he has some measure of privacy."

"Graham, I'm not sure what I think about being monitored all the time while here."

"We have had the same crew now for years. We feel like we are part of Paddy's family, and we never discuss what we see. Never. Not even with each other. Some of the men, and women, on the team have families that don't even know they are security for Paddy May. Trust me, you'll want the protection here."

"Am I going to have to deal with trespassers?"

"Try not to worry."

Stepping into the house was like stepping back into England in the late 1800s. Wooden floors, flowery wallpaper, low ceilings, and wandering hallways leading to rooms both tiny and grand.

On some walls, the original paper had been removed and murals were painted. Murals of fairies and magical kingdoms. J stood looking at one that covered the walls of the sitting room.

"Those are Paddy's paintings," Graham informed him.

"They are stunning."

"Yes. Unfortunately, he doesn't paint anymore. He did most of this when he first bought the house. Did you know he bought this place when he was just nineteen?"

"No!"

Graham nodded. "Paddy was already a wealthy man before The Crashers. People forget he was a top session musician and a young workaholic. He usually worked six, often seven days a week and eight- and ten-hour days. He's on thousands of records and soundtracks for hundreds of artists."

"This doesn't seem like a place a young, single, good-looking teenage male would buy."

"Paddy's an old soul."

"Yes. He is." J paused. "So is Lexi."

The two men closest to Paddy and Lexi looked at one another. Each wanting to discuss the budding relationship of the ones they cared for, but hesitating.

Graham broke the silence.

"I know I don't have to tell you to not talk about Paddy, or this house, to anyone other than Lexi. We have notified the local authorities that you're staying here. Before I leave, I'm going to introduce you to the local villagers at the tea house, grocer, pub and other places you might visit so they know you're legitimate. They won't ask, and you won't tell, about your life here."

J was starting to wonder if the gift of staying at Paddy's Thames House was going to be worth the cautions and protections necessary. What a life Paddy May had lived since he was a kid. No wonder he became an alcoholic and drug addict with all the expectations and pressures.

Graham spent most of the day showing J around the house and property. They went into the village to meet the retailers, buy groceries, and orient J to the area.

That evening, the two sat on the back deck having takeout dinner. Across the Thames was a farm with cows, and the water gently lapped against the dock.

"This sunset is gorgeous. I think I might never leave this deck."

"This deck is perfect regardless of the weather. The sunsets are beautiful. It's meditative when it rains. We have the heaters for when it's cold. Yes. I think you'll be out here frequently."

"I'm still not sure why Paddy offered this place to me, especially since it is such a private haven for him."

"He trusts you and Lexi. I haven't seen him trust like that since Sofia."

"How long were they married?"

"Long enough to have two children. And he's a wonderful father."

The men didn't want to violate the "we don't talk about Paddy" rule and sat quietly until the sun was completely gone.

"Jarius, I'm going home now. You have my cell, and here's the one for my man who'll be nearby. Do you feel good about staying now?"

"I think so. I'm sure it will take a while to get used to the sounds, both inside and outside the house."

"Don't hesitate to call, regardless of the time. That's what I'm here for."

The men shook hands, and J waved as Graham drove away.

J returned to the back deck and walked out onto the boat dock. Stars were peppering the sky already.

"This is crazy," he said out loud.

A soft light from the moon reflected in the calm waters of the Thames. More stars appeared in the sky. J hadn't turned on any house lights, and the area was dark. The only sound was waves lapping against the dock.

J slid his hand down the front of his pants. It was completely dark and he was shielded from any onlookers. He was hard and just wanted to caress himself. It seemed to be the right thing to do in this serene setting. He had to unzip his jeans to get a better grip.

He thought of Lexi and how they had shared lovemaking that one day in New York. He loved how she pulled him inside her with a suction he'd never felt. Her breasts, swollen so full. He couldn't believe they could change so much in excitement.

J thought of Paddy. He'd never thought of a man while pleasuring himself before. He thought of how Paddy would one day, probably soon, finger Lexi and wondered how they would first experience penetration: would she be on top with her breasts bouncing in joy, or would he be on top, his bottom thrusting up and down, or maybe doggie-style.

He rubbed himself harder and harder into a strong, intense orgasm that lasted longer than usual. He imagined Paddy and Lexi having sex the entire time of his pleasure.

CHAPTER 23

Lexi spent a few days visiting her son at his New York prep school. Her feelings about him being there remained conflicted, but Jack was a hockey prodigy, and this was a way for him to pursue his passion while still receiving an excellent education.

Jack seemed okay with his mom's "possible relationship" with Paddy May. He was mature beyond his years, always had been.

Her upper-west side apartment felt very empty without J. He had his own room there, and she walked around it one evening, looking at his drawings pinned to the wall. Drawing was his hobby, but could be his profession with a little more effort. Feeling guilty about being in his private room, she forced herself to not open his closet door to inhale his scent.

I wonder how the Thames House is going for him?

Ha. She knew. He'd sent her photos of the place.

"No fair. I should have stayed there."

"Well, come back, you can't believe how incredible it is to live at the Thames House," J replied. "I'm sure Paddy would be thrilled."

Paddy.

Lexi and Paddy texted or called every day. The five-hour time difference wasn't too difficult to manage. They'd text a quick note about their day in the morning, and then, most evenings, they would talk.

Most of her days were spent writing and talking with her agent.

"What are you writing now?" Lexi's agent was happy her client was back in New York because she liked grabbing coffee with her star writer. She knew that Lexi was writing something different, and she started asking Lexi about her work.

"You'd be surprised how much I'm writing, Michelle. It's nothing I've ever written before, but it's really flowing, and I'm just going to let it go where it wants to go."

Michelle Abrahamson knew not to probe, although she was concerned. Lexi's fan base was used to a new book in the *Cally Summer Adventures* murder mystery series every year; she wondered how much this new book was different from the Cally series.

Lexi had told her nothing of Paddy, but Michelle knew something had changed—especially when Lexi's constant companion, J, had stayed in London.

Her pattern was to walk an hour around Central Park after breakfast and her morning texts with Paddy. She'd enter the Park near the American Museum of Natural History and then just wander about.

Interacting with Paddy made her feel sexual. It didn't matter if they were discussing their children or the weather, she felt her body fill with a sexual energy.

She used that sensation while on her walk to start thinking about what she was going to write that day.

She was at her desk by nine, where she let herself dream of Steve again. She missed his touch. She missed him as her best friend even more. She was writing her grief about Steve's death by remembering all the moments of fun, joy and sexual intimacy they had shared. And she wasn't holding back on the descriptions.

The writing was so different for her and the judging editor in her head was constantly screaming, *What are you doing? What will people think?*

She hadn't figured out the format of this book, and she'd write a scene each day of something she and Steve had done.

She wrote about the time she and Steve had climbed up the light towers near the runway at DFW Airport. They were in high school, and there had been a massive security breech in the fencing around the east runway that some of the kids had discovered, or probably made.

On weekend nights, teens would go out to the dark field and climb up the light tower to its platform. Once on the platform, they'd wait for the jets to fly overhead. The noise was so loud that their bodies literally vibrated. They were overwhelmed with sound and vibrations, plus the thrill of doing something wrong.

Lexi once said, "You know, if a plane crashed into this platform, nothing would remain of us."

Steve simply replied, "Well, they would find my car over there and eventually figure it out."

Most of the teenagers just sat on the platforms smoking weed, but some, like Steve and Lexi, would have sex on one of the platforms and try timing orgasms with the jets landing above.

The signal that you were sexing on the platform was to tie a kerchief around the bottom rung of the ladder.

Lexi and Steve stopped going there after the time another couple decided to join them anyway. It was a couple in their twenties, and they knew what the scarf tied on the ladder meant, but they said, "We thought it'd be fun to share this, makes it more nasty, huh?"

Steve and Lexi were already naked and the couple laid their mat down right next to theirs since there wasn't that much room. Then they got naked. The man stood up with his very large erection and lifted his arms in the air like a conqueror.

Clearly, the strangers wanted Lexi and Steve to watch them.

And they did.

And then the couple watched Steve and Lexi.

Everyone smoked weed together afterwards.

The other guy said, "Wanna switch?"

"Huh?" Steve didn't know what was being asked. He thought it had something to do with using different drugs.

Lexi knew what the other couple wanted. "Oh, I don't think I'd be good at that."

The man said, "Oh, I don't know about that, little lady. I was watching you just now, and I think you're very good at it."

He tapped Steve on the shoulder. "And my lady is really good at it, too."

A huge jet flew over, shaking all four. Part of Lexi wanted to switch. The whole thing of it: on the platform, jets shaking you to the core, being with someone you didn't know, and watching your boyfriend have sex with another.

Steve was already pulling on his pants. "No, that's not us. Thanks for the offer though."

"It is tempting," said Lexi. She could see the grin on the twenty-something man. He knew she wanted it.

"Maybe another time," he said. We'll be out here next weekend. Maybe you'll feel more adventurous."

Steve and Lexi never went back to the airport runway lights.

Lexi wondered about that night as she looked out her window at the leaves blowing from the Central Park trees.

Would I have really done it? Have sex with an absolute stranger on that light platform?

Her practical side kicked in. *What if I caught a disease?*

Yeah, it's better we didn't do that, but it is kind of thrilling to think about. Maybe that's why it's called fantasy—you don't actually do it.

Lexi spent the day writing about all the unusual places she and Steve had sex while dating.

She wrote about sex on the golf course when they slipped under the fence late at night. They were naked waist-down and enjoying the moment when the sprinkler system kicked on. Laughing and stumbling, they were completely soaked by the time they dressed, rolled back under the fence and ran to Lexi's car parked down the street.

She wrote about the time she and Steve had sex in the back seat of her car. They were driving back from some school function and knew there would be no privacy at their parents' homes, so Lexi said, "Let's just park the car on some street. It's late, it's dark. It'll be so obvious and common to have a car parked on a street that no one will notice us."

"We'll have to be fast," was all Steve said. He liked it.

They had sex under the pool cover of her neighbor's house. It had snowed, *real* snow, not sleet as was usual in Dallas. Lexi and Steve had been watching TV at her parents' house. Her parents kept walking through the den, making snide comments about the movie, so they decided to bundle up and take a walk.

Arm in arm, the high school seniors walked in the middle of the street. No one was out. The silence from the snow was unexpected and unknown to them. They knew they wanted to make love, but how? Both their families were home. Her car was in the garage.

The Stanleys lived on a corner lot and their pool could be partially seen as Lexi and Steve walked by. There was an enormous cover protecting the water and steam was drifting out the sides.

"It's heated," was all Steve said.

"I think they're gone for the holidays," was all Lexi said.

The Stanley house was dark, as was the backyard. The gate was unlocked.

The pool cover was low, but clearly designed to allow for winter swimming. The heated water and steam made it warm and comfortable inside. The pair stripped and swam, weaving their arms and legs in and out of the other in a mating dance.

Lexi remembered Steve's kisses feeling more fluid that night. It was as if he was tasting her for the first time. The steam was so thick that they couldn't see the other if one moved more than three feet away. Steve started teasing her. He'd dive under and surprise her by emerging at different places around her.

They made love on the steps coming into the pool.

Lexi and Steve returned to the Stanley's pool for the next three nights, but stopped when they found the house lights on during one of their walks. It was late, but they heard giggling from inside the pool cover.

"I wonder if Mr. and Mrs. Stanley had the same idea as us."

Lexi wrote about how, in the summer, she and Steve would have sex in his childhood treehouse. He and his father had built it when Steve was barely six years old. It wasn't a flimsy platform tucked between branches like other kids' treehouses. This was a real fort in the sky with a retractable ladder, a waterproof roof, walls, and screened windows that could open to throw things at the "enemy" during child warfare. He didn't know it then, but building that treehouse was what sparked Steve's interest in becoming an engineer.

He and Lexi would climb into the fort in the middle of the night and make love on the mat he'd placed there for such occasions. Once, he could tell the mat had been removed, laundered and replaced. His mother never said anything about it, but he knew she knew. His family always loved Lexi.

Lexi and Steve learned about all the creative places to make love and explore sex because there was no privacy inside either of their homes when they were teens. It was a funny game because both sets of parents knew their teenage children were having sex. And each of their mothers had, in their own way, commented to "be sure you're using birth control."

The birth control worked just fine, until it didn't, during their sophomore year at University of Texas.

Lexi knew exactly when she conceived Jack. She and Steve worked temp at the school co-op, unpacking and stacking textbooks to earn enough cash, and then took turns standing in line for almost three days to buy tickets to see The Crashers, who were coming to Austin for the first time.

They bought floor seats and were able to maneuver their way to the front of the stage. Lexi felt a jolt of lightning when Paddy looked down at her during one of his guitar solos.

Steve noticed the guitarist was playing directly to Lexi and shouted over the music into her ear, "Lexi, it's like he's making love to you with his guitar."

After the concert, she and Steve made love multiple times back in her dorm room. Her roommate was always at her boyfriend's apartment, and Steve essentially lived with Lexi in her dorm room.

The next morning, Lexi woke and rushed, barely making it to the toilet to vomit. There wasn't much to discharge and so it was more dry heaving.

"I feel like I have the flu," she said as Steve pulled the covers over her.

The "morning flu" was Jack forming in her body.

My god, Paddy May, what is it about our lives being entangled? Steve and I were turned on by you when I conceived my son.

Lexi looked out the window of her upper west side apartment. Snowflakes drifted around outside.

Snow. It's not even Thanksgiving. Maybe Jack and I could go to London for his school break.

Lexi stopped writing and started checking airfares.

CHAPTER 24

Paddy was at Ceal Maith Studio laying tracks with his long-time engineer, Amanda Carvajal. Paddy had established the Studio when he was barely twenty-four. He knew from listening to artists during his session musician days that an artist needed to own, and control, his work. He and his manager insisted the band had their own record label within the bigger, well-established company. Paddy and Nigel set up the band as a five-part ownership with the manager being an equal fifth owner.

Paddy, however, wanted to have access to a recording studio at will and purchased a church being abandoned when its congregation needed a different location. Ceal Maith meant "good music" in Irish, and Paddy wanted to honor his mother's side of the family with the name. It became known as "the Maith," the studio where established and emerging musicians clamored to record.

Paddy had practically begged Amanda to move to London from her Caribbean Island home where she lived. Nigel had insisted on the island recording since "all the huge groups are going there," and the Maith was still being renovated.

Paddy was quoted years later saying, "The island vibe was

Nigel's vibe, not The Crashers. However, it's clear to us, or at least to me, that it was meant to be. We would never have met Amanda without going there. She grew up in that island recording studio but was never allowed to be the engineer in charge because she is a woman. She's in charge at Maith, and we are forever grateful she was willing to give up the eternal sunshine of her island for our lovely rain in London."

Paddy bought a home near the Studio and gave it to Amanda on her thirtieth birthday. She knew from the day he invited her to London that he wanted someone who would meet him at any time of the day or night to record. One room was always kept available for just such occasions. "Paddy's Room" was photographed as a kind of shrine by every artist who came to the Maith.

Paddy's sobriety both pleased and surprised Amanda. Paddy was drinking and drugging heavily when they first met. No one ever knew, but she was the reason he stopped his heavy drug use and just switched to weed only.

"I'm not staying in London if you're drugging like you do, Paddy. You are opening the portal to the devil with those drugs, and I won't have it. If you want me as your engineer, then nothing more than weed."

Paddy's Irish mother taught him to believe in fairies, spirits and the reality of portals into the other world. He kept his promise to Amanda and had a sign posted in the reception room at the Maith that said, "Nothing more than weed here."

Amanda often wished she'd also told Paddy to stop drinking too. She believed he would have stopped if she'd asked. Now he had stopped, and she felt it had something to do with meeting his favorite writer, Lexi Maxwell, but he wasn't revealing too much. She understood that as well. Sometimes when you talk about early love, it dissipates in the air.

Paddy was recording all acoustical tracks. The tunes had a tenderness Amanda knew was at Paddy's core, but he usually would cover up a quiet piece of music with his trademark guitar blast.

It wasn't yet dawn and just the two were in the studio. One light was on Paddy, and the lights from the monitor lit Amanda's face in the recording booth. She knew not to speak. She and Paddy had a creative flow at times like these.

This was the quiet Paddy. The introvert Paddy. The sweet boy Paddy whose childhood as a musical prodigy had jolted him into a world too grown up for him to handle at such a young age.

Amanda noticed an unlit cigarette hung from his lips.

He's smoking less and not drinking. I need to meet this Lexi.

Around noon, Paddy emerged from his creative fog and looked at Amanda through the glass. She'd been recording him almost continually for nine hours, unusual only because he never touched an electric guitar.

"I don't know what I want to do with all that, Amanda."

Amanda smiled gently.

"Are there any parts better than others?" Paddy wore jeans. His black curls were a strong contrast on the shoulders of his simple white t-shirt. His muscular arms were accentuated because he was so slim. Amanda imaging this is what he looked like when he was a young teen and first recorded.

She flipped on the mic to talk to Paddy.

"Patrick Edward May, this is some of the best you've ever played. You've transported us to a different layer of reality."

"I'm not sure it's Crashers music."

"Yes, it is. It always has been in the soul of The Crashers. You guys always push it down, though."

"True. I wonder what kind of lyrics Eric will create with it."

"Maybe take him to the Thames House and play the tracks for him."

"Hmmm. Well, I have someone staying at the Thames House."

"What? Who?"

"Jarius Harjo. He's Lexi's—Lexi Maxwell's—friend and companion. Work companion, a sort of manager, but more really kind of like family for her."

Amanda was truly stunned. The Thames House was his portal, a sacred site for him.

"Jarius?!"

"Something's changing in me, Amanda. I like it, I think. I'm feeling things I only have memories of."

Amanda knew to just sit in the recording room and listen. She'd kept the "DO NOT DISTURB" sign on so no one would enter.

"You know, I stopped drinking the day I met Lexi. Just stopped. She didn't ask, and she and I've not talked about it. I knew I couldn't be with her if I was a— well, if I drank the way I did. It's kind of like when you told me I couldn't continue hard drugs if I wanted you in my life."

Paddy looked at Amanda, and the two friends grinned.

"What is it about powerful women in my life?"

"You're lucky to have us."

"Yes, I am."

CHAPTER 25

Lexi was about to buy the plane tickets to London when her son texted: *Can I go skiing with Tori and her family for T-giving break? Her uncle has a ski resort in Salt Lake, and I only have to buy my plane tickets. Please.*

Jack had never asked to spend a holiday away from her. She knew it would happen one day; after all, he was seventeen, and in his post-grad year at the boarding school before going to university. He'd talked about Tori several times all fall and now Lexi realized how important this young woman was to her son.

Lexi took a deep breath then texted, *OK.*

She looked at her laptop, switched the airline search to *one passenger*, then reset the search to *Dallas/Fort Worth.* She wasn't sure why she was changing plans from London, but she needed to go to her home in Dallas. The one she and Steve and Jack and their cats and their dog lived in for the years after university and before Steve's death.

She kept the house, partially because she didn't know what to do with all the stuff. The house wasn't cluttered, but there was too much to move to a New York apartment, which wasn't really home for her anyway.

Plus, Steve's parents, brother and two sisters still lived in Dallas. They, along with Jack, were her family. Her parents dumped her when she became an "unwed mother." Truth was, Lexi's parents never thought Steve was good enough for her. Of course, for them, no one—including Lexi—was ever good enough for anything. A characteristic of alcoholics that Lexi learned in Al-Anon.

"Why don't you come to London? You can't believe this house. I can see you in front of this gigantic fireplace, writing day and night."

J was begging Lexi to join him instead of going to Dallas.

"Are you lonely, J?"

"No. No, actually Paddy's engineer has a sister about my age, and I've started hanging out with her and some of her friends. She's at Oxford."

"Oxford. Is she a smartie?"

"Yes, but also a creative. Did you know Paddy was the first major star to use a female engineer, and Amanda co-produced The Crashers' last record with Paddy. It was..."

"Yes, I know, J."

"Of course you do. Well, he's definitely more than his over-the-top rock star image. You should see the books in his Thames House."

Lexi wanted to change the subject for some reason she didn't understand but would later.

"Are you writing, J?"

"Tons. Mostly poetry and I've done some readings at Waterstones. Waterstones Bookshop in Piccadilly, can you believe it? I know it's because I'm your friend, but still, I'll take it. And it's giving me all kinds of ideas about what we can do to promote your next book."

Lexi was happy, but felt the two young men in her life, Jack and Jarius, were moving on, and she was stuck.

"J, I'm happy for you, but I need to go to Dallas. I'm writing something I've never written before."

J waited.

"It's a memoir, sort of, but is laced with poetry and imagination, and a lot of sex. I'm in a fog while writing. There's an elegant sadness to it."

"Are you writing about Steve?"

Now Lexi was silent. J knew her so well.

"Yes. I guess I'm writing my grief, but in a different way than before."

"Good. That's good, Lexi."

The two stayed in silence over the call for longer than most people would.

"Does Paddy know?"

"Know I'm writing about Steve?"

"No. Well, yeah, that too. I meant does he know you're going to Dallas alone and not coming here. But, yeah, about your writing too."

"I only just decided about Dallas. I've told him my writing is very different from what I usually write and that it has me a bit off-kilter."

"How would you define your relationship with Paddy now?"

"A long, slow foreplay."

The two laughed so hard that Lexi snorted.

"There it is. I hear that Lexi snort!"

"Okay. Talk soon, J."

"I love you, Lexi."

"I love you, J."

CHAPTER 26

Lexi's house in north Dallas was in a transitional neighborhood. They had reluctantly left the beloved area where they lived when they first moved from Austin. The new neighborhood was transitional in the sense that people who bought the area's upscale homes only saw them as a stop on the way to an even more affluent neighborhood just three miles south.

As a result, people weren't that friendly.

She and Steve bought the house for the good local public schools. They didn't want to be locked into using private schools, and the nearby public schools for first through twelfth grades were walkable for Jack. No one walked their child to school in the neighborhood, though, except her. People drove even if they lived on the same block as the school. Sometimes she wished she and Steve had bought a house in east Dallas, a less affluent area, but one with people more aligned with their beliefs. They did the "practical thing" with the house being a "good location, good schools and will hold its value." True, but it had no soul.

Steve's engineering job gave them a comfortable income and the ability to let Lexi stay at home and write. She was disciplined and would write non-stop while Jack was at school.

Sometimes she'd apologize that the house was a wreck, and no food was prepared, but Steve always said, "Writing is your job, Lexi. I don't expect all that other stuff to be done. In fact, if it was, I'd wonder why you weren't writing."

Standing in her house now, three years after Steve's sudden death, made her feel as if she was an anthropologist visiting an ancient culture. Some things were familiar, but others felt distant to her.

She still hadn't cleaned out the clothes from Steve's side of the closet. Her mother-in-law had offered several times, but Lexi said, "I'm not ready." Sefarina respected her "oldest daughter's" request. She always introduced Lexi as "her oldest daughter married to her oldest son." It confused people until she explained it. Lexi really was deeply and sincerely loved by Steve's family.

Lexi opened the closet door and was overwhelmed with Steve's scent. She slammed the door closed.

Tears flooded her eyes.

"Okay, Steve, okay. I'll stay with you. I'll complete you, us. I will honor you. I will keep writing about us."

CHAPTER 27

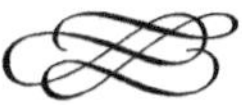

Paddy felt rejected at first when Lexi said she was going to Dallas instead of London. It was made worse when he learned Jack was going skiing and not going with Lexi.

"Would you like me to join you? I've only seen hotel rooms and the concert arena on my trips to Dallas."

Silence.

"Lexi," he continued, "I think I've been obvious that I want to be with you."

The split second of silence on the call stabbed Paddy with fear that he had misinterpreted the daily calls with her.

"Yes, Paddy. I want to be with you, too. In fact, that's why I need to be in Dallas, alone. Being with you is waking emotions in me that I have suppressed, some for a very long time."

"Lexi, we've each awakened things in the other. We don't have to process them alone."

"No. And I don't think we are. We do talk every day. I don't know exactly what is happening to you now that you're not drinking. It must be something, though, right?"

"Right."

"But you've not talked about it really."

"That's because I don't even know. I'm taking it day by day, as they say."

"Me too, Paddy. I've realized I never let myself grieve about Steve's death in the way I am now. I couldn't."

"You had to take care of Jack."

It always amazed Lexi how much Paddy understood about parenting.

"Right. And now I need to let those deeper feelings about Steve surface."

"Yes. I understand, Lexi. I do. I'm being selfish. I miss you."

There was a pause again, too long for Paddy's comfort.

"I miss you too, Paddy. I dream of you, you know."

"I didn't know. I'm so glad, Lexi. I've never stayed with a woman. And the one I would have stayed with, Sofia, left me because, well, you know."

"She has let you stay involved with your children, though. I think that says a lot about her, and what she thinks of you. Trusting you with your children is enormous, and I'm starting to see all the reasons she would want you to be in the lives of Evelyn and Julien."

Lexi was standing in her back yard. It was a typical late November day in Dallas, shorts and t-shirt weather with a freeze predicted by the weekend.

"Paddy, there may be some days when I don't talk as much or when I don't immediately answer your calls. I'll call later when you do call, but if I'm in the middle of writing..."

"Lexi, I totally understand. Remember, that's why I have the Maith so close."

"And Amanda."

"And Amanda."

The two talked about Amanda, J, and Amanda's younger sister.

"Yeah, that one seems to be a budding romance. I hope J's good to her because Amanda will eat him up otherwise."

"Jarius will be perfect, I'm sure."

They ended as all their calls did now, with a long silence, each listening to the other's breath, and then one finally saying, "Okay, well, tomorrow?"

This day was different. Paddy wanted to throw something across the Atlantic to tether them together. He was worried she might be slipping away, even though her words said she wasn't. He decided to take a risk.

"I love you, Lexi."

A thousand words and a million thoughts rushed into her as she looked at the backyard she had made with Steve over the years. She could feel Paddy's fear as he, once again, felt that her pause was more of a hesitation about him. She wasn't quite ready to say the same to him, not over the phone, but knew that, sometimes, you have to do what your partner needs.

"Paddy, I love you in more ways than I expected. I cannot imagine my life without you."

Lexi could feel Paddy's relief all the way across the Atlantic ocean.

CHAPTER 28

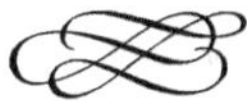

The Dallas house was a museum of Steve and Lexi's life.

She walked along the back fence looking at all the different rocks with names of their former pets painted in different colors. It was the family pet cemetery. They had several cats and two dogs. Tiger, Sarah, OJ, Tipper, Ashley, Trey, Doodle, Smokey, Joe, and Mike. The last two were dogs they rescued from her grandfather's farm when her parents brought him to Dallas to a nursing home. Her parents had just left the dogs to fend for themselves out on the remote country farm.

That's when she and Steve rented a U-Haul and brought back the dogs, along with her grandparents' furniture, rather than letting it rot or be stolen.

The furniture was what they used in their house. As a result, every room was filled, not with just stories and memories, but the energy of her ancestors. The dining room table and hutch were what her grandparents bought after they had been married five years. Before that, they only had a card table.

The rocking chair in Lexi's bedroom corner was the one her

grandparents bought on their first wedding anniversary and gave to Steve and Lexi on their first wedding anniversary.

The French doors hanging between the living and dining rooms once hung between the "parlour" and dining room at the farm. They had been made by a friend at her grandparents' church. The church where her grandmother played piano every Sunday morning, Sunday evening and Wednesdays, and her grandfather was a deacon. The church where the preacher and parishioners never made the long drive out to the country house after her grandmother became ill. No one in the church community ever came to help her grandparents because "they live so far out in the country." That was the beginning of the end of traditional church life for her family.

Lexi's grandparents were her saviors. Her maternal grandparents gave her summers, wandering for hours in the fields and creeks, taking only her spiral notebook, pencil, and the bird dog for companions.

She learned to breathe with the rhythm of nature. It's where her love of walking started. It's also where she learned to pay attention to the unseen beings living in the shadows. She believed in portals to other worlds because she experienced the shifts in temperature and energy around certain crevices in trees and holes with no visible ending in the ground.

She learned later that Paddy had similar experiences visiting his family in County Sligo, Ireland during his early childhood summers.

Lexi's paternal grandparents lived on the historic Swiss Avenue near downtown Dallas. Grand old homes, some with former carriage stables in the back, now converted to car garages or extra rental property.

Her city grandparents were "old money" from Boston and moved to be near their son and his family. A son, who they once confessed to Lexi, "Seems to have, with his wife, lost their souls to Dallas flash money."

Lexi escaped to her grandparents as often as she could on

weekends. She had her own corner room upstairs that overlooked the wide, tree-lined boulevard of Swiss Avenue.

Lexi wasn't able to rescue much from her dad's parents' house before he and her mom put everything up for auction. In fact, her parents didn't even tell her they'd sold the historic house until after it was complete. It stunned her when her mom told her as an afterthought on one of their few calls.

"Oh, I didn't think you'd care about anything from that old place," was all her mother said. Lexi knew that her mother just wanted the money from the estate sale.

These memories flooded Lexi as she walked around the home she and Steve bought after university. They never thought they'd leave Austin, but Steve's job offers were only in Houston, Dallas or LA. The cities were all the same to the young couple: car-oriented, and all about work. Dallas had Steve's family, so that's where they moved with their four-year-old son.

They were young parents with an almost-school-aged son, living near family. All reasonable and practical. Well-respected. Safe.

Lexi was too busy to really pay attention to the gnawing tug that woke her in the middle of the night saying, *Is this it? Really?*

There was nothing wrong with the life they'd created in their north Dallas home. Steve liked his job. It challenged him, was rewarding, and gave him flexibility to be an engaged father who coached Jack's sports. Lexi was writing and publishing a book a year on average. The *Cally Summer Adventures* series was starting to gain a market of loyal readers. Jack was smart, athletic and extremely energetic. Labeled ADHD like all boys were it seemed, Lexi and Steve frequently had to meet with the school principal to defend his actions.

Lexi often told Jack, "Remember, Jack, all your teachers are female, and if you notice, the girls in your school don't get into trouble as much as the boys. I'm not a traditional female, and you weren't brought up in a home that's uptight about your high energy the way the teachers are at school."

Jack's hockey was his savior, not because it gave him an outlet for his high energy, but because it took him away from the increased pettiness of his school's administration and other parents. He was on one of the top youth team in the States by age eight, which required daily afterschool practices and travel out of town most weekends during hockey season.

Lexi looked at all the hockey sticks in the garage. Steve and Lexi both learned to skate and took lessons from one of Jack's coaches just so they could go to "stick time" with Jack when he was very young. Hockey became the family obsession.

The only thing Lexi liked about the hockey years was watching her son on ice.

Compromise. The word kept talking to her as she walked through her home looking at the history of her married life.

"Compromise is co-promise." Lexi started talking out loud to create energy in the house that had been absolutely silent for months. She knew a house would crumble over time when abandoned. She'd seen it happen to her grandparents' farmhouse.

"A co-promise means each person gives up something he or she wants in order for the two to agree on other elements of a disagreement. At least I think that's the definition. When is it too much, though? Did I compromise too much here? And why would I think that? Steve ran the house and made the money we mostly lived on."

She stood in front of the bookcase, moving her fingers along the row of her published books. "I love you, books, but I could not have supported myself with just you for most of these years."

She missed her cats. They'd always had cats, either adopted from the shelter or found stray. She, Steve and Jack always talked to the cats, and they responded. They knew that people who thought cats were aloof simply didn't engage their pets.

She kept walking through the house, continuing to let the memories and emotions affect her.

She took her laptop outside to sit under her live oak trees. She knew the green November grass was about to get a punch of ice in a few days. Hopefully, her trees would not be covered and the limbs would not sag. If they did, she'd take one of Jack's old hockey sticks and gently scrape the ice off the limbs, as Steve had done many years. Once it was so cold, Steve had dressed in his ski outfit complete with mask and stood outside at 2 a.m. slowly scraping the ice that had accumulated on the branches. He stayed outside most of the night. Theirs was the only house on the street that didn't have a yard full of broken limbs the next morning.

Steve was the steady protector of his house and his family. He loved the differences between himself and Lexi. "You amuse me," he would tell her.

"What does that mean, exactly?" she wondered, sitting out under the oaks.

Lexi sat her laptop aside and pulled out her journal to write haiku. She often started her writing sessions by composing several haiku. It had become the signal to her brain that she was now going to separate from the ordinary reality around her and go into her imagination.

> *Did I merge too much*
> *lose myself in you and son*
> *what is family?*

> *Two merge into one*
> *how much should we blur the lines*
> *to make a marriage*

> *The trees are talking*
> *They wonder where I have been*
> *I abandoned them*

> *They are returning*
> *Spreading the news that she's back*

To her outside friends

Lexi looked up a saw the bird bath she filled with water full of birds, several squirrels chasing each other through the trees. One was sitting near her, looking at her while munching on his acorn.

"Are you my old buddy?"

The squirrel put the acorn in his mouth and walked toward Lexi, where he dropped it at her feet.

Lexi burst into tears.

"Paddy, I think it's time to bring the band in after Christmas."

Amanda and Paddy had been in the studio every day for weeks. Paddy's tracks reflected a gentleness and poignancy his engineer had only seen him reveal in glimpses before. Now, everything he played was a gentle Paddy. The Paddy she said "yes" to years ago.

She was an anomaly, because of Paddy defying the norms and hiring a female engineer in an industry where women just didn't exist anywhere in production or management. More women were artists now, and they started traveling to Paddy's Maith Studios just to have Amanda engineer and Paddy produce their work.

The Crashers were always Amanda's priority, and she knew it was time to bring them into the studio to develop the songs Paddy was birthing.

"Oh, I'm not sure my mates are going to know what to do with these tracks."

Amanda noticed how good Paddy looked. He'd always been handsome, sexy, but the recent years of his heavy drinking made his face muddled and puffy and gave his belly a bit of a pouch. That was all gone. He was trim, and his face literally glowed, especially under the soft lights of the recording studio.

He's so happy; no, he's so content, thought Amanda. "Paddy, I think the guys will actually like change."

"Ah, but will our fans?"

The two started organizing the rooms to leave for the evening. They both were fastidious and could never leave the studio without guitars back in their cases or stands, wires wound up and hung, chairs pushed into their proper place.

"What are you doing for the holiday? Going home?" Paddy asked Amanda.

"No. My parents are coming here, with all my siblings and cousins."

"You're going to need to rent a hotel," joked Paddy.

The two laughed.

"What are you doing? Do you have your children with you this year?"

"No. Evelyn, Julien and I will celebrate this weekend with my parents, but Sofia is taking them to her parents in Paris. I think they're also going to go skiing."

"So come to my place for Christmas Day. It'll be quite a festive scene."

"Thanks. Actually, Jarius and I are going to Dallas to be with Lexi, her son and her late husband's family, and then I'm going to Ireland to be with my parents on Christmas. At least, I think that's the plan."

"Is it time to meet the family? The whole family? All at once?"

"I want more with Lexi. Or at least, I want to see if we can make it more. I want to be family with her."

Amanda stopped what she was doing and looked at Paddy. "I've never heard you speak about anyone that way, not really even Sofia."

"Yeah. With Sofia I was able to become a dad, but not a husband.

With Lexi, I feel like I will become a full partner." Paddy hesitated, then added, "A husband, but not a dad."

"Won't you become a father to her son? Wouldn't that be possible?"

"I guess I'll find out in Texas, huh?"

"Yeehaw."

CHAPTER 30

Paddy insisted on buying J's ticket to Dallas. First class.

"Business class is fancy enough for me, Paddy."

"Yes, but you've never traveled with 'the Paddy May.'" Paddy used his fingers to air quote. "Trust me, we will have a better chance of being left alone a little bit in first class, but even there we will not be completely left alone."

Paddy's arrival with J at Heathrow ignited a firestorm of fans. Paddy hadn't let his manager arrange a private entrance, which Paddy soon regretted. Fortunately, it wasn't long until airport security came and escorted Paddy and J through the back hallways to a windowless room where they waited until they were escorted to their gate and became the last two people to board, enabling them to avoid letting the entire plane know that they were traveling with a global superstar.

Paddy was right about not being left alone. Within minutes after the plane reached its flying level and the seatbelt light had been turned off, a man in a suit across from Paddy and J leaned over and asked for an autograph. Paddy was against the window, so the businessman had to reach across J to hand a piece of paper and a pen to Paddy.

That started a cascade of first-class passengers taking turns for their moment with fame. The flight attendant tried to stop people, but Paddy waved her off, smiling and signing for everyone in first class, hoping they would then leave him alone for the rest of the nine-hour flight.

When everyone finally settled down, Paddy said to J, "Now you see why so many of us use private planes."

"No kidding. I don't think I'll ever ask for anyone's autograph again." J then pulled out a piece of paper and turned to Paddy, "But before I do that, can I have your autograph?"

The men laughed so hard that Paddy snorted. Stunned, J looked at Paddy and said, "Lexi has that same snort when she laughs hard."

Wiping his nose, Paddy looked at J and confided, "I'm not sure where she is about us, J."

Paddy was fishing for J to confirm that he knew Lexi wanted Paddy in the same way he wanted her. But J remained silent. Finally, he said, "Paddy, you just keep being you and staying sober. Lexi's going through her own processing. I'm not going to..."

"No, J. No, I don't want you to be in the middle."

"No. I don't feel that way, and I won't be. I love the relationship with each of you. And I do hope you two take it to the next level. I will say that much."

Arriving at DFW Airport was less dramatic than leaving Heathrow. An airline representative escorted Paddy and J off the plane before the other passengers, and then slipped them through an unmarked door just off the jetway. They wove through long, beige, windowless hallways.

Paddy carried his guitar case with his favorite Gibson.

"We have a private waiting room for you while we retrieve your checked bags, Mr. May, and yours, too, Mr. Harjo," said the airline representative.

J was fascinated by the entire process. "I knew there was an entire world behind the walls at an airport, but I've never been in it."

Paddy spent most of his travel time in the secret world behind the walls of airports, hotels, concert arenas and retail stores. "I rarely see the front of any place. I'm always taken behind the scenes. It's drab, isn't it?"

J found out where to tell Lexi to meet them. Again, it was a "who-knew-it-was-here" special parking area for VIPs.

Lexi was standing next to her sporty SUV, as red as her hair. She wore jeans, a flowing white poet's blouse and dangling celtic earrings. He stopped walking to try and absorb everything about this moment.

"Well, look at you Mr. Dark-haired Santa," Lexi said to Paddy. He touched his stomach, thinking Lexi was referring to it.

"No, Paddy, I'm referring to your beard. Wow, you can grow one."

The two hugged and paused, trying to decide how long and deep a kiss to share while J put the bags in the back of the vehicle.

Paddy whispered to Lexi, "We'll snatch a better kiss when we're alone."

Paddy noticed that Lexi kept the conversation light and somewhat superficial.

"Do you always have to arrange for this special treatment when flying?" Lexi asked.

"No. Well, Nigel usually arranges something for us, but when I try traveling like a normal person, it gets crowded really fast."

"Heathrow almost became a mob scene before the airport realized it was Paddy and took us down the secret hallways," reported J. "Even the people in first class didn't leave him alone until they all got their autographs and pictures with him. And that was with me sitting on the aisle trying to block them from Paddy on the window."

Paddy was studying everything out the window on the forty-minute drive to Lexi's home in north Dallas. "The grass is still green here." He kept glancing at Lexi, perplexed that she behaving more like "just a friend" rather than a committed couple.

"Welcome to December in Texas. Just wait, though, we're supposed to have some ice this weekend."

"Ice?"

"Yeah, it sleets here. No snow really."

J asked, "Is Jack in?"

"Yes. Came in last night, along with his three large suitcases."

"That guy. I've never seen anyone travel with so much stuff. He does look good, though. An outfit for every occasion."

Paddy's stomach tightened when Jack's name was mentioned. He had been so focused on seeing Lexi again, that he hadn't thought ahead that he was about to not just meet Lexi's son and the rest of the family, but he was staying at her home with her son and J. He wasn't even sure where he would be sleeping. He knew he wanted to sleep with Lexi, but suddenly things didn't feel so romantic.

Jack put the issue up front and center when he carried Paddy's bag into the house.

"Where shall I put Paddy's luggage, Mom? Your room or the guest room?"

Lexi's 6' 4" son stood in the living room grinning, knowing he was embarrassing his mom.

Both Paddy and Lexi blushed.

"The guest room, Jack."

J and Jack cut knowing glances at one another and refrained from giggling like schoolboys who'd just learned about sex.

The house had four bedrooms. Jack and J shared a "Jack and Jill bathroom," and the guest room was off the kitchen with a bathroom right outside its door. The master bedroom was on the backside of the house. It was large with windows across the entire back of the house overlooking the yard. You had to walk through the main den of the house to reach any of the bedroom areas.

Paddy slowly walked through the house. Almost every wall was a bookcase. Lexi had converted the dining room into her office long ago. He wandered into her office, looking at her books and noticing that one entire bookcase was lined with red books that appeared to be journals.

"Are these your journals? Actually, should I even be in here, Lexi? I'm sorry."

"No, stay. It's fine."

"Your grandmother's?" Paddy pointed at the stand-up piano with ornate wood carvings on the upper panel.

Lexi nodded and watched Paddy move his long slim fingers along the front of the piano, as if drawing the energy of anyone who had played it before.

"And you don't play?"

"No. Jack does a little. I always wanted to. I would spend hours at this piano at my grandparents' farmhouse, playing whatever I could."

"You didn't want to take lessons?

Lexi looked at Paddy and held up her left hand and right arm as if to remind him she had one hand.

"That's no excuse."

Paddy leaned over and played a beautiful composition. Lexi had forgotten that he played—the Crashers' lead singer, Eric, usually played in concerts and on videos.

"Maybe I can play Christmas carols, and we can have a family sing-along. And I'll show you how to play with one hand. No more excuses, Red."

"I'd love that."

Lexi sat down next to Paddy. He leaned down and kissed her. The frostiness he had felt from Lexi before was gone now. They were turning to one another when the doorbell rang.

Lexi sighed.

"Here comes the family. Are you ready?"

"Probably not, but it's part of you."

Steve's entire family arrived. His parents, his brother and two sisters with their spouses and Jack's eight cousins. They all carried bags of food, games and presents to put under Lexi's tree, which was up, but not decorated.

Paddy was not expecting to be hugged and kissed by all thirteen. It felt as if he'd been in the family forever. Steve's mother, Sefarina, kissed him on both cheeks. "I am so happy you are with us, but prepare yourself."

"Excuse me?"

"Prepare yourself. Lexi has accepted you and so we do, too. That means we will treat you just like family, which means you are fair game!"

Sefarina's eyes twinkled, and she laughed. Paddy hugged her again.

"That's the best news."

People were everywhere. The TV was on with heated discussions about what shows and sports to watch. Food was spread throughout the kitchen and Paddy noticed the family just ate as they wished. Disputes were handled quickly and easily with a "rock-paper-scissors" technique.

Lexi said, "I taught the family that."

Steve's brother said, "And thank God she did. Steve and I were the worst about arguing over stupid stuff."

It was turning dark, and Lexi noticed Paddy standing in the backyard, his back to the house.

J said, "You might go see how he's doing."

Lexi put her arm around Paddy, who seemed to be in a trance thinking about something far away. He had an unlit cigarette dangling from his lips. He put his arm around Lexi's shoulders and took out his cigarette with his other hand.

"You okay?"

"Yes. I'm actually feeling good. Very full."

"Full?"

"I'm trying to describe it."

"It's a lot at first. Steve's family. You and I are only children, and so to come into a home where's there's always motion and energy and talking and feeling…"

"…and hugging and kissing."

"Yes. Sefarina created a family of affection and love."

"I'm in love with your mother-in-law. You know, I think she and my mam will really like each other. There's a bit of magic in both of them. Actually, a lot, I think."

"How is it with your mom, um, mam?"

"She and Papa have already gone to the house in Ireland."

"You'll be there in time for Christmas, yes?"

"Yes. You're still coming for New Year's, you and Jack?"

"And J."

"Oh." Paddy thought Lexi knew already. "Well, J has decided to go to London. He and Amanda's sister are going to celebrate on the Thames."

Lexi got very still. It wasn't that she didn't know about J's change of plans, it was that Paddy did.

Paddy noticed she was a little upset.

"I'm sorry, I thought you knew."

"No, it's okay. He really must like this girl. Woman."

"I guess. I don't know her as well as her sister, but I think she's a good person."

Lexi clearly wanted to change the subject.

"Tell me more about your mum, mam."

"She's full Irish. From Yeats country, where the house is. It was her family home. I bought it when I got my first record deal. And I've added to it over time to make it possible for my children and me to visit my parents there. They go back and forth from there and London."

Paddy was smiling, thinking of his mam. "She honors the fairies and lives the mysticism that is County Sligo. She brought that to London and added her witchy friends."

"Witchy friends?"

"The UK has a rich history with witches, you know. Remember the Scottish play? Bad witches, but good ones, too. Good witches doing good things. It's said there was a coven that met at Buckingham

Palace during World War II to save London from total destruction during the bombings."

"I've heard that."

"How much do you let your witchy side out, Lexi?"

"What?"

Paddy just looked at her.

"You're right. I've learned from Sefarina that magical realism isn't just a literary style."

"But it's not your natural way of being. Yours is probably more Celtic, but you don't let yourself explore it fully. At least not yet."

Lexi felt as if Paddy had pierced her most private thoughts.

"How much do you..."

"Remember, my mam's full Irish. Never underestimate the Irish."

It was totally dark now.

Lexi's father-in-law opened the back door. "We're all leaving now, you two."

The house felt like a morgue after Steve's parents, siblings and all their children left. There had been so much energy for so many hours. Now it was just Lexi, Paddy, J and Jack.

"I'm going to bed." Jack kissed his mom and walked to Paddy, who was sitting on the couch. He opened his arms for a hug. Paddy stood and the two men hugged. Jack kissed him on the cheek. "I'm glad you're here."

J followed Jack back to their bedroom suite area, closing the doors to the den behind him.

Someone, probably Jack, had built a fire in the fireplace earlier, even though it was still t-shirt weather, the last blast of hot weather before the storm.

Lexi and Paddy were alone for the first time since his arrival. He put his arm around her and their bodies started turning into one another. Paddy was about to kiss her when the den doors banged open. It was Jack.

"Are we doing our tiny family Christmas before Paddy goes to Ireland?"

Paddy withdrew his arm from Lexi without thinking.

"I hadn't thought it through, Jack."

"Well, we need to because J just told me he's going to London and not Ireland with us for New Year's. Can I go to London too?"

"Jack, remember, Paddy was coming here to meet our family and we're going to Ireland to meet his parents and his children will join us."

"But why Ireland? No offense, Paddy, but don't all of you really live in London? That sounds more fun."

"Jack." Lexi's tone was sharp, and Jack backed off.

Paddy explained, "It's my family tradition to be in Ireland for the holidays."

Jack was thinking about Ireland now. He looked at Paddy.

"You grew up Catholic, didn't you?"

"Yes. I was even a choir boy, but I have a lot of problems with—"

"Oh, don't worry," interjected Jack. "We have a lot of problems with the Church. Dad grew up Catholic, but he and his family seem to disagree with most of the rules. Wow, the Irish Catholic Church really has issues."

Jack sat down on the fireplace hearth, clearly settling in to talk with Paddy.

Lexi knew her son hadn't intentionally interrupted what might have been a romantic evening between her and Paddy. She also knew he needed to connect with this man his mom was seeing.

"I'm going to bed so you two can talk." Lexi kissed Paddy and they gave each other knowing looks. "Good luck," she whispered to Paddy.

"Night, Mom."

Paddy and Jack talked all night long. They never slept.

CHAPTER 31

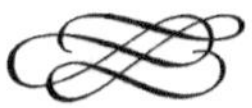

Paddy was only in Dallas four nights. He and Lexi were safely affectionate, meaning they held hands, sat close to one another with Paddy's arm around her and kissed, sometimes passionately, but they never were sexually intimate.

"Can you tell me what's going on, Lexi?" Paddy asked the night before he was to fly to Dublin.

"It's hard to feel romantic with Jack and J in the house."

"It feels like it's more than that, Lexi."

They were walking in the neighborhood. The weather was cooler, but only required light jackets. Lexi wasn't even comfortable holding hands, not wanting to deal with what the neighbors might think. Some had stopped by to visit and meet Paddy. They all knew who he was, but thought he was there as a friend of J's, not her boyfriend.

Boyfriend. Is that what Paddy is now? she wondered.

"No, you're right," she admitted. "It's something else."

Paddy braced himself to be dumped. He just knew his favorite writer, his crush, the woman he was starting to feel real, adult love for, was about to say she didn't feel the same.

"Paddy, I'm in love with you, and I love you. I mean, look at us, we are bringing our families together, and it feels like the most natural thing. This isn't a passing thing."

"It's been so easy. At least, with your family."

"Yes."

"So, what's the pull-back about? You keep pulling away."

"My loving you has made me realize I haven't gotten over—no, I don't want to say that. All these feelings I have for you, especially the sexual ones, make me realize I haven't grieved Steve. Not fully. All these emotions keep bubbling up. I almost feel guilty."

"Do you feel like you're cheating on Steve by wanting to be with me? Wanting to love me. Wanting to make love to me."

They were standing in front of Lexi's house.

"Yes. That's it. It surprised me. It's what I've started writing about. I'm processing."

They stood in the dark, looking through the front window at Jack and J, who were yelling at the football game on TV.

Paddy looked at Lexi.

"I want you to process this. I want to support you, but I also want to start moving toward a romantic us. I want us to sleep in the same bed. To make love. I want us to be a couple, not just dating, but a forever couple. I'm afraid if we just keep going along at this level too much longer that we'll never go deeper. I don't want that."

Lexi turned to Paddy.

"I don't want that either—just being friends. That's why I'm coming to Ireland to be with you, your parents, and your children. Paddy, I do dream about you being inside me. About us having complete union. About us being a forever couple. I want that, too."

They kissed, their bodies pressed tightly. Paddy always easily had a full erection with Lexi, and tonight's felt especially large and strong pressed against her. She felt her panties become wet.

The front door flew open. It was Jack.

"Aren't y'all coming in? We've made dinner."

Paddy said, "He has amazing timing."

"Yeah, it's a talent he's had since birth."

CHAPTER 32

Samantha Peters knew Paddy May went to Ireland for the holidays, every year without fail. He even did so when he was doing drugs heavily.

"A fallen choir boy," she would tell people.

The way he had confronted her outside Paddington Station when Lexi left London confused her.

Paddy really didn't confront me. In fact, he was...what was it? He was kind. He wished me well. What is going on with Paddy May?

She was determined to find out and tell the world.

It had been months since her photo of Paddy sleeping in Hyde Park on a warm day in the fall was on the cover of The Sun. That photo had been good for business. Several celebrities, a couple of actors, and a hot new band had all booked her both in the studio and on location for photos. She was a good photographer and business was thriving, once again because of her photos of Paddy.

She wanted the scoop on Paddy. If he was still a sloppy drunk and druggie she wouldn't care. She had the iconic photo of Paddy in that condition and another one just wouldn't have the same punch.

Paddy was obviously sober now. His face was clear, and his eyes were vibrant. He took her breath away when he spoke to her on the sidewalk that day. His sexy swagger was back. The sexy swagger he had as a teenager, only now he was a wildly successful man and his power more potent.

God, I'd love to bed him again, she thought while she booked the ferry to Dublin. She wasn't sure why she chose the ferry instead of taking a short flight over. Then she remembered. Years ago, Paddy had told her how he would take the ferry to see his family in Ireland. He could easily afford a plane ticket, but, as he told her, he could feel himself transitioning from an Englishman to an Irish poet on the short ferry ride. In fact, the crashing of the waves is really what gave him the idea for the band's name.

Samantha knew something was different when she caught Sofia leaving Paddy's Thames House more than a decade ago. A few weeks after first spotting her, she saw the baby bump and thought Paddy had settled down. Eventually they had two children, and it seemed all was well. Paddy was never home, though. Nigel kept the band on tour constantly, and they were recording during their "off" days.

Samantha could never approach the band, their hotels or concerts, Nigel's ban on her being so strict. She did learn, to her surprise, that Paddy was no longer hanging out with groupies. He seemed to be faithful to Sofia.

However, Paddy's drinking was out of control. The rumor was that Sofia took the children and left Paddy the day she came home to the Thames House to find Paddy passed out in a deck chair while their toddlers were swimming in the indoor pool.

Sofia put the children in their clothes, grabbed their favorite toys and walked out that moment, leaving an unconscious Paddy May wondering the next day why he was alone.

That was not Paddy May of today, and Samantha Peters wanted to know if it was this new, red-headed woman in his life that was the cause of his sobriety. His engineer, Amanda, inspired him to get off hard drugs. Did this new woman issue something similar about alcohol?

Sammie knew a person can't stop drugging or drinking for someone else. Not really. She had her own challenges with hard drugs and alcohol to know that. So she was off to Ireland to see who Paddy was holidaying with this year.

CHAPTER 33

The days around Christmas in Dallas meant Lexi's house was full with family, and Paddy was in Ireland. She needed to keep writing, and packed up her backpack with her laptop and journal and walked to the nearby coffee shop every morning to sit for two or three hours and write.

Somehow, she could tune out all the people and noise in a very busy coffee shop, but wasn't able to tune out her house full of family. The family understood this. After every writing session, she'd come home to a house that had been cleaned, where the laundry had been done, and food had been cooked for the day's meals.

Jack and his best friend since third grade were hanging out with Jack's cousins. While there was a busyness to it all, there was an easiness to it as well. Lexi's family with Steve never had too much drama or stress. She credited her mother-in-law for setting that tone. The result was that everyone wanted to be together at one or another of the family homes at all times. "Our family posse" is what they called it.

The weather turned frigid overnight with a vengeance. Typical for Dallas. The coffee shop was chilly, and Lexi kept her coat draped around her shoulders as she settled in to write.

She still wasn't sure what this book was. Was she just writing her grief, and it would remain private, or was she actually going to publish these thoughts and feelings? She knew it was a memoir because she was not fact-checking parts and didn't want to. She was going to let herself stay in a flow of feelings. She usually outlined her books before writing, but not this time. This time she was just going to write what came.

The previous night was the first and only time she was alone in the house. Jack stayed with his grandparents. It was his only time to be alone with them. J had taken the quick flight up to Tulsa to see his family.

Before she came to Dallas, Lexi had spent a few nights alone in her New York apartment, and Steve had started talking to her then. It was faint, but she knew he was trying to connect with her.

She walked back home after her morning writing session at the café. She was finally alone. Steve's presence was close, as if he was still alive. She was putting something into her closet, the large closet that was divided into two parts by cabinets in the middle. She could smell Steve, even with the partition. She walked around to Steve's side of the closet. Three years after his death, and she still hadn't cleaned out his side.

His scent was stronger than before.

"You're here, aren't you?"

Lexi pressed her face into his clothes. She pulled out her favorite coat of his. It was a dark purple, so dark that it could be dark navy or black in certain lighting. It was not at all the type of jacket Steve normally wore. He was, after all, an engineer. He surprised her when he came home with it explaining, "I thought I'd be a little adventurous for a change." He grinned like the Cheshire cat, his dimples winking at her. They threw the jacket on the floor, along with all their other clothes that day, and made love quickly, knowing Jack would be home any minute.

Lexi had never been able to completely turn off her mom radar and totally relax sexually after Jack was born.

Holding the purple jacket, standing in Steve's side of the closet triggered regrets about how many times she resisted Steve's desire to cuddle because she couldn't drop "mom mode."

"Sorry, Steve. I wish I'd said 'yes' more often."

"It was more than just that though, Lexi."

Steve's voice in her head was as if he was in the closet with her. She closed the door and sat on the floor among his clothes.

The tile floor was cold, and she pulled down the blanket he used to spread across his side of the bed at night. She sat on his blanket, put on the purple jacket, and sat in the dark closet.

"I've never really grieved you, have I, Steve?"

"No. You went straight into mom mode, taking care of Jack."

"I'm sorry."

"Don't be. You needed to do that. He needed you to do that. And, Lexi, you did a good job with Jack. You still do."

Lexi was speaking out loud to Steve. For her, he was answering as clearly as she was talking, but to anyone observing her, it looked like she was alone, sitting on the floor in a dark, cold closet, talking to herself.

"Steve, do I need to help you?" Lexi paused, afraid to use the word. "Do I need to help you transition?"

"No, Lexi. I need to help you."

Lexi stiffened. She panicked.

"Am I about to die? What about Jack?"

Steve laughed.

"No, Lexi, no. You're not going to die. Not now, and neither is Jack."

Lexi's eyes filled with tears, and she blinked repeatedly, in part because she thought she actually saw Steve now in the dark, sitting across from her.

"What transition do I need to make?"

Steve just looked at her.

"Think about it, Lexi. What's new in your life?" Steve waited. "Who's new?"

Lexi blushed in the dark, but she knew Steve could see her. She started to sweat in the cold.

"Lexi, it's okay. It really is. Paddy May. Your dream, but now he's real. He's here."

"I'm sorry, Steve."

"Why?"

"I don't know. I feel—it feels like I'm being unfaithful to you."

"That may be part of it, Lexi, and thank you for that, by the way. I admit a little part of me likes that you feel a little guilty."

The two looked at one another in the way that only long-time deeply connected lovers can. A knowingness that surpasses other relationships.

"What do you mean, it's only a part of it?"

"I'm not here to give you answers, Lexi. I'm here to ask questions and hold your hand while you process through the answers."

"You know the answers though, don't you?"

"That's not the point."

"Ugh, you're like a therapist now!"

The two laughed.

"I'm better than a therapist. We're deeply connected spiritually, always will be. That doesn't mean, though, that you can't have another deep love, Lexi."

Lexi started crying. She hadn't even cried at Steve's funeral because she was afraid to lose control.

"But what about you, Steve?"

"I am in a great place. You know, Lexi, my spirit is about supporting you, both while alive and in this presence now. I've always known it somehow, that a big part of my existence has been to serve you."

Lexi looked around in the dark for a towel or something to wipe her nose. She found a towel Steve always sat his hiking boots on. She was a mess of tears and snot.

She felt Steve push her hair off her face. She reached to hold his hand and realized there wasn't a corporal hand to hold, instead there was just shared energy. She held her hand still, eyes closed, and felt the warmth.

"Lexi, I will tell you that a place to start your exploration is to ask yourself why you use Jack, your mom mode, as an excuse to not be fully sexual. Fully intimate. You held back with me, and you're definitely holding back from Paddy."

Again, Lexi blushed and flashed hot at the mention of Paddy. They sat in silence for a long time.

"I guess I have used Jack as my excuse. Why would I do that?"

"That's your place to start." Steve stood up. "And speaking of Jack, he's home."

"What?"

"It's late now. We've been talking for hours."

"Don't go."

"I'll be around. For a while longer, at least. I love you, Lexi."

"I love you."

"Mom!" Jack yelled, coming in from the garage door.

Lexi wiped her face and left Steve's closet just as Jack walked into her bedroom.

Jack looked at his mom. Her faced was splotchy from crying.

"Hi, Jack."

They kissed and hugged.

"You okay, Mom?"

Lexi thought about lying to protect Jack or, maybe, herself.

"I'm okay, Jack, but I do have a lot of emotions flooding me these days."

"Mom, I'm okay with, you know, you and Paddy. He seems like a good guy. And you have good judgment. You're still young, Mom. Don't stop loving. Dad will understand."

"Yes. I think he does, Jack. I think he does."

CHAPTER 34

The drive from Dublin to County Sligo was almost three hours from east to west across the upper part of Ireland.

Paddy knew not to arrange for a private plane to pick up Lexi and Jack from Dublin and fly them to Sligo. The flight would have been about forty-five minutes, but he knew Lexi would have thought it too much. Instead, Paddy drove three hours to Dublin and three hours back, bringing his beloved Lexi and her son to meet his parents and children.

Only minutes outside Dublin, the landscape changed into rural rolling hills on either side of the highway.

"Where's the snow?" asked Jack.

"Well, Jack, surprisingly, Ireland doesn't have as much snow as you'd think."

Paddy glanced at the teenager in the backseat and wondered how he would fit in with his younger children. Jack was seventeen. Paddy's daughter, Evelyn, was fourteen, and his son, Julien, barely thirteen. All seemed mature beyond their years, probably because each had to deal with major circumstances regarding their fathers:

death, in Jack's case; extreme addiction, in the case of his own children.

"That's a bummer about no snow." Jack continued commenting on what he saw out the window. "Lot of sheep here."

Paddy laughed.

"Yes, Ireland is very pastoral."

It was cold, wet and dark, and Lexi loved it. She was hoping Paddy's mother's childhood home had a fireplace where she could sit and write. She asked Paddy about how cramped the house might be with everyone there and suggested she and Jack secure a hotel.

"No need, Lexi, I bought the houses on either side of Mam's childhood home long ago and connected them all. Actually, I bought three houses on one side and two on the other. Mam jokes we have six houses in Ireland, they're just all connected into one!"

Even though it was six houses connected into one, none of the houses was Texas-size large, and so it was still a warm and cozy property.

Paddy's parents had been watching out the window and came outside the minute Paddy pulled into the front drive. Paddy's father was tall, lean and dressed like an English gentleman. Paddy's mam was petite, red-haired, with dancing green eyes. She seemed like an Irish version of her mother-in-law, Sefarina. She hugged Lexi and Jack as if they were already part of her family. His father was more reserved, but his warm smile showed his pleasure.

Evie and Julien came running out of the house, both barefoot.

Classic teens, thought Lexi.

They shook hands with Lexi and nodded to Jack.

Julien looked exactly like a teenage Paddy May, while Evie looked like her mother. Lexi had seen photos of Sofia many times, wondering what she was like.

The house was a maze of disjointed hallways and uneven floors between the different houses. It was quaint and charming.

"This really feels like a home," Lexi said to Paddy as he sat her bag into what would be her room.

"It is home. We all love it here. Mam and Dad come here the most, obviously, but Sofia and my children come here a fair amount, too."

"And you?"

"Not as much, but always on the important days. Always."

Paddy's mam, Cara, took Jack on a tour of the houses, showing him a secret passageway that linked two of the houses. Speculation was that once, years ago, one house was sheltering members of the IRA.

"I'm going to shower off all the airplane germs," Lexi said as Paddy went to his room across the hall to play guitar.

Lexi was showering more than airplane germs. Steve's spirit had talked with her the entire nine-hour flight from Dallas to Dublin. The man seated across the aisle from Lexi and Jack could have been Steve's doppelganger.

"Jesus, mom, he looks just like Dad. That's creepy."

The man turned and smiled at them. Lexi knew from the look in his eyes that he was a spirit with some kind of message for her. It had happened once before, when Jack was about eight and could not sit still or quiet on a plane. His fidgeting became worse and worse on the four-hour flight until finally, a woman across the aisle broke the chaos when, in a firm but not angry or loud voice, she said, "Young, man, you must learn to find your inner peace."

It was as if lightening had struck Jack. He looked at the woman, took a deep breath, and completely relaxed. From then on, Jack always knew how to calm himself.

Lexi had that same feeling about the man on the flight to Dublin. Somehow, he was there to help her continue the conversation with Steve that she'd started in the closet of her home in Dallas.

This time, they weren't going to talk out loud, though. She was to continue the conversation by writing. This was going to be her book. "A Conversation with My Dead Husband," but with a better title.

The man across the aisle was either just the trigger for her or indeed a spirit to channel Steve. It didn't matter to her really. While

Jack alternated between watching movies and sleeping the entire flight, Lexi wrote and wrote and wrote.

Here you are again
I am waiting for your words
Help me complete this

Lexi wrote haiku to transition from the world around her into her writing world.

"I see you figured out the man across the aisle." Steve opened the conversation and Lexi wrote down both his words and her responses.

"Do you think it's too early for me to bring Paddy into Jack's life?"

"Here we go again. You keep thinking and doing everything for Jack."

"I am his mom, and he is still young."

"All that is true, but he's emotionally steady, Lexi. I give you the credit for that."

"Well, you too, Steve. You were a totally hands-on dad."

"So, let's jump into it, Lexi."

"It?"

"Yes. There's something about deep intimacy—not just sexual, but that, too. You were so free with everything when we were first together, and then it was as if doors started closing to parts of you."

"Think about it, Steve. What happened?"

After a long pause, Steve replied, "We had Jack."

"Yes. We had Jack, and we were barely twenty and at university, and then my parents disowned me, and I had no money and..."

"...and I married you, and my family helped us. We didn't fall apart, Lexi. We actually made it."

Now Lexi paused for a long time.

"There's something else there, Steve. I don't know what it is, or why it is, but there's a place my emotions won't reach. They stop. It's like hitting a glacier, a cold place that just won't move. Rather, it barely moves. No, it doesn't move. I don't know why."

"That's where you start, Lexi. Explore that."

"You really have become my therapist."

Lexi laughed out loud, breaking the absolute silence of the plane. The man across the aisle opened his eyes, gently smiled at Lexi, and then closed his eyes.

Shit, he is channeling Steve's presence.

Lexi's body temperature shot up several degrees, and she pushed off the jacket she'd draped across her lap.

Steve's voice was quiet while Lexi wrote out her thoughts.

"Steve, I think I was at capacity."

It felt as if she woke Steve from the place where he was far away.

"Capacity?"

"Capacity. I think I started pulling back after Jack was born because I'd reached my emotional capacity. I just couldn't be a mom, a student, wife, a part-time student aide, a person, a..."

"So you think a person doesn't expand. You think a person is a finite container and only so much can go in, and if more comes in, something has to go out?"

"Yeah."

"Bullshit."

Steve's reaction stunned her. Steve rarely cursed. In fact, he was known for essentially never cursing.

Silence.

Lexi dozed.

She woke with a start and didn't know where she was at first. She looked at Jack, asleep beside her. She looked at the man across the aisle. His eyes were closed, but she knew he wasn't sleeping.

She opened her journal and wrote, "Let's resume, Steve. I think I was angry those first years. Mad I got pregnant, and my plans for my life were turned upside down. Embarrassed and shamed by people. Dumped by my family. Angry with you because you didn't have any of that happen to you. You didn't have a baby making you throw up every morning for almost nine months straight and then clinging to your breast non-stop for, for forever."

Lexi's hand wrote furiously across the paper.

"But it's more than that," Steve pushed.

Lexi waited for her next thought. Steve waited, too.

"I hold back because I want to. It gives me power over others. No one can totally know me. Have me."

"Use you."

"Use me."

"Hurt you."

"Hurt me."

"Not everyone is out to use you or hurt you, Lexi. Your parents, yes. But you also had some early blessings. First, your grandparents. They were your first Earth angels. Then me, Lexi. Me. Then my family. A large family of people who embrace you with unconditional love. Then Jack, who worships you and will continue to love and care for you as you age. And now, Paddy. Yes. Now, Paddy.

None of us use you. We just love you."

CHAPTER 35

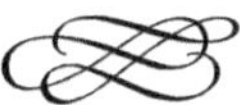

Jack knocking on the bathroom door jolted Lexi from her dream state, thinking of her conversation with Steve on the plane.

"Mom!"

"Yes, Jack. Wait, I'm showering."

"Yeah, you've been in there forever. I'm going with Paddy's dad to the store."

"Okay. Thanks for telling me."

Edward had immediately embraced Jack as if he was one of his own grandchildren.

Lexi turned off the shower and dressed in her flannel pajamas, wondering why she brought PJs into the bathroom instead of clothes. She wondered why she didn't bring something sexier. *Because the house is full of children.*

She heard Jack run down the stairs and a door slam.

She towel-dried her hair and stepped into the hallway. She could hear Paddy playing guitar and walked to his room. He was sitting on his enormous antique four-posted wooden bed, totally absorbed in his music. Lexi stood and listened until he looked up. He smiled the smile that charmed millions of fans. *He's adorable,* she thought.

"Do you have a hair dryer?"

Paddy rested his hands on his guitar, then pointed to his bathroom on the other side of the room.

"Top drawer. Left."

Paddy resumed playing while she dried her hair. She was aware he had not taken his eyes off her. She looked at his reflection in the mirror. He saw her and they just stared as if trying to talk with their eyes.

Lexi sat beside Paddy when she was finished. He kept playing.

"Oh my, I'm really tired all of a sudden." Lexi looked out the window. "It's only four o'clock in the afternoon and pitch dark."

"Do you have much jet lag?"

"All of a sudden, I think I do. I need a nap."

"Why don't you get under the duvet. It's a great bed. I'll play softly for you. A lullaby, maybe."

Paddy was right. The bed was lush, and she sank under the covers. Lexi had no idea what he played for her because she was asleep immediately.

Paddy played for another hour just watching Lexi's face. *That is a happy woman,* he thought.

Paddy closed his bedroom door when he left and then closed the door to Lexi's empty room. *It doesn't need to be obvious to the children where she's sleeping.*

He went downstairs to be with the rest of the family. Everyone was in the kitchen, either cooking, setting the table or moving things into the main living room to make more room at the table.

"Lexi coming down for dinner?"

"I don't think so, mam. I think jet lag caught up with her, and she's sound asleep."

"Why do you call your mom mam? That seems pretty formal," asked Jack.

Cara put her hand around him and said, "It's Irish, Jack. We call our mothers mam or mammy here."

Jack admitted that he, too, was feeling tired and went upstairs after dinner. He opened his mom's bedroom door and smiled at her empty bed. He wasn't sure what he felt, but it wasn't a bad feeling. It felt a little like he was about to take a big trip somewhere exciting.

Paddy wasn't sure what to do when he came to his room much later. He showered, thinking the running water might wake Lexi, and they could decide sleeping arrangements together. They had agreed she wasn't ready to sleep together in Dallas, but things felt different now in Ireland.

Lexi didn't wake.

Should I go sleep in her room? he wondered.

Paddy decided to take a risk and slipped into bed beside Lexi. The bed was wide enough that four people could sleep in it. He could sleep next to her without touching her without her permission.

He watched her and listened to her deep, slow breathing then fell asleep himself.

Paddy didn't know what time it was when he woke to soft moaning and the sheets and covers rubbing back and forth. Lexi was having an orgasm in her sleep. The power of such an intimate act stimulated Paddy, and his body temperature made him uncomfortably hot.

Lexi stopped with a jerk. Her breathing quickly changed, and she was rigidly still.

They both lay beside each other in the dark, neither moving and each listening for the other's breath to determine who was awake.

Lexi suddenly turned toward Paddy and propped up on her elbow.

"You're awake, I know."

Paddy opened his eyes. They could see each other in the dark room.

"Yes. I didn't know what to do."

Lexi buried her head in her pillow, saying, "It's so embarrassing."

"No. No it's not. God, Lexi, it took everything I had not to hold you and caress you."

"Why didn't you?"

"I didn't want you to wake and think I was taking advantage of you."

Lexi realized she had been dreaming of both Steve and Paddy. In her dream, she started making love with Steve, but as she reached orgasm, he morphed into Paddy. It was an undulating orgasm that rolled deeper and deeper inside.

Lexi reached out to Paddy's hand under the covers. They turned toward one another and kissed.

"Wait. I need to be on your other side," Lexi said as she rolled over Paddy to lay on her right side so her left hand would be free to touch him.

"Oh, I see. I didn't think of that," Paddy said as he pulled her closer to him so she could now caress him too. They kissed as if they never had before, slow, exploring, tongues tickling and bodies pressing.

"I want you inside me, Paddy."

Paddy sat up, pulling off his t-shirt. He then pulled off Lexi's top and put his mouth around her breasts. The firm softness excited him more. Her nipples were responding, and he nibbled on them.

Lexi squirmed playfully. "You're tickling me, Paddy May."

Paddy rolled off her pajama bottoms in one motion. He kneeled upright and Lexi pulled his pajama pants down. When he was exposed, she took him in her hands, and nibbled and licked him into an even bigger erection. He moved completely out of his pants and started trailing kisses down her body.

She opened her legs so he could taste her and feel her wetness.

He lifted his head and kissed her more. She guided him inside her. Just before penetration, Paddy stopped and looked at Lexi. They knew there would never be another "first time" with each other.

Lexi spread wide and Paddy entered her. His arms were straight, and he arched his back as he pushed his hips as close to her as possible. He was so deep inside her, but moved carefully to let the feeling linger.

Then he closed his eyes and tilted his head back. Lexi had seen that look in him. It came on stage when he was lost in his guitar solo.

"God, I love you, Paddy."

He thrust in and out, and she wrapped her legs around his back. She didn't have orgasms in this position, but felt a tingle, an almost orgasm. She knew she would have her turn next and looked at Paddy, smiling at his enjoyment.

His chest and back were wet with moisture as he moved up and down, faster and faster now, trying not to come, but wanting to, so badly. Finally, he exploded.

He wanted to cry out, but remembered where he was with children down the hall and parents downstairs, so he buried his face in the pillow beside her.

"Oh-my-God." Each syllable timed with a last thrust. Then he collapsed on top of Lexi and held her close, his breathing slowing.

They drifted not to sleep, but to some other land where lovers go when they let go of the separateness and become one in union. The place where there is nothing else but the other. The place neither had been for a long time. Not since Sofia. Not since Steve. Now, it was Lexi and Paddy. In union. In love. But not knowing the chaos about to happen around them and how it might separate them.

CHAPTER 36

Lexi and Paddy made love the rest of the night. Lexi showed Paddy how she liked to lay on her side with him inside. "It's like a lazy doggie-style tipped over," she said. The tease excited him even more.

Mid-morning, they heard the noise of everyone else in the house being awake and knew it was time to get up.

Downstairs, the children were all excited. It had snowed quite a bit the night before. The children were searching for baking sheets or something to use to sled down the neighborhood hill. Paddy's father went to the backyard shed and came back with cardboard boxes laid flat.

Paddy's mother searched closets looking for more clothes, none of which were for staying dry in the snow.

No matter. There was snow in County Sligo. That rarely happened and everyone decided they were going to enjoy it to its fullest.

Lexi and Paddy bundled up, and all seven walked to the neighborhood hill and joined what looked like everyone in town. Lexi was completely hidden underneath her hat, dark glasses and scarf wrapped around her face. Paddy was heavily bundled, but still recognizable. No one bothered him. He was one of them, and they knew this was where he came to not be famous. Everyone treated him like a regular neighbor.

Everyone except Samantha Peters, who was hiding across the street with a long lens, taking pictures of Paddy, his parents, his children and now, a woman and what seemed to be her son.

Lexi was so bundled, though, that none of her face showed.

"Who are you, lady?"

Somehow, the endlessly resourceful photographer still had not figured out Lexi's identity. Was it because she couldn't, or perhaps didn't, want to realize Paddy had finally found his true mate?

CHAPTER 37

Paddy and Lexi spent their mornings taking walks, then working after breakfast. Lexi sat in front of the fireplace in the main house, while Paddy cloistered himself upstairs in his music room. Music from his acoustical guitar drifted throughout the entire house. It was soothing.

Everyone was responsible for their own lunch. Lexi noticed Paddy's parents both made sure the kids had food and frequently took them to the main part of town to shop, see other relatives, and show Jack historic sites.

Everyone came together in the afternoon, and evenings were spent playing games and talking, with Paddy playing guitar. Some days, they all piled into the large SUV and drove to historic sites. One day, they drove down to Galway because Jack had seen photos of the rugged cliffs along the Atlantic Ocean and the Spanish arch in town. That night, they chose to find a hotel rather than make the two-hour drive back home in the dark and rain.

"It's okay if you and Paddy get a room together, Mom," was all Jack said at check-in. He and Julien shared a room while Evelyn was with Paddy's parents.

Back in Sligo the next day, Paddy's mam said to Lexi, "Would you like to walk through the fifth house with me?" The houses were referred to by the order in which Paddy acquired them.

"Fifth house?"

"The one where I keep all of Paddy's memorabilia. Everything since he was a little boy. Would you like me to show you my favorite parts?"

Lexi thought that area was just storage because Paddy had dismissed it with a wave of his hand when he first showed her and Jack around the property. "Oh, that's where Mam keeps stuff."

Lexi wasn't sure what "everything since he was a little boy meant," but she was definitely interested in being with Cara May. Paddy was playing music, and Edward had taken the kids to the movies.

Cara and Lexi walked through the hallways until they reached the house storing all the early recordings, films, photographs, tickets stubs, posters, news articles...anything about Patrick Edward May and his career as a child prodigy, session musician, global rock star, and music producer had been saved by his mam.

"Oh my gosh," Lexi slowly said as she walked through the first room. It was overwhelming. She noticed it was the only house that had security bars on the windows, and there was a different feeling to the air. She also noticed Cara had kept the door to this house closed and separate from the rest of the houses.

It was a museum to Paddy.

"Edward said I was over-the-top saving all this when Paddy was little, but now, he agrees it was a great idea to save it all. Who knew Paddy would become so accomplished?"

"You have to be so proud."

"We are. But there have been tough times, too."

Lexi looked at photos on the wall, a timeline from when Paddy was a choir boy, to his early performances on the BBC entertainment shows, to when he performed in clubs with his uncle when he was barely fourteen, to when he was a session musician at sixteen.

Lexi was a careful observer and noticed how Paddy changed physically over those years, and it was more than just growing from puberty to late teens. She was the child of alcoholics and knew how to read body language, dull eyes, changes in complexion. She had survived by knowing how to adjust behavior based on how much she could tell her parents had been drinking.

Looking at the chronology of Paddy's life displayed in pictures, she could see exactly when he had changed.

She kept walking through the ground floor rooms, the wall photos following Paddy through the years.

"Cara, have you noticed how Paddy's posture and hair changed based on whether or not he was performing?"

"What do you mean exactly?"

"When he was a choir boy and the very early years on the BBC, he stood tall, and his hair was brushed off his face, still longish, but not covering his face. That changes when he was playing clubs with your brother, Pat. See? He's slouching on stage and his hair, still the same length, is hanging over his face."

"That's being a teen, isn't it?"

"Maybe. But it seems more because, look here. When he's a session musician, he's standing tall and sitting straight, and his hair is pushed behind his ears. These photos of him in the sessions look like he's confident, relaxed. It's like he's with his buddies and they're just playing music."

"Those session musicians took such good care of Paddy. The closest in age to him was still ten years older. All except Paul, you know, The Crashers' bass player. He was there with Paddy. They were so young. They didn't even have peach fuzz, much less real facial hair."

Lexi walked into the next room that was filled with all the press and photos from the first years of The Crashers. Paddy's hair was long, covering much of his face. He was often bearded and slouched over his guitar when on stage.

Cara said, pointing to a photo of one of the Crashers' first concerts, "It took Nigel, his manager, a couple of years to stop Paddy from spending most of the concerts facing the drummer and bass player. In fact, Nigel had to start kneeling behind Owen and motion to Paddy to turn around and face the audience."

"Didn't Paddy used to get sick all the time when he was with Pat's band playing clubs?"

"Yes. That's why he had to quit and become a session musician."

"Did Paddy drink so heavily before The Crashers?"

"No. I know he sipped from my brother's bottle, but he wasn't drunk. Not like later. What are you thinking, Lexi?"

Lexi studied the photos on the walls. A visual timeline of Paddy's life.

"Paddy's afraid of performance. Think about it. He slouched over the guitar to make his hair hide his face and hide the audience. And when that didn't work, he just turned his back on the audience. And when Nigel wouldn't let him do that anymore—"

"He started drinking, and drugging."

"It sure seems that way, Cara."

"I can't believe I never made the connection. It is so obvious now." Paddy's mam started crying. "How did we not make that connection? We could have helped him."

Lexi put her arm around Cara. "You can't blame yourself for someone else's behavior."

The two women looked at more recent photos of Paddy. Photos on stage. Photos where it was obvious he was drunk, but able to perform. The blistering rock star who danced across the stage only came out when he was drunk or stoned.

They were silent a long time when Cara said, "Lexi, what happens now that he's sober?"

"I don't know. I don't know."

"I wonder if he's thought about it."

"I don't think so, Cara."

CHAPTER 38

It was their last night in Ireland. The bags were packed, ready for the cars to pick them up early the next morning. They were flying out of Dublin rather than the County Sligo airport to make it easier for Jack to catch his flight back to New York.

Lexi was already missing her son.

Jack, never shy about speaking his mind, asked, "Mom, are you visiting Paddy in London or are you moving in with him?"

Everyone at the dinner table paused for a moment, then resumed eating, pretending nothing was said, while Lexi thought about it. Paddy's dad, Edward, was grinning broadly. He and Jack had bonded during the stay because Jack's demeanor reminded him of Paddy's cocksure confidence when he was young.

Lexi looked at Paddy who said, "That's a good question, Jack."

"Yes, son. It's a good question, and we really haven't discussed it quite like that."

Jack continued, "And what about J? You're always with J. I know he's got a girlfriend now, but are you going to live with J, or with Paddy, or your own place?"

Paddy daughter said, "Yeah, what is going on, Papa? You never

have women here or at your other homes. You use that apartment."
Evelyn liked Lexi, but still kept a little distance. She liked Jack quite a
bit, though. Something Lexi and Paddy noticed with some
nervousness.

Paddy was beet-red now.

"Okay, okay, okay." Paddy looked at Lexi. "I guess we are going to
talk about this in front of the whole family."

"Yes, I think we are," she said, looking at Paddy's parents, his
children, and her son. "I can't speak for Paddy, but..."

Paddy put his hand on her shoulder. "Let me speak first if I may
please, Lexi."

"Okay."

"Clearly something changed for me when I met Lexi." He looked
at his mam. "I've stopped drinking entirely after being, uhm, having a
huge problem with it since, well since I was close to your age." He
motioned to the children and the eyes of his mam and father filled
with happy tears. "I just stopped."

"But Papa," asked Evelyn, "why couldn't you stop before? We
asked you so many times. I begged you."

"I know, Evie, and I'm so sorry." Paddy looked at his daughter,
wanted to say more, but didn't. "I just don't know why I couldn't stop
before, and I don't know why I have stopped now."

"Do you think you'll start again?" asked Jack.

"I hope not. I take it day by day."

Jack continued, "Back to you and my mom."

Lexi noticed Paddy was still blushing and having a hard time
talking. "Let me answer," she stepped in. "Paddy and I want to be
together. And we want to be with all of you as much as possible. We
haven't discussed whether or not we are now officially living together
or..." She looked at Paddy, and the whole family burst out laughing.

Paddy's mam said, "I think you two are living together, and I
haven't been this happy for my son since, well, for a long time."

CHAPTER 39

J and Sofia were both waiting at the Paddington Station when Paddy, Lexi, Evie, and Julien arrived. They didn't know they were each waiting for the same group.

Introductions were friendly. Paddy's children had been telling their mother about Lexi. Sofia was cautiously excited that her ex was sober and with a woman who wasn't a groupie.

Sofia noticed Graham wasn't there to meet Paddy, but suspected he had some of his security somewhere nearby. They all took the same tube toward north London. The family sat on either side of Paddy and across the aisle, trying to minimize the number of fans approaching for an autograph. It helped some.

"Are you sure you're ready for this?" he whispered to Lexi. "All these photos of you and me will be everywhere by the time we get home."

"No. I'm probably not ready. I have fans, but not like this."

Lexi sat still, wondering if she really was ready. She knew in the next moment she could lose her privacy. Forever. Being noticed because she had one hand was something she lived her entire life.

Occasionally readers recognized her and wanted to talk, take pictures and obtain an autograph.

Lexi knew, however, that she was about to step off the tube at Hampstead and her life would never be the same.

Do I really want this? she wondered.

Sofia said, "Paddy, I think we'll stay on the train to guard you until your stop."

"Thank you, Sofia. That will help some. Do you want Graham to take you home?"

"No. It'll be faster to just backtrack on the tube." Sofia looked at Lexi. "I look forward to knowing you better."

Everyone had quicks hugs as the train pulled into the north London station.

Sofia said, "Paddy, I am so happy for you." Then to Lexi, she said, "And I'm so happy for you. He's a lovely human being." The women hugged.

Graham and two other men were waiting at the station. The security men who had been on the train had texted him, saying fans were increasing on the train, and they might need more help with protection. Indeed, they did. The station was packed with fans jostling for photos and autographs.

Paddy whispered to Lexi, "Do you want Graham to take you home while I sign and pose?"

For a fleeting moment, Lexi thought about draping a coat over her arm to hide it so she wouldn't be so uniquely recognizable. She'd never hidden her arm before in her life and decided she wasn't going to now.

"No. I'm with you now. This is my new life."

Paddy put his arm around her, kissed her, and turned to sign and pose.

"Thank you for welcoming me home. I only have ten minutes, so please understand." Paddy was smiling and signing whatever was handed to him. When finished, he turned to Lexi and together they started walking toward his London home. J, Graham, and Graham's security team followed while fans looked on, taking hundreds of photos of Paddy May holding Lexi Maxwell's hand.

Samantha Peters watched the photos of Paddy and the mystery woman explode on social media. She was stunned he was taking the tube and not being driven by Graham. She had left Ireland without any decent shots of Paddy with his new lady and her son and wasn't about to miss out on breaking the story of Paddy May's new life.

She sat down at her laptop and started her facial recognition program. If Sammie hadn't been isolating herself in her narrow world of rock stars and celebrities, she might had figured out who the "one-armed red head" was by now. But Sammie kept her world narrow and wrestled with her own substance abuse.

Time for me to find out who you are, lady.

Lexi's identity popped on her screen immediately.

An accomplished writer? A widow? A mother? Educated? The author of the Cally's Summer Adventures *series!*

Samantha quickly searched through all the posts from the tube station and found one she especially liked. It was a perfect photo of Paddy, with his arm around Lexi, kissing her. There was no mistaking they were a couple.

She messaged the fan who took the photo, offering to buy it. Quickly she transferred him money and a legal release to sign, before the young fan knew that he could have sold the photo for thousands more to the London tabloids—which was exactly what Samantha did. The kid had sold his rights to a photo that Samantha used, once again, to have her name associated with getting "the shot" of Paddy May.

CHAPTER 40

"What are you doing with Paddy May?!" Lexi's agent was on the phone. The photo that Samantha Peters had bought from that young fan was everywhere.

"Gee, happy New Year to you too, Michelle."

"And are you living in London now? When are you returning to New York? Are you still working on your book? When will it be ready?"

Lexi was usually amused by her long-time agent's stereotypical rapid-fire abrupt New York questioning, but this felt like an attack. And it was. They had never had a warm relationship, which Lexi had heard some writers had with their agents. But Michelle believed in Lexi's writing long before others, and it had been a successful business arrangement.

"Michelle, can you ease up a little, please?"

"Well, you're the one who has always said you don't want to be famous; you want your books to be famous. You've never wanted to lose your ability to move around in public, observing people, and not being bothered. Dating Paddy May, this picture, changes all that. You've just lost your anonymity."

Lexi was silent a long time.

"You still there, Lexi?"

"Yes, Michelle. I understand what you're saying, but, I, he, this moment..."

"Lexi. You have the right to date, to be in love. After all, it's been three years since Steve. But being with Paddy thrusts you into global celebrity overnight."

"I thought you'd be happy, Michelle. Afterall, this probably means my books will sell even more, and to a new group of fans."

Michelle relaxed her tone. "Yes, but there may be a loss of privacy I know you have always cherished. Jarius is still with you most of the time, right?"

"Of course."

"He's good at taking care of you. In fact, I've been trying to convince him to join my agency to help with other writers, but he's too dedicated to you right now. Anyway, I'll talk with him about how we can try and protect you. Somehow. Not possible with Paddy May, but, still, we can try."

"Thank you, Michelle. I know you mean well. I think this might be my new life."

"I'm happy you're happy, but I don't think you really realize what's about to happen to you."

CHAPTER 41

The day after he returned to London, Paddy called the band back into the studio. Paul and Owen were excited to be back playing. It had been months since they were in the studio. Both recognized that the "old Paddy" from when they were in their late teens was back. He was focused, creating extraordinary music. They liked this sober Paddy but knew not to discuss it. They did, however, not drink while in the studio, even though Nigel had laid out the usual equivalent of a full bar on a side table in the recording room. Nigel, with his own substance abuse issues, hadn't noticed how totally sober Paddy really was.

Paddy and Eric had been the two in the band with heavy drinking problems. Eric said he was glad to be back in the studio, but he arrived late every day and immediately started drinking. Some days he showed up already drunk and added more to his stupor by continuing to drink.

Once, Paddy asked Owen, "Was I that bad?"

Owen's shrug told Paddy everything.

Paddy and Eric were the main songwriters, and it was different now with Paddy not drinking.

"Come on, mate, we've always slammed a few together when writing. It's our process." Eric was not thrilled that his bandmates weren't drinking while in the studio. "Thank God for Nigel," he said. "He'll drink with me."

Nigel stopped by to check on the band. He looked around and assessed that something was very different, and he wasn't sure what it meant. Finally, he realized that not only was Paddy not drinking heavily—he was not drinking at all.

Eric held up a bottle of bourbon and motioned to the other bottles on the table. "You can have your very own bottle it seems, Nigel. Cheers." Eric leaned back, bottle to his lips and chugged nearly a third of it.

Nigel took a bottle but only poured a small amount in a glass. "Cheers."

He lifted his glass to Eric and then to the rest of the band, who returned to working out a change in a section Paddy had shared with them.

Paddy would usually huddle with Nigel when he was on-site, since they were the two that really drove the management of the band, but not this day. Nigel knew Paddy was creating music and wasn't going to talk business.

"Okay. I'll see you later." Nigel left.

The engineer, Amanda, was sitting silently in the recording booth, watching the dynamics of her beloved band and their manager. She knew that with Paddy sober, Paul and Owen wouldn't drink as much, if at all, because they were never comfortable with the excesses of Paddy and Eric. Indeed, after the last tour, there had been a band meeting with the bass player and drummer insisting on a break of at least three months to be with their families, and away from the debauchery of their two other band mates.

"Oh lord, what happens now?" she muttered to herself while watching to see when to press record. Paddy was in a magical place with music, inspiring Paul and Owen to a level they'd not been in a while, and Amanda was not going to miss a moment to capture the sounds on tape.

"Hey, Paddy, isn't your latest squeeze coming for a visit today?" Eric was slurring his words, and it wasn't yet noon. He had been walking around the studio, drinking, sometimes listening to the music, and occasionally chiming in with lyrics.

"Her name is Lexi, and she's stopping by on our lunch break."

"Oh, I didn't know we were back to having a schedule. Just like the early days, huh, when you had everything so organized?"

"Well, Eric, we all agreed we'd try and finish this record in a month—"

"—like in the early days."

"Yes."

"There was a good energy that came across when we used to do it that way, you know," Paul chimed in, trying to reinforce focus and order.

Owen sat silent at his drum kit.

Eric took another bottle and went and sat at the piano. He was the accomplished pianist of the group, but sat just pressing random keys like a child on a toy piano while the rest continued building on Paddy's compositions.

The musicians in the band - Paddy, Paul and Owen – focused on laying down tracks while Eric literally stumbled around the studio drinking, swaying to the music but not writing any lyrics.

Lexi was nervous. She'd managed to write two hours of "good pages" after Paddy had left the house for the studio, but she was now about to officially enter his rock and roll world by visiting him in the studio with his band, the Crashers, guys who were as famous as Paddy, only in a different way. Paddy was the leader, but he always said he wouldn't be who he was without these "master musicians" alongside him.

Lexi was going to meet her favorite band.

The receptionist expected Lexi, but didn't expect her to look the way she did.

"*You're* Lexi?" the young woman said with obvious surprise. She might as well have said, "You're kidding me. You can't be Paddy May's girlfriend; you don't look like a groupie or a model."

She pointed Lexi down the hallway to the second room on the left.

Amanda was in the booth, and the first to greet Lexi. Lexi noticed that, like the first time she met Paddy at the bookstore, Amanda extended her left hand to shake instead of the typical right hand.

She hugged Lexi long and hard. "I love you. I do. You created the opening in the portal for Paddy to find his soul again. Thank you."

Amanda then kissed Lexi on both cheeks. She turned to the console and flipped a switch, opening the mic to the studio.

"Lexi's here."

Paddy, Paul, and Owen stopped playing and looked at the attractive redhead standing in the booth next to Amanda. Paddy waved for her to enter.

The bass player and drummer were happy to see her. They didn't want to just shake hands with the woman who meant so much to their mate—they hugged Lexi, pleasantly surprising Paddy.

"Where's Eric?" Paddy asked.

"He's sleeping behind the piano, I think," said Paul.

"Passed out, more likely," said Owen.

The guys and Lexi walked to the back side of the piano, where Eric was laying on the floor. His lips were blue and skin gray.

Lexi pushed Paddy aside and squatted down next to Eric with her hand on his neck.

"Amanda, call an ambulance."

Lexi started CPR on the lead singer of the Crashers, who was unresponsive. She had worked summers in high school as the cashier at the community pool. They didn't allow her to lifeguard, even though she had the training and first aid certificate to prove it. "Lexi, what are people going to say if we have a one-handed lifeguard?" was all the college-age manager could think of saying.

Rescue depended on how long Eric had been lifeless. Lexi knew, once she started, she was not to stop until someone official pronounced him dead. She opened his mouth to clear it of anything, then tilted his head back in the cup of her arm to open his throat air passages, put her hand on his chest and pumped rapidly several times for a minute, then put her mouth to his and blew several short breaths. Nothing.

She repeated the process. Left hand on his chest, pressing multiple times, then lips on his to blow short breaths several times. Still nothing. Eric was not breathing.

"Come on, Eric." Owen and Paul were anxious.

Paddy watched Lexi and said a silent prayer. "God, please guide her."

The guys and Amanda were scared, as nothing seemed to be happening.

Suddenly Eric convulsed, his body violently projecting a stream of yellow-green bile of toxins straight onto Lexi's face, hair and clothes.

The stench caused everyone to gag.

Lexi was covered in thick slime. Eric coughed some but did not regain consciousness. He was alive, though.

Paddy reached out to wipe the goo from Lexi's face. Owen brought paper towels from the booze table, and Paddy wiped what he could off Lexi while she continued to care for Eric.

"Paul, Owen, I need you to sit here and keep Eric on his side. You cannot let him roll on his back. And keep his head like this."

Lexi showed the musicians how to keep Eric from rolling back and possibly choking on his own vomit.

The receptionist was leading the ambulance workers into the studio. Her eyes showed how stunned she was. A few musicians who'd been in the other studios were standing near the entrance to Paddy's studio.

Paddy asked the receptionist to go lock the front doors. He looked at the musicians who had been recording in other rooms and said, "Can we stay quiet about this for now, mates?"

One musician, who was the lead singer for a band Paddy helped form, said, "We're here for you, man."

One of the paramedics asked what happened while the other two lifted Eric and strapped him onto a stretcher, being careful to keep him on his side.

Paddy pointed to the empty bourbon bottle on the piano bench.

Owen said, "I think that was his second one, just since ten this morning."

"Two bottles in two hours?" The medic held up two large bottles.

Owen nodded yes.

Paddy said, "Owen, can you go with Eric?

"Of course."

Paddy asked Paul if he would go to Eric's house, tell his wife, and take her to the hospital where Eric was being taken.

Nigel burst into the studio just as Eric was being wheeled out. "Jesus! What happened?"

Without looking at Nigel, Amanda said, "He died, and Lexi saved him."

Everything had happened in minutes, and now Lexi was exhausted and covered in the toxic goo from Eric's stomach.

Paddy guided her to the restroom down the hall. He walked past Nigel and the other band musicians gathered in the doorway. Lexi started shaking. She knew this feeling. It always happened after she had handled a crisis. She'd handled her drunk parents more than once, including when they were retching on themselves from too much booze. She had been the one caring for them. Now, Paddy was caring for her after she saved Eric.

Paddy sat her on the restroom countertop. He wiped her face with wet paper towels and wiped as much of the gunk out of her hair as possible. The smell was still so strong that they each had to pause to suppress gagging.

Paddy removed her blouse, careful to not let the soiled part touch her skin. He had her stand her up so he could remove her soaked jeans.

Amanda entered and saw Paddy gently holding Lexi as he continued to wipe away all the vomit. "I brought my gym clothes for Lexi. I was going to work out later." She opened her gym bag and helped Paddy dress Lexi, who was calm, but dazed.

Amanda gathered Lexi's ruined clothes. "Lexi, I'm just going to throw all this away, dear, okay?"

"Okay."

Nigel was waiting in the hallway.

"Jesus, Paddy. What happened? The press is already buzzing me."

Paddy held Lexi, uncertain how he was going to walk her home. Just then, Amanda said, "Graham's out back with the car. I called him."

Paddy kissed his longtime engineer and friend on the cheek. "Thank you." He turned to Nigel. "Try not to say anything to anyone until we know Eric's condition. We don't know how long he was... out. I'm taking Lexi home."

Graham wrapped Lexi in a warm blanket that Amanda gave him and put Lexi and Paddy in the back seat. He told them, "I'm going to drive around a bit because there's already a crowd starting out front. Will that be okay, Lexi? Do you need something else, sweetie?"

Lexi smiled, focusing on what was around her. "Graham, can we go to the Thames House instead?"

"Good idea." Paddy knew Lexi would need nature to recover. "I'll need you to return to the London house to get clothes for Lexi. Is that okay, Graham?"

"Makes sense. We need to tell J we're coming."

"I'll call him now."

Paddy called J while Lexi closed her eyes and slept. The Bentley slowly made its way through the busy streets of London and out to the leafy green outskirts.

Lexi was aware that Paddy and J were whispering and that Graham was with them now at the Thames House. She'd fallen asleep on the drive.

Lexi wanted to sleep on the couch in front of the fireplace instead of sleeping in Paddy's bedroom. J used one of the guest rooms as his own, not wanting to encroach too much on Paddy's most personal rooms.

Paddy came over and sat in the chair beside Lexi.

"You need to go see Eric, Paddy."

"I spoke with Owen about fifteen minutes ago. Eric's in a coma. The doctors aren't sure yet of the damage."

"Well, you need to be there."

"I think I need to stay with you."

"I have J." Just then, Amanda and her younger sister, J's girlfriend, came in. "And now I have Amanda and Cissy. I'm okay. I just need to rest and eat and rest again. I'll be one-hundred percent in the morning. You need to go take care of your mate. Your band. You need to calm Nigel down."

"She's right, Paddy," Amanda said. "It's blown up all over social media. The rumor is that Eric's dead."

Paddy sighed heavily and looked at Lexi. "You sure?"

Lexi nodded. They kissed. Paddy whispered, "Please don't leave me over this."

His words startled her, but more for the fact that some part of her was thinking, *I can't do this, I can't be part of this wild life.* Did Paddy know she'd been thinking this? Of course he did. His instincts were heightened and especially when it came to understanding Lexi, sometimes better than she knew herself.

CHAPTER 42

Lexi woke completely confused where she was. Her phone pinged, but she didn't know where it was. It was very dark, but slowly the main den at Paddy's Thames House came into focus. She was on the couch covered in a big warm comforter, and Paddy was asleep under several blankets in the large leather club chair beside her, his feet propped on the edge of the couch.

The phone pinged again, and its light revealed its location.

It was Jack texting. *WHAT is going on? News says Eric is dead. WHY didn't you call me?*

It was 2:00 a.m. in England.

Paddy stirred but didn't wake when Lexi reached for her phone.

Sorry son. So much so fast. I did CPR on him at the studio. He was alive when they took him to the hospital. Then Paddy brought me to the T-house where I've been asleep since, so I don't know current status. Paddy's here sleeping. Try to lay low and not talk about it. I'll text you as soon as I know more.

OK, Mom, but it's ALL over media.

OK. Again. Sorry. Love you.

Love you.

Lexi's eyes had adjusted in the darkness, and she looked at Paddy. He looked like a deflated version of himself. He was sunken, thin, gaunt, and exhausted.

Lexi carefully slid out from under the comforter. It was cold in the house. She looked around, saw Paddy's coat on the floor and put it on. She remembered everything about the day before.

She walked to the kitchen, where a light was peeking out from under the swing door. Graham was sitting at the long wooden table with two other men and a woman. She recognized them as part of Graham's security team. Graham jumped up and without saying anything hugged Lexi.

Lexi asked, "What's the latest? I'm afraid to ask."

"He's still in a coma. I think an induced one to let his brain heal."

"Jack texted me saying the whole world knows about this."

"Yes. That's why I've brought more of the team here, Lexi. They're here, at the London house, at Paddy's parents' house, at the Ireland house, and I've had to put security at Sofia's for her and the children."

"And the other band members?"

"Everyone is covered, but, as usual, the public wants Paddy."

Lexi made coffee.

Graham looked at Lexi's bare feet, left the kitchen and returned with a suitcase. "Elga packed your clothes. I bet she put some socks for you in here. Your feet look cold."

Lexi kissed Graham on the cheek and understood he wasn't just Paddy's driver and security chief; he was family. He'd even brought Paddy's two cats. They were rubbing against Lexi's legs and trying to jump on the kitchen table.

Lexi sat at the table with the others. Graham continued discussing the security plans with his team. Graham always had women on his team, but now had more who could be available to follow Lexi, Sofia and Evelyn into the womens' room when they were in public spaces.

The kitchen door opened, and Paddy walked in holding his

phone. He looked worse than in the pictures Lexi had seen over the years when he was in his full addiction.

"Eric's awake."

Lexi walked to Paddy, who put his arm around her and pulled her close.

"How are you doing?" he asked.

"Okay."

No one spoke.

Finally, Lexi asked, "Who called you?"

"Sylvia."

"How's she holding up?"

"I think she's expected this day her whole marriage to Eric."

"What is Nigel saying about how to handle this?"

"Right now, I don't give a fuck what Nigel thinks."

Graham's security team left the room, but Graham stayed with Paddy and Lexi.

"Sorry about my language." Paddy sighed. "I don't like how Nigel has been about this, and so I told him I'm in charge now."

"Haven't you always been in charge, Paddy?"

Graham smiled at Lexi's observation.

Paddy made his tea. Elga walked in, kissed Paddy and Lexi, and started making breakfast. The sun was barely thinking about waking, but the pink sky revealed its purpose.

J, Amanda, and Cissy walked in.

"It's a party." Lexi lifted her mug in salute, then quickly added, "I'm sorry. That was wrong of me to say."

Paddy gave the update on Eric. "I'm going to the hospital."

Lexi stood up, taking a last sip of coffee. "I'll go with you."

"No. No, Lexi."

"I'm okay now."

"I know." Paddy hesitated. "Sylvia asked for you to not come."

Everyone froze. Lexi felt as if a knife was plunged in her gut. "Oh. Okay. Did she say why?"

Paddy shook his head no.

"Are the wives going to the hospital?"

Paddy just pursed his lips, not wanting to answer.

"I understand. Y'all have been together basically your whole lives." Lexi's Texas twang surfaced when she was stressed, and it was prominent now. "I'll just hang out here. Walk and write."

Paddy looked at Graham. "I haven't briefed her yet," Graham said.

Lexi asked, "What?"

Graham continued, "Lexi, I've surrounded the property with security. I even have two teams in boats on the Thames opposite the house. You can walk on the property, but just know, every camera in England will be on you."

Paddy added, "Every camera in the world. Let's talk."

Paddy had his arm around Lexi and led her out of the room. The rest of the group in the kitchen looked at each other.

J said, "And so begins, the reality for Lexi of what it really means to be in Paddy May's world."

Amanda said, "This will be a huge adjustment for her, won't it, J?"

Jarius looked worried. "I think she can handle the lack of privacy better than she can handle band mates dying from being drunk. She grew up with alcoholics and long ago promised herself she wasn't going to live that life anymore. I'm certain she wouldn't be here now if Paddy was drinking, even a little bit."

Paddy walked Lexi to the indoor pool. It was a beautiful room with floor-to-ceiling windows overlooking the Thames on one end and Paddy's English garden on the other. The lights were antique chandeliers reminiscence of health spas in the 1800's.

They sat on deck chairs facing each other, their knees intertwined. The wicker chairs looked straight off ocean liners from the era of grand voyages.

Paddy looked as if he could barely stand, he was so gaunt from exhaustion. He took her hands in his and sat quietly.

Finally, and speaking more softly than his usual gentle voice,

Paddy said, "Lexi, I almost lost my childhood best mate yesterday, and he still may be mentally gone, we don't know, but I don't also want to lose you. I know that this..." He paused. "...situation could cause you to leave. I know your history with your parents. I know..." Paddy's voice choked up. "I know yesterday was horrific. Eric would be dead if it wasn't for you."

Lexi wanted to wipe the tears from Paddy's face, but didn't.

"Sylvia and the other wives haven't met you and, as far as they know, you're just—"

"Another Paddy May groupie."

"No. They know you're not that, but they don't know you, and we're barely handling the crisis and—"

"A deathly crisis I handled yesterday, and I think I can help you handle what's coming next." Lexi bit her bottom lip. "You're right." She paused. "I'm not sure it's a crisis I want to continue to be part of. Maybe yesterday was my big role in our relationship, and I've fulfilled it. Maybe that's the greater purpose, the cosmic scheme of our relationship, I'm here because I had the wherewithal to know how to save Eric. I've done it, and it's time to go."

Paddy knew to be careful next because Lexi had a look in her eye he had not seen. A look that was cold and distant. A door was shutting, and he was trying to wedge a foot in the jam to keep it open.

Lexi continued, "Look, I get it. Sylvia has her husband on life support, not knowing tomorrow. I'm a stranger. You have your best friend in an unknown condition. Your band—your whole world—could be ending. Your manager is very much responding in his obsessive-compulsive way that you don't want anymore, and your girlfriend, me, is thinking about leaving."

"Are you seriously thinking about leaving? Now?"

Lexi took in a long, deep breath and let it out slowly and with a long, deep, sad sound.

"Paddy, we've talked every day since we met. We've made love every day since Ireland, except for today."

"At least so far." Paddy smiled sheepishly, dimples showing and curls wrapped around his face.

God, he's gorgeous, she thought. "What I'm trying to say, Paddy, is I have bonded with you. I'm in union with you now."

Paddy was visibly relieved. "But?"

"But you have two addicts very close to you, Eric and Nigel, and that's not going to work now that you're sober. I don't think Paul and Owen are addicts."

"They're not."

"So, you, Paul, and Owen have tough decisions to make about how you go forward. That's assuming Eric is capable of going forward. I don't want the chaos of alcoholics in my life. With you, comes Eric and Nigel. I guess I wasn't thinking clearly and somehow thought they'd be less addicted now that you were sober. Maybe Eric's death and resurrection will be the turning point."

Graham tapped on the door to the natatorium. "Sorry to bother, but Nigel is calling incessantly. Eric is out of his coma and asking for you, Paddy."

Lexi and Paddy hugged, with Paddy holding her longer.

"Stay with me, Lexi. Please. I will sort this out. Somehow. Some way. My parents, my children, and now you, Jack, and J are the best things in my life. Please, please, please, let me make this work for us."

CHAPTER 43

The crowds and chaos around the hospital were so intense that Graham had arranged for Paddy to helicopter onto the roof, where the care flights typically landed. It was decadent, but the streets leading to the hospital were blocked for miles. Ambulances were diverted to other facilities around London and beyond.

The roar from the crowds below could be heard over the engine when the copter carrying Paddy, Graham, and two security people landed. The fans knew that was Paddy May landing on the roof.

Police and security were on every floor. Family visiting relatives were now trapped in the hospital. Some grimaced at Paddy as he walked by, while others expressed delight and a desire to touch the rock star.

Nigel rushed up to Paddy. He had a cigarette hanging out of his mouth that he had been chewing on since smoking wasn't allowed.

"Jesus, Paddy, I'd thought you'd just stay here the whole time and not go home."

"I have Lexi to care for too, Nigel."

Paddy hugged Owen and Paul and their wives, who were standing by Eric's door.

Paddy looked up and down the hallway at all the families, doctors, nurses, and orderlies. Most were trying to go about their business, but clearly, all eyes were on the door to Eric's room.

"Nigel, does the hospital have a dining hall?"

"What?"

"Is there a place to eat here at the hospital?"

"How the fuck do I know. Are you hungry?"

Owen figured out what Paddy intended. "Yes, there's a restaurant and a snack bar."

"Great. Nigel, you go tell hospital management that we are going to pay for everyone in the hospital to have free food and drink. We've trapped them here. We can at least feed them."

Nigel stood in disbelief.

"Now Nigel. Please go do this now. We'll be here when you return."

Paddy turned to his bandmates and their wives and said in a low voice, "Let's get Eric stabilized. Let's get through this, but we need to talk about how we can be a sober band." Paddy looked at the wives. "I'm sorry for all the shit you've had to tolerate because of my addictions over the years. I can't tell you how thankful I am that you have let Owen and Paul stay with the band. With me."

Paddy was openly crying. His bandmates and their wives circled him in a big hug. Someone said, "Thank God." Someone else said, "Thank Lexi."

Lexi and J spent the day at the kitchen table. Each with their own laptop, writing.

Her agent back in New York was texting constantly. *Is he dead? Are you with the band? What's happening?* Lexi had answered one of her multiple calls, only to be told to "don't be associated with any negative press." Lexi knew her agent was not really worried about her number-one client's emotional being. She was worried about preserving Lexi's wholesome reputation and reliability in producing best-selling books every year.

Lexi's book about Steve, their love, and her grief had become mystical. He hadn't appeared to her since the first night in Ireland when she was making love to him in a dream, and he gave her his approval to love Paddy.

She was certain now that night in Ireland when she woke in the middle of an orgasm was Steve's way of telling her it was okay to move on to Paddy. That, too, saddened her because she didn't feel Steve's presence the same way after that.

Where are you going, Steve? she wondered.

She didn't hear his voice like before, but felt that he told her he'd be around, but maybe not as closely.

He's moving on.

She asked him to stay around and share where he was going. What it looked like. Felt like.

Nothing.

Now, she sat with her longtime buddy, Jarius, while they each worked on their books. It would be J's first, and they talked at the beginning and end of each writing session about where they were in their stories.

"Does Michelle know what your novel is about?" Jarius asked. "I guess it's a memoir of sorts."

"No. It's mystical. Erotic."

"I don't think 'the agent who discovered Lexi Maxwell' is going to like it. Especially the very erotic parts."

"No. She won't."

"By the way, your erotic writing is such a turn-on."

The two remembered the twenty-four-hour period in New York when they shared love.

J reached out and squeezed Lexi's hand. "Paddy's very lucky."

Lexi squeezed back, "And so is Cissy."

"You'll like her."

"I already do. She and Amanda are like you."

Paddy returned to the Thames House long after dinner. Graham had more security around the property. So far, no one broke through the security lines. Most were holding candles and photos of Eric. There still was no public information offered about Eric's condition.

Lexi was napping in Paddy's bed and heard the shower. The large bathroom was already steamy when she entered. Paddy's jeans, paisley shirt, long thin signature scarf and jacket were crumpled on the floor next to his socks and shoes.

She could see his tall, lanky body through the frosted glass door to the shower. She took off her pjs, opened the door and stepped inside.

They didn't speak. Paddy seemed to melt into her arms when he saw her. There was a bench at one end of the shower, and she steered him to it to sit. Lexi took the shampoo and washed his long curly hair, letting the suds flow down over his body. She washed his arms and torso, and kneeled to clean his legs and feet. She moved slowly to massage him, rolling the stress of the last two days out. He held onto her the entire time, one hand on either side of her waist as she stood in front of him.

She rinsed him over and over and then lowered her head down over his lap. She took him in her mouth, her tongue rolling around his tip and up and down. Paddy laid back against the wall and released everything he had into her hand. His body shook. Lexi held him until the tremors of his climax stopped. She rinsed him and herself. She turned off the water, dried both of them, and they went to bed.

It was raining and dark when they woke, but they knew it was mid-morning. Paddy entered Lexi for what had become their "little morning love." It was an easy intercourse. A way to say, "We are one." And they were.

"Eric's talking."

"That's good."

"It is. He has some memory of being saved by you. He's embarrassed and ashamed."

Lexi wanted to say, "He shouldn't be," but couldn't.

"I've not been watching the media, Paddy. Have y'all said anything yet?"

"No."

"You need to. It's time."

"I know."

"What's Nigel's advice?"

"He's not talking much. He's really shaken by this. And I've been short with him. He even asked if I blamed him for Eric."

"Do you?"

"No. We three enabled each other all these years."

"He's uncomfortable now that you're clean. Have you talked with

Woody about all this? His band didn't all clean-up at the same time. How did they do it?"

"Good idea. He's been texting me, encouraging me. Offering help."

"Take it. Is Eric close to Woody?"

"Oh yeah. We've been mates since we were thirteen, fourteen."

Elga had food, coffee, and tea prepared in the kitchen. She and Graham were sitting at the table. Old friends who shared a life caring for Paddy May.

The rain bounced off the Thames, and winds blew trees back and forth. Paddy's phone rang.

"It's Sylvia." Everyone in the kitchen feared bad news. "Sylvie..."

Paddy listened.

"Yes. I was just eating and preparing to come. I agree. Yes. I'll prepare the statement. No, not Nigel. I'll ask Lexi to help me."

Paddy listened more.

"Yes, she'd like to meet you, too, Sylvia. Okay, love. It'll be a while, but I'll get the band and we'll be there. Love you, too."

Paddy texted Paul and Owen while talking to Lexi, Graham, and Elga.

"Graham, can you arrange for the mates and their wives, Lexi, and me to arrive at the hospital at the same time?"

"By copter?"

"No. It'll be challenging, but can we arrive in cars at the same time? I want to show the fans we three are all together, unified, supporting Eric. I want our wives to be with us, showing we are a family."

Everyone caught that Paddy included Lexi as a "wife," but no one commented.

"Lexi, can you help me write a statement, please?"

Lexi opened her journal to a fresh page. She knew not to ask about Nigel and if he should be included in the plan as the group's longtime manager. Paddy was the one who originally brought Nigel to the group; he could dismiss him if needed, but he wasn't going to do anything without talking to his bandmates.

Paddy looked at Lexi, stumped for words.

"How about we keep it extremely simple, Paddy. Something like, 'Our bandmate and brother, Eric, suffered cardiac arrest while in our recording studio earlier this week. Fortunately, CPR saved his life. Eric is awake and talking now. We will keep you informed of his progress. You have been with us all these years, and we can't thank you enough for the love and support you are giving us now. If you wish to help, we ask if you consider a donation to the Red Cross who teach CPR to so many. Thank you.'"

Paddy read the statement over and over, thought about changing a few words then said, "It's perfect. We'll run it by my mates before asking the hospital to release it."

"I think you should read it aloud. I think, you, Owen, Paul, their wives and Sylvia should stand together, and you should read the statement."

"Only if you stand with us."

Paddy and Lexi hadn't noticed that Graham had left the room. He returned and said, "Your car is ready, and we are coordinated to join the cars carrying Paul and Owen and their wives. The hospital and police know what we are doing and are preparing."

Lexi went to the restroom before leaving. For a moment, she actually thought about how she looked, knowing it would be her first official time before the world's media with Paddy May. She was in jeans and a poet's blouse with a scarf tossed around her shoulders. She grabbed her jacket on the way to the waiting car.

Paddy smiled and nodded to the long line of fans waiting on the road leading to the Thames House. He and Lexi held hands in the back seat.

Fans lined the road to the hospital for more than a mile. It was stunning to Lexi. People were crying, holding hands, and holding signs with Eric's photo.

Graham's team coordinated the cars carrying the band with

military precision. They formed a line of black SUVs, the first carrying several of Graham's security team, the second car with Paddy, Lexi, and Graham, the third with Owen and his wife, the fourth with Paul and his wife, and a fifth car with more of Graham's security team.

Fans clapped as the cars slowly drove through the streets. A deafening cheer erupted when the cars stopped in front of the hospital and the band stepped out of their cars.

Paddy insisted on opening the door for Lexi, something Graham had learned to let him do. They stood together while the others left their cars. Everyone stood together for a moment. The men each had an arm around their loved one's waist. The band mates lifted their hands in acknowledgement, but not really a wave.

Paddy let everyone else go into the hospital first, keeping his arm around Lexi. He stopped just before entering, turned around so he and Lexi faced the crowd, and said, "Thank you" while crossing him arms over his chest as if receiving a hug. Lexi looked up at Paddy with love in her eyes. It was the photograph that made the cover of every media source instantly.

Inside, the hospital public relations and executive staff had prepared the media room, which was already jammed with press. Television networks and news outlets from all over the world were there.

The group was escorted to a private room where Sylvia was waiting. Paddy had called her during the drive to the hospital, and she agreed to stand with the band while Paddy read the statement.

"Everyone, this is Lexi. Lexi Maxwell, my, my..."

"Your best love ever," Owen's wife said as she hugged Lexi. Everyone hugged Lexi. Sylvia was the last to do so, and she held Lexi the longest, whispering something to her that no one heard.

Paddy read the statement and asked if everyone was okay with it. "We will just go out, stand together, read the statement and then we will leave. I don't think any of us want to take questions, right? Okay. Owen, Paul, which of you can read the statement?"

Lexi had noticed Paddy's upper lip was wet with sweat and that he was fidgety, uncomfortable. The bandmates looked puzzled. Their wives laughed, thinking Paddy was joking.

Lexi remembered how Eric had always been the primary spokesman for the group. Now, without him, Paddy was expected to speak, and that scared him.

Finally, Owen said, "You're serious, Paddy?"

"Yes." Paddy was pale and started scratching his arm nervously. He looked around the room like a caged animal searching for the escape—*or looking for a drink to escape*, thought Lexi. She knew that look. This was probably Paddy's first real test of sobriety.

Paul said, "Should we call Nigel? He can do it."

Paddy's hair was wet along his neck, causing his curls to puff out even more. He kept taking deep breaths but still couldn't calm himself.

Lexi put her hand on Paddy's elbow and led him to a corner away from the group. She positioned him so his back was to his mates, and he could only see her.

The couple stood looking at one another. Lexi had learned to do this with Jack when he was a boy and his hyperactivity was about to send him out of control. She didn't have to say anything. She just synchronized her breathing with his, in and out, in and out, slower and slower, deeper and deeper.

Paddy was following her lead and calming down.

"Just read the statement, Paddy. You don't even have to look up. If you do, just look over the top of their heads. You will be surrounded by your best mates in the world. Those men over there have been with you through, well, everything."

Paddy nodded. He and Lexi kissed. He nodded at his life-long mates and, holding Lexi's hand, walked into the hospital conference room.

The large room was dangerously crowded. The click of cameras reminded Lexi of cicadas sounding off on Texas summer nights. An all-consuming and overwhelming sound.

The three band mates stood bunched closely together at the podium, everyone with an arm around another. Paddy had Sylvia on one side of him and Lexi on the other.

Paddy thanked everyone and then read the statement. At the end, he emphasized that they'd keep everyone informed. They stood for an extra moment for more photos, then slowly walked out of the conference room while reporters shouted questions.

Reporters shouted louder as the band left.

"Paddy, what caused his heart attack?"

"Was he drunk?"

"Who saved him?"

"Is his brain functioning?"

"Will the band continue?"

"Did Lexi Maxwell save him, Paddy?"

Paddy knew the voice of the person asking the last question. It was Samantha Peters. He glanced at Graham, who had also recognized the voice.

Graham mouthed, "I'm sorry" to Paddy, who just shrugged.

Paddy thanked everyone again, and the group left for the special room that had been set up for them near intensive care where Eric was.

Away from the crowd, Sylvia said, "Lexi, Eric wants to talk with you, alone."

CHAPTER 45

Eric and Lexi had technically never met, since he was already dead on the floor when she entered the studio.

He was now in his hospital bed, wires and tubes connected to multiple parts of his body. He was sitting up, which surprised Lexi. She was stunned to see how good he looked.

Damn drunks, she thought. *So often it's others who get hurt when they drink.* She was thinking of her parents.

Eric's eyes were closed when she entered the room. She stood at the foot of his bed and waited. When he finally opened his eyes, it took him a moment to realize it was Lexi and not a nurse.

His face turned red. He was embarrassed. He lifted his hand to shake hers. Lexi twisted her left hand around to shake, a maneuver she had done hundreds, if not thousands, of times in her life. It was the first time Eric saw her, and he hadn't known she had one hand. He held her hand with both of his to make it less obvious that he didn't know what to do. Lexi appreciated his sensitivity.

"I'll never be able to thank you enough for saving me. I'm sorry, I'm sorry for everything." The Crashers lead singer looked away from Lexi.

"Eric, both of my parents were raging alcoholics, so I'll warn you that I don't have a lot of patience, unless someone is actively working to stop their addiction. Sorry."

"Don't apologize."

"Have you had withdrawal pains? It's been a while since you've had alcohol."

"Hard to tell, since I'm hooked up to so many other drugs and fluids."

The two chuckled. The mood lightened.

"Well, your mind seems to be working."

"Well, there wasn't much there to save."

Now they laughed, and Lexi moved to the chair near Eric. The room was not like private hospital rooms in the States. It was bare, beige, and designed for function.

"Did Sylvia tell you about the statement the band just released?"

"Yes. Paddy told her you wrote it."

"Well, I am a writer."

"Maybe we can write a song together sometime."

That stunned Lexi. She studied his face, trying to understand his mental state. She decided to push. "What are you going to do about your alcoholism?"

A nurse opened the door. "Just a few more minutes, Miss."

Lexi stood, and Eric grabbed her hand, holding on tightly.

"How did you get Paddy to stop?"

"I didn't. We never spoke of him stopping. He just stopped the first day we met. It was as if a switch just flipped and he was done drinking. It can happen. You should talk to him and Woody."

"Woody?"

"Yes. Eric, there's a hallway full of people who love you deeply. You all have been together since you were children. I'm the outsider."

"Not according to Paddy."

Lexi paused. "Well, I'm the newbie, and I'm going to lay it out to you. I believe you're going to destroy The Crashers, and worse, lose all those people out in the hallway, unless you sober up. No one has said anything, but I can tell they're done with it. They may not even know it, but I do. You were given another chance at life. What are you going to do with it?"

Lexi patted his forearm and left.

She was shaking as she walked straight to the restroom without talking with Paddy or any of the group standing in the hallway. She wondered if she was too strong too soon with Eric. She was angry and needed to feel into it to understand why. Was it memories of her parents? Was it anger that Eric's addiction might ruin her favorite band? Was it that suddenly her life seemed to be the hurricane of drama called Paddy May's life?

Have I done it again? Focused on someone else's life and not my own?

Back in hallway she told Paddy, "I want to go to the Thames House now. Can Graham arrange a car, please?"

Everyone in the group was completely silent and still, as if to make Paddy and Lexi forget they were there.

"Of course. Are you okay? Do you want me to go with you?"

"Stay here. I need to write. I've neglected my writing for days and need to write."

Paddy understood what it felt like to need to create your art. It was why he always had a guitar nearby. He knew, though, that this need in Lexi was something different than simply her desire to work on her book.

Graham had a team of his security detail, one man and one woman, take Lexi back. Graham always stayed with Paddy. She realized just before stepping outside the hospital that she needed to think about the expression on her face, since hundreds of cameras would be waiting for her, and there would be photos of her all over the world before she reached the Thames House.

Should she smile? Wave? She couldn't look happy because of what happened to Eric. She couldn't look sad because that could send the wrong signal. She wasn't part of The Crashers. Did people think she was just another of Paddy's temporary flings? Would it cause more of a scene if she left now? Should she stay and wait to leave with Paddy?

Lexi stopped just inside the front door. Her security detail waited.

The female guard said, "We'll get you in the car pretty fast, and the windows are blacked out, so you'll have some privacy."

Lexi smiled and stepped outside to a roar of screams and confusion that it was her and not the band. She neither smiled nor frowned. She held her hand to her chest in a half Namaste, the Hindu greeting saying "the god within me salutes the god within you." Then, just before she entered the SUV, she turned to the crowd and surprised herself lifting her thumb up in the worldwide signal that "everything's okay."

CHAPTER 46

J was standing on the porch when Lexi arrived at the Thames House. It was dusk, and the sun peeked orange rays through the clouds. They sat in the back of the house listening to the gentle waves lapping against the dock. They didn't talk for a very long time. Long-time friends, just being together, reconnecting and understanding.

J wanted to ask so many questions about Eric and the band but knew that was exactly what Lexi did not want to talk about. He wanted to ask about her book but knew that was often the last thing an author wanted to be asked when they were stalled in the writing process. He didn't know if she was stalled but assumed so since he hadn't seen her writing for long periods of time.

They sat watching the bank of the river on the far side lose color in the setting sun and turn black. J and Lexi knew there was high probability that people with cameras stood on the opposite side of the river, taking pictures. Paddy had tried buying the property opposite his house for years to have some privacy.

Elga came outside, gave blankets to J and Lexi, set a pot of tea and snacks on the table, lit the firepit and left. She didn't say a word.

"Thank you," Lexi and J said at the same time.

The silence was broken. Time to talk.

"J, I've done it again. I'm focusing on someone else's life rather than my own."

J opened his mouth to speak, then decided no.

"I focused on Steve early on to be sure his career took off. Then, of course, I was consumed by Jack. It's only been since Steve's death that I've focused selfishly on me. And that's only been the last year or so."

"Hmmm. Let's think this through a bit more, Lexi. Yes, you were huge in always supporting Steve, and you earned undergraduate and graduate degrees while being a great wife and a mother of a baby. Oh, and then there's the matter of becoming a well-respected and popular author while taking your son all over the States for his hockey life. So, I'm a little confused why you think you've only focused on others. Looks to me that you've been, I hate to sound trite, but you've kind of been a super woman. Maybe, let's say, a bad ass."

Lexi reached out and touched J's shoulder.

"Thanks for that perspective."

"I do admit, though, Lexi, that being with Paddy is wildly different. It's going to be tough to not be consumed in his world. I mean, that's a bullet train you're either on or off, no in between, especially now with the Eric thing. Can you update me on that?"

"Yeah. He asked to meet me privately. He's awake and seems fine. He's still hooked up to everything."

"How hard did you blast him about drinking?"

The flames from the firepit made it possible for the two to see each other. J lifted an eyebrow at Lexi as if to say, *I know you.*

"I wasn't patient. Didn't coddle him, that's for sure."

"I bet you didn't!"

"I told him that I thought he'd lose everything and everyone if he didn't stop. He actually asked how I made Paddy stop drinking."

"Did he understand that you can't make someone stop?"

"I don't know. I told him to talk to Woody."

"Woody has really done so much to help so many rock stars and regular people, too, with his social media. I've been amazed at how many famous people, big time people, come to his house for meetings."

Lexi looked at J, wanting more information.

"I've been going to Woody's for AA meetings. Just keeping it solid. Supporting others. This new life has been a lot for me, too, Lexi." J paused, then asked, "So how is the book coming along?"

"I'm almost done. I'm close to sending it to Michelle."

"Good. I had no idea. I thought you were struggling."

"I was, but mostly it was about some edits I made, but knew I had to put them back in. It's way out there for me, J."

"I'll be curious what good ole Michelle thinks."

"Oh, she'll hate it. She'll want me to publish under a pseudonym."

"Will you?"

"Hell no."

"Why not? Many famous writers do that when they write in a different genre."

"Because this is me. This is the spiritual, maybe mystical, me. This is what I've been hiding. And you know what?" Lexi was sitting up, energized in the strength of her full Self. "You know what? I think I like being in this Paddy May world. It, he, is now part of my world and me, his. Thanks, J. This has been a great talk."

Lexi stood up. "I need to call Paddy. Thanks again for the advice, J."

"Happy to help," J said as she walked into the house, where she couldn't hear him say, "I did nothing, but that's how you and I do it, Lexi Maxwell."

CHAPTER 47

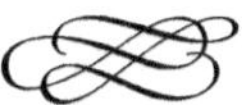

The next several weeks were about Lexi listening to her literary agent telling her all the ways this "almost pornographic book and Paddy May" were risky. Maybe too risky. Paddy was in the studio with Paul and Owen laying down tracks, wondering about Eric's return.

Lexi and Paddy moved back to the London home so Paddy could be close to the studio. Lexi walked to Barbara's Tea Shoppe every morning before sunlight, sneaking in the back door to avoid the crowd of fans that were still holding vigil in the neighborhood.

Paddy insisted on walking to the studio. Graham and his team walked with him, an SUV always nearby for escape if needed. It wasn't. Somehow, Paddy being more visible, more physically approachable, calmed the fans. In fact, they protected the entire band and their loved ones. They would intervene if another fan became too intrusive. The troop of regular fans would surround media who wanted to hound the rock stars and their families, blocking their chance at good photographs.

The public thought that Eric had relocated to his farm in Scotland to recover, but he, his wife, and three children had moved in with Woody. The house was full of people: Eric's family, Woody's family, morning AA meetings with famous rock stars and locals. It seemed to be exactly the intense, twenty-four-hour support Eric needed.

Paddy, Owen, and Paul had several private visits with Eric. Nigel wasn't invited to any of them.

"Paddy, what's going on? We've been together for years," Nigel pleaded with Paddy one night when he dropped by the London House unannounced. Lexi could hear the panic in Nigel's voice from the other room.

Paddy's softspoken voice made it too hard for her to hear his full reply, but she did hear him tell Nigel, "The band needs time to heal and decide how we want to move forward."

"Will I still be part of that, Paddy?"

Lexi couldn't hear Paddy response.

A few days after Nigel's visit, Lexi had an equally tense conversation with her agent about her book.

"The publisher's not printing this, Lexi."

Before writing the book, before being in her new world in London, before Paddy, Lexi would have panicked at her agent's words and pleaded for acceptance. She probably would have reluctantly agreed and ditched the book.

That was before. Before she lived in her full Self. The Self she'd always been, but now was refusing to hide.

"Okay," she said to her agent, "I'll find someone who will."

"Lexi, this book is just too much. Too different from anything you've done before. You have detailed sexual scenes combined with talking to the dead in your closet and imagined night flights to mountain tops to listen to the full moon. It'll be a shock to fans who buy it thinking it's another *Cally Series* book by Lexi Maxwell."

There was silence, and Michelle smiled, feeling that she'd won, that she'd convinced her longtime client, her most successful author, to return to writing the type of novels her fans followed.

"Okay. You don't have to be part of it anymore, Michelle. Life goes by faster than you think it will, and so you shouldn't do something you don't want to do." Lexi's voice was calm and detached.

Michelle Abrahamson sat in her office overlooking the Hudson River. It was a glorious, sunny day in New York City. She knew she needed to either support Lexi or lose her.

"You won't consider a pseudonym? So many of the great writers do that, you know."

"No. Are you embarrassed by me now, Michelle?"

The two women sat in silence on either side of the Atlantic.

"No, Lexi. I know a wonderful indie publisher in London who will be perfect for this book, and this new writing of yours. Give me a few days."

"Thank you."

CHAPTER 48

Lexi was fascinated by Paddy's London House. It was historic with wooden floors, three stories and a basement, two turrets, a garden in the front and another, much larger one, in the back.

The top floor of the London House was in two parts. One was Paddy's bedroom with the large four-posted bed nestled in the turret. The other half was the reading room. An enormous stone fireplace separated the two areas.

Lexi still hadn't brought much of her belongings into the house.

"It concerns me that you've not really settled in, Lexi. Does this feel temporary?"

"No. I feel very comfortable here."

"I meant us. Our relationship. Does it still feel temporary, Lexi, because it doesn't feel like you've made this your home yet."

"Well, it isn't really my home, you know."

They were lying in bed. The room was not completely dark because Lexi had pulled the shades all the way to the top of the windows to allow the full moon to shine down on them. They were naked, lying on their sides facing one another, legs interlaced. Their hands slid up and down each other's bodies, reigniting their connection, waking them for the love being shared.

The tips of Paddy's fingers were rough from callouses. He was so gentle, though, that the touch tickled her rather than feeling like a scrape. Tender. That word best described Paddy for Lexi.

He cupped Lexi's breast and rolled his tongue around her nipples. She stretched out on her back so he could see her full body in the moon's rays. She loved that fact that he loved to look at her naked body. She was convinced that he didn't even need to penetrate her because he seemed so satisfied just looking at her, letting his hands and mouth explore her.

"I love your red hair and that you've not shaved between your legs." He lowered his head between her legs, his tongue nudging through her hair to her vagina. She felt herself swell and knew her clitoris was full and erect. It always happened now with Paddy and, when he found the hardness of her excitement, his passion surged.

He knelt over her, full, strong and surging to be inside her. Lexi wrapped her legs around his back and pulled him toward her. He slipped inside her and then did what she always loved seeing: he tilted his head back, closed his eyes and opened his mouth in a silent sigh of ecstasy. With Paddy, Lexi had learned how to have orgasms in this position, in addition to all the ways she knew before.

Afterwards they lingered, letting Paddy naturally relax out of her body. He rested his head on her chest, and she stroked his hair. They let the sexual energy subside before talking about what Lexi called "the administration of life."

"Is it okay if Jack comes over for his school break?"

"Yes. Of course. You don't have to ask, Lexi. See, this is what I meant earlier about you're not living here yet, at least not emotionally. Please, Lexi. Aren't we family now?"

"Family."

"Yes. Family. You, me, Jack, my parents, Evelyn, Julien. Even J. Family. This is how I think of us. But you don't."

Lexi twirled some of Paddy's curls, then kissed his forehead.

"You know, I actually do think of us as family, it's just that I…"

"Do we need to be married to be family?"

Paddy sat up.

His question made Lexi speechless. Then she wondered.

"That's interesting. What is different from what we have now from if we were married?"

"Well, I wouldn't know, Lexi. Sofia and I weren't even together four years. I was on tour most of that time anyway." He sat quietly. "So, what would it mean for us to be married, Lexi? How is it different from what we have now?"

"I married Steve because I was barely twenty and pregnant. I loved him, and he was my best friend. I have no idea if we would have married otherwise. I think so. I do love his family. That was a big part of the success of our marriage. Steve knew how to love, how to be in relationship, how to care and how to just declare we were a forever couple. I think that's a lot of it. All of that."

Paddy said, "I know how to love my parents. I know how to love my children, even when I was messed up. I love my band mates. They are part of my family. I imagine you as my forever…"

Just then, a blinding search light shined in the room. The couple was disoriented, then realized some kind of spotlight was beaming into the bedroom, revealing their naked bodies. Paddy covered them, and they slid off the bed onto the floor.

"Jesus! What is that?"

"I don't know."

The two crawled out of the bedroom with the bedsheet covering them like a tent. They were the only ones in the house that suddenly felt very large and empty, unprotective.

The light went away. Paddy put on pants and lowered all the shades in the bedroom. He peeked outside to see if he could determine what caused the light. He felt like he knew, but wasn't sure how. It was Samantha Peters somehow, taking pictures of her favorite person to stalk.

CHAPTER 49

Eric returned to the studio without telling the band he was coming that day. It had been weeks since his accident. He wasn't sure when he would return and so didn't want to say anything and then not make it.

Amanda saw him first. They hugged, and then he walked into the studio where the band was working through a section of music Owen had initiated. They stopped when Eric came in. He waved his hand and simply said, "Carry on."

The band smiled. Eric looked healthy. He slowly walked around the room over to the piano, the place where he had downed two bottles of bourbon in less than two hours, laid down and died.

He sat at the piano and listened to his mates play a slow piece. The yearning in the music was so heartfelt. When they stopped, Eric asked, "Do you have lyrics?"

Paddy said, "We've been waiting for you."

Amanda turned on the studio mic and said, "I have your writing pads here, Eric."

Eric retrieved the pads and pens, then sat in the middle of the musicians and started writing as they played.

Eric wrote "Lazarus" across the top of the page.

It was the first song in what was about to become The Crashers' next album, *Resurrection*.

The band was back on schedule like the very early days when they didn't have much money for studio time. They stayed focused and completed so many great songs in less than a month. Paddy was always the producer and Amanda the engineer on all except the first two albums.

Amanda let her tears of joy flow as she looked through the glass to the four men sitting close to one another, surrounded by cables and microphones. She noticed they were sitting closer to Owen's drum kit than usual. It was as if they were one body with a missing part having returned.

The studio receptionist had arranged lunch without being asked.

"I thought we might go out to lunch," Paddy said.

The receptionist said, "You haven't looked outside. The whole world knows Eric's here. Graham has added a wall of security around the building. Let me know if you want something else." She stopped before leaving the room. "You know, I work here, but I'm also a fan of The Crashers. I can tell you that you guys being together, Eric being okay, is hugely important to us. You are a part of our lives whether or not you know it. We fans really think of you as family." She looked at each band member, stopping at Eric. "I think everyone needs to see Eric now. They know he's here and will feel left out if you don't at least come outside and wave."

The band sat quietly.

Eric spoke first. "This is where we need Nigel. He does all that so we can just make music."

Paddy still had his Gibson guitar in his lap and his fingers unconsciously played new chords. Amanda turned on the recording without telling the band. She turned it off when the band spoke, then turned it back on when Paddy played. Back and forth, back and forth.

Owen started the conversation the band needed to have.

"We can't do things like we've always done. The constant touring,

I mean. I've wanted it to stop for a couple of years now. I want to, need to, be with my family. And it's literally been killing you, Paddy, and Eric. Literally."

Paul added, "Yeah. I love this band. Us. You're my best mates, but I need to be home more than we've been for, for almost a decade now—we've always been on the road. There's been too much chaos. Too much drugs, booze, girls we don't know."

Paddy said, "I understand. I understand it, probably for the first time ever, mate. My life has changed so much these last months. But I still want this band."

"Yes, we do too, Paddy."

Paul, the bass player, who was the quietest and most stoic, said, "We need to talk with Nigel and tell him what we want now and give him the choice to stay with us the way we want to work now or..." He let his voice trail off.

None of them could imagine being without Nigel. He was the fifth member of the group, figuratively and legally in the corporation Paddy had established in the early years.

Everyone looked at Paddy.

"Let's call Nigel."

"Now?"

"Yes. Let's bring him here and discuss this now. We told our fans at the hospital we'd keep them up to date on Eric. Let's see how Nigel advises us on that. And then let's have the real talk."

CHAPTER 50

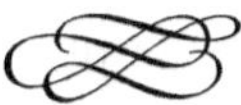

Paddy didn't arrive home until almost eight, much later than usual. He and Lexi made a point of having dinner together every night. They both were deep into their work. Paddy in the studio, and Lexi now meeting with her new London publisher.

Paddy had texted her the news that Eric had arrived unexpectedly at the studio. Nigel was summoned to help handle the crowd gathering and announce Eric's status.

Paddy came in through the front door, waving to the fans who now kept constant vigil at his house. Lexi noticed his "five o'clock shadow" was much heavier than usual, and she wondered if he'd shaved before leaving the house in the morning.

They hugged, kissed and held one another. It was their habit. They had learned that taking extra moments each time they greeted one another helped erase the craziness of their external world and enveloped them in their own protective bubble.

"Elga made us a nice dinner. It's in the conservatory. I thought that might help us both relax. We've had quite the day, haven't we?"

"Yeah. I really want to hear about yours. Can I take a quick shower first? I feel like I need to shower first and remove all the dust from being on the rooftop."

"The rooftop?"

"Yeah. Nigel had us go on the rooftop to show off Eric."

"Like the Beatles long ago."

"Blasphemy, my lady. No one is like the Beatles."

"Go shower."

Lexi looked at social media while waiting for Paddy. There they were. The Crashers on the rooftop of their three-story studio, waving and smiling at the hundreds of cheering, crying and screaming fans. Video showed dozens of police helping to manage the crowd.

The BBC reported the story with delight. "Hundreds of fans screamed and cried in joy today as Eric Hunter, lead singer of The Crashers, made a surprise appearance on the rooftop of their Maith Studio. Mr. Hunter had died just nine weeks ago in the studio and was revived by CPR. He has not been seen since, but certainly looked healthy and strong in his rooftop appearance today."

Lexi was looking at the social media posts when Paddy walked into the garden atrium. He took her breath away. He was wearing tight-fitting jeans over his long legs, the Scully western shirt she'd bought him in Dallas and was barefoot. His hair was wet and started curling and waving in the way that had excited Lexi since her youth when she stared at posters of him in her bedroom.

She held up her cell and said, "I had no idea this happened today."

"It happened fast."

"Nigel's idea?"

"Yes."

"Did you invite him back?"

"Yes. It was time. The guys and I discussed everything. Owen started it, saying we really need to address the situation, but I want to talk about your day first."

The couple sat in the middle of the atrium at the long wooden table they had recently bought so Lexi could write among the flowers, plants and trees on days when she wasn't at Barbara's Tea Shoppe.

"I think I have a new publisher."

"That's great. Who?"

"It's called Meru Press. They are a small, but very successful, indie press. Michelle arranged a meeting, and I had lunch with them. A four-hour lunch."

Paddy stood up and leaned over to hug Lexi, kissing her.

"This sounds promising. Meru? Isn't that a Yeats poem.?"

"Paddy May, that's why I love you. You are a man of many talents and knowledge."

Paddy grinned. He was clearly happy for her. "What's next?"

"She asked me to have my attorney send her the contract I want."

"What?"

"Yeah. She said, send me what you want, but, remember, we are an indie press and so the budgets may be different. At least at first."

"Cheers."

The two lifted their water glasses.

"Now, tell me about your day on the roof."

The atrium was dark, and they left it that way. They still didn't know for certain who, or what, had flashed a search light in their bedroom several days before. They kept their routines as much as possible, but they knew turning on lights in the atrium at night made them easy targets for pictures. So, they sat in the dark with the moon providing a soft light.

"Eric's back. He just slipped right back in with us. Started writing lyrics while we worked out tunes. It feels like our first days when we practiced at my Thames House. We all just flowed together. We really didn't even have to talk."

"But you did."

"When we were told us an even bigger crowd was gathering because word was out that Eric was at the studio, we agreed we needed to talk about how we want to be as a band now. Owen said it best. We had been on an addictive high the past several years. We've been recording, touring, recording, touring with Eric, Nigel, and me heavily fueled by our addictions. Owen and Paul have asked us to slow down many times, and we've ignored them. They made it clear today that they are not going back to that pace."

Paddy stopped.

"Did they threaten to quit?"

"Oh, it was no threat. They'd been talking to each other, and said they are out if Eric and I don't stay sober, and if we don't change the schedule. They've talked with their families, and all feel that Eric's death was the warning to us all."

"And Nigel?"

"And then there's Nigel." Paddy shifted uncomfortably in his chair. "We asked Nigel to come to the studio to hear his ideas about Eric being back, which turned into the media circus on the roof. He showed up smoking non-stop as always and eyes looking like he was coked-up."

"Yikes."

"Yeah. Yikes."

"We did the media thing and then sat in the studio and told him what we want as a band from now on."

"Which is?"

"First, we have to have the booze and drugs out. Eric and I can't have it around, and Owen and Paul have never had the problems with it. They could care less about that stuff. Next, we aren't going to tour all the time."

"Oh, I bet Nigel didn't like that."

"No. He actually broke into a visible sweat when we said that one."

"Who led the discussion?"

"We all did. It wasn't me leading the business talk like usual. Owen and Paul really spoke up. A lot. Eric, too."

"Did Nigel understand? Did he agree?"

"He agreed for sure, but I could tell he's thrown. He kept trying to get us to elaborate on what reduced touring means. You know, that's where the huge sales come and the huge publicity."

Lexi's former media relations days filled her mind. She was quiet and obviously thinking.

Paddy smiled at her. "All right, Miss Former Publicity Person, what are you thinking?"

They laughed.

"Why not do multiple nights in the same place?" Lexi suggested. "Maybe live broadcast one night, film the rest and release the film? Or mix it up. Several nights here, say at the O2 and then go to Madison Garden in New York and maybe Tokyo. The film shows a mix of all the regions. Maybe even like a documentary. I bet you could get the BBC to broadcast the opening night live. Make it for charity. Staying in one place for several nights gives fans time to travel to see you. Maybe have Nigel arrange for discounted rates at hotels for those with tickets."

"You've got quite a plan."

"Just thinking out loud. No one's done something quite like that. The Crashers would have another first. And, the band won't kill itself anymore. You can have lives. Lives with all your loved ones."

Paddy reached out and squeezed Lexi's hand.

"What time does Jack's flight arrive tomorrow?" he remembered.

CHAPTER 51

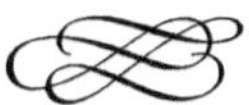

Graham discovered who had shined the light on Paddy and Lexi's bedroom that night.

Samantha Peters had arranged a camera on a drone and had photos of the couple naked in bed. She was selling them off her website. Graham was looking at them. While their most private parts were not visible, the pictures showed Paddy clearly sitting up naked in bed with a woman's legs around his waist. The top of her head and the curves of her naked body visible. By now, the world knew it was Lexi Maxwell, but this was a very intimate photograph.

Devoted fans claimed their disgust, but everyone seemed to have copies of the photos.

Graham called Paddy's lawyer to discuss what legal actions could be taken. He wanted to know all the options available before talking with Paddy. Graham had started doing things Nigel typically would do for Paddy because he'd noticed The Crashers' manager was floundering.

He paid the fee on Samantha's site and downloaded all the pictures. He used his own name, putting the photographer on notice.

Paddy's daughter, Evelyn, told her dad about it before Graham had the chance. "Gee, Dad, looking pretty good there all naked and such."

"What are you talking about?"

Evelyn and Julien were at the London House. They wanted to go to Heathrow with Paddy and Lexi to meet Jack. Evelyn showed her dad the photos on her screen. She, too, had paid to see the "private sex photos of Paddy May."

Paddy turned red, more from anger than embarrassment.

"You can't really see the most personal stuff," his daughter said, trying to help.

Paddy snapped the photos off. Lexi walked into the room and could tell something was wrong. She thought it might be with Paddy and his children.

"Should I come back?"

"No. Samantha Peters was the one responsible for the lights in our bedroom that night. She's posted and is selling photos of us."

Evelyn opened up the pictures to show Lexi, who studied them all slowly.

"I gotta admit, Paddy, if I wasn't with you, I'd buy these too. Damn, you look good naked by the moonlight." Lexi wanted the photo of Paddy. His smile was soft, and he was looking at her with pure love.

The teenagers laughed with Lexi. After all, they'd grown up knowing about Samantha Peter's iconic postcoital photo of their Dad when he was nineteen. They'd also seen all the photos of him with various groupies and knew all the stories. Their mother never hid the reality of their father.

Lexi eyed Evelyn careful to be certain she really was okay with all this. Sofia had recently talked with Lexi about how her daughter was beginning to realize Lexi was here to stay and that her role as "Papa's favorite girl" was evolving.

Paddy wasn't laughing. Just then Graham walked in. "The car's ready."

Then Graham saw what was going on. "I'm sorry, Paddy. I was

going to talk to you about those. I've contacted the attorneys to see what rights you two have."

Everyone stood quietly.

Julien finally said, "Don't we need to go pick up Jack?"

Paddy and Lexi were in the middle seats and Graham in the front passenger seat, with a security man driving. Graham had arranged such a quick pickup with Jack that fans were unable to realize Paddy May was there.

Evelyn couldn't wait to show Jack the photos of his naked mom. Clearly, she wanted to cause a stir. She opened up the pictures the minute Jack got into the far back seats of the SUV with her and Julien.

Paddy was furious with Evelyn. "Stop that, Evie. Why do you think that's the right thing to do right now?"

Jack looked at the photos of his mom and Paddy.

"It's okay," Jack said, calmly handing the phone back to Evie. "I'm with your dad. Why did you feel the need to show me these first thing, without even giving me a heads-up that I was about to see our parents naked? And obviously just after they made love."

Lexi turned around and winked at her son. Though Jack was only a couple of years older than Evelyn, he had clearly not had the same exposure to sex, drugs and rock and roll as Paddy's children. But he was far more comfortable with adult actions.

The car was quiet the rest of the ride back to their London home. Lexi reached out and held Paddy's hand. It took him a few moments to truly notice. Finally, he smiled and squeezed her hand.

Jack had been to London other times before. A favorite memory of his was taking photos from top of a red double-decker bus when he was about seven. He kept saying "got it" with each snap of the camera Lexi had surprised him with on the flight over.

There were a few fans on the sidewalk across from the London house.

Jack asked, "What's going on?"

Julien answered, "Welcome to your new life, Jack. These are

some of Papa's fans, usually American tourists, who come to take a photo of our famous house."

Paddy's parents were waiting inside. Lexi had invited them. The mood lightened and the happiness of the winter holiday in Ireland returned to the group. J came for dinner that first night.

Lexi whispered to Paddy after dinner, "This is close to pure bliss, isn't it?"

Paddy wrapped his arms around her. "Thank you. Thank you for this. This is how I dreamed my life would be when I was fifteen. I was going to be a rock star with a beautiful wife and perfect children. And I have it."

She felt his body tighten.

"But?" she asked.

"But I'm petrified I'm going to lose it."

"Paddy, what we focus on expands. Look at this." They turned and looked at the kitchen full of their loved ones, who were cleaning dishes, laughing and putting a board game on the table. "Look at this, Paddy. You and I created this. This is ours."

"We made a real family didn't we, Red?"

Paddy played a few games, but was clearly distracted.

"I need to go downstairs and play for a while, is that okay?"

The family knew to respect Paddy's need to play his guitar at any moment. They knew Lexi was the same way with her writing.

The lowest level of the London House had some recording equipment, but it was more where Paddy retreated to sit with an acoustic guitar and left his fingers roam over the strings. It was meditation for him.

After a while, Lexi walked downstairs to say goodnight. She stood at the bottom of the stairs, her breath literally taken at the beauty of Paddy's music.

She stepped inside the room. Paddy stopped playing as she walked to him. He held his guitar to his side and motioned for her to sit on his lap. He then put his arms around her with the guitar on her lap.

"I'll be your right hand and you be my left. We will play together, as one."

"As one." Lexi could barely speak, she was so deeply touched by Paddy's action.

Nestled on his lap, his arms around her, holding the guitar on her lap, Paddy May held Lexi's left hand to teach her chords. She moved her right arm, resting it on his right hand while he stroked the strings.

She closed her eyes, leaning into Paddy and feeling the vibration of the guitar that they were now, in a way, playing together as one.

Sometime before dawn, Paddy set the guitar aside. Lexi turned around in the chair, and they made love.

CHAPTER 52

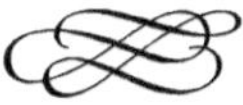

"An entire album of quiet music?"

Nigel was in the studio with the band, listening to their latest production. Paddy and Amanda had spent the night fine-tuning tracks. Nigel stopped by to tell the group that the BBC was very interested in the live concert for charity concept at the O2 that Lexi had suggested.

"We are calling the album *Resurrection*," Owen answered. "And the lead song is 'Lazarus.'"

Nigel looked at the band that was his life. He was chewing his gum so fast that he bit the inside of his mouth. "Damn."

The band looked at each other. Their manager had clearly changed his habits, at least when he was with them. He had multiple nicotine patches on his arm, chewed massive amounts of gum, and had started attending Woody's morning AA meetings. This band was his life, and he didn't want to lose it. It was still a huge struggle for him. "Why didn't it seem as hard for Paddy and Eric as it is for me?" he asked his wife one night as she poured another drink for herself.

The music world was anxiously waiting for The Crashers' new creation, and the publishing world was equally curious about Lexi

Maxwell's forthcoming book. The gossip press loved capturing photos of the couple as they walked throughout London, often with their children, including Jack, when he was in town.

"Paddy and Lexi in Love" was the frequent headline. They'd become the couple that made people feel good, and their willingness to walk about publicly endeared them even more. Of course, it was a huge challenge for Graham and his security team. Graham knew it only took an instant from one person to change everything.

Paddy and Lexi decided not to pursue charges against Samantha for the nude photos. "We don't need that negative energy in our lives, Paddy." While the attorney disagreed, Nigel released a statement saying, "Ms. Peters is a talented photographer. Of course, Paddy and Lexi wish she didn't violate their private life so inappropriately, but they wish her a good and decent life."

Good and decent life. The phrase Paddy used with Samantha the year prior when she followed him out of Paddington Station.

Presales for Lexi's book were the largest of any book, not just in the UK, but also throughout the EU. US sales were also strong, although a much harder market to top. J decided he wanted to be Lexi's manager full-time.

"What about your writing, J?"

"I'm still writing. Slower. But this is a ride I want to be on, Lexi. You, Paddy, this life, Woody's morning group, my girlfriend. I feel like I was made for this."

Nigel gave J an office at his production company. It was much easier to coordinate the couple that way.

Things seemed to be flowing well, but Lexi noticed subtle changes in Paddy as the band started practicing for the shows at Wembley Stadium. Plans changed from the O2 because the ticket agency said that venue at 20,000 seats was too small to meet the demand they knew was already building. Wembley held 90,000, and the band sold out seven shows in less than an hour. That was 630,000 people, with more than 500,000 trying to buy tickets if more dates were added.

Paddy had started growing a beard and was quieter. The band had decided they weren't going to release *Resurrection* until the night of the first show and that first-day sales were all going to charity.

On the surface, everything was going well for both The Crashers and best-selling author Lexi Maxwell. Lexi's gut told her, however, that Paddy was starting to stress about the shows. She remembered looking at the photos at the house in Ireland with his mother. The photos of his career where, the more his fame increased, the more he hid behind his beard, slumped during performances, and drank until almost blackout.

Wembley would be the first time, probably ever, to play sober.

Lexi decided it was time for a "walk and talk," as they called them. They enjoyed walking. It was, after all, how their relationship began. They discovered if they each tucked their distinctive hair—his long curls and her vibrant red—into hats, they had a decent chance at walking longer without being recognized. Graham's teams were masterful at staying close, but not being intrusive, allowing Paddy and Lexi to feel somewhat normal.

She surprised Paddy and the band by showing up at the studio during their rehearsal time.

"Let's walk and talk," she said with a smile, handing him his hat.

Paddy knew to accept her request. She'd never done anything like this before. The band just nodded as he put on the hat.

Outside, the couple had to handle the celebrity part of their lives and "sign and pose" as Paddy called it. Paddy's fans had become Lexi's, and hers his.

Some fans followed as they walked down the street, but eventually other fans policed the followers, saying, "Hey, give them their space." Graham's team was always surprised and relieved at how the hard-core fans protected the couple so fiercely, especially from any paparazzi.

They walked around North London in silence for a few minutes, then Paddy asked, "What's up?"

"Your beard."

"Huh?" Paddy instinctively stroked his bushy growth. "You don't like it?"

"That's not it, Paddy. And I think you know that. Remember what I told you I discovered with your mam in Ireland? About your photos over the years…"

"That I hide behind my beard."

"It's not the beard I worry about."

Paddy held her hand, and they kept walking. He was looking ahead, not at her.

"Lexi, I've never performed sober."

"Never? Not even when you were on that BBC variety show where you were eight?"

He stopped walking and looked at her. "Not even then. The guys in the band gave me a shot of whiskey to calm my nerves."

Lexi wanted to hug him, but knew he was already feeling exposed emotionally and that might be too much for him at that moment. Paddy looked like a little boy, his eyes sad, pleading for help.

Instead, she turned to keep walking. She'd learned from living with Steve and Jack that sometimes you had to focus on something else for the conversation to open up. That was why she learned to shoot hockey pucks in the garage with them.

"So, what are your thoughts about how you're going to prepare for this, Paddy?"

"I. Have. No. Idea," he said, slowly emphasizing each word.

The couple walked for more than an hour, eventually returning to the London House neighborhood. They were in front of Woody's house just as his car pulled into the drive. A rear window rolled down, and Woody popped his head out saying, "Are you two stalking me?" He laughed his smokey voice laugh and jumped out of the car.

"I didn't stage this, Paddy," Lexi said, knowing that Paddy wondered if she'd discussed his fear of performing sober with his longtime mate.

"It must be divine intervention then, Lexi."

Woody was laughing as he hugged each of them. "Come in for tea?"

"I need to go read the gallies of my book one last time. You two go on, though."

Paddy said, "I'll let the band know what I'm doing."

"I don't want to keep you from your mates, Paddy," said Woody.

Paddy kissed Lexi goodbye and turned to his childhood mate.

"It's okay. I need to talk with you, Woody."

CHAPTER 53

Jarius was waiting for Lexi on the top floor of the London House. Paddy had surprised Lexi weeks earlier by having her favorite round, wooden Empire table shipped from Dallas to London. He converted the second half of the top floor into her writing room. The master bedroom on one side of the house and her own writing room in the other half. He positioned the round table in the turret. The floor-to-ceiling bookcases lining the walls had been rearranged to include her personal books, which he had also had shipped. J and Steve's mother had helped select what they thought she wanted.

J was spending more time in the London House now that he was officially representing Lexi and arranging for the launch of her much-anticipated new book. His girlfriend, Amanda's sister, was back from Oxford, and she was also staying in town. The Crashers family was expanding with Lexi, Jack, J, and Steve's family. Paddy was in regular communication with Steve's mother and the rest of the family in Dallas, which surprised and delighted Lexi. The family had been terrific taking turns going to New York to see Jack's games. Lexi flew to New York about every third or fourth weekend, usually with Paddy. She still couldn't understand how a parent could just ship a child away. Of course, she noticed that was the common practice among a certain economic class in Europe.

J was at the round Empire table with Lexi's book manuscript spread before him. "You sent a copy to Steve's family, right?"

Lexi gazed out the window of the turret at the loyal fans out front. They never bothered anyone coming or going to the House. Paddy and Lexi learned some of their names, and J would often stop and have conversations with them. Lexi suspected he was going to write a book about them.

"I've never sent them gallies before."

J put his pen down and stared at his mentor and friend.

"Lexi, this is personal. Very personal, about their son and brother." He paused. "What's really going on? Why haven't you sent it? Have you even given them a heads-up?"

Her silence told him the answer. He pushed away from the table and leaned back in his chair with his hands wrapped around the back of his head.

"Talk to me."

Lexi sat down. "Should I really be doing this, J?"

J leaned forward on the table and reached out to put his hand on Lexi's arm.

"Yes. Period. End of sentence. Yes."

"Why?"

"This," he motioned to the papers on the table, "is how you move on. And it's the fullest, most emotional, deep writing you've ever done. It takes you to a new level, Lexi." J paused, worried if he should really say what was next. "Lexi, this is full-woman writing. Everything before has been good-girl writing."

J waited. The two just looked at each other. Not in a stare-down, but in a way that traveled back all the years they'd known one another, and maybe further back than that.

Lexi broke the silence first. "Will my readers stay with me? This isn't *Cally and Her Summer Adventures*."

"Some won't. But your social media shows you're attracting more fans. It may be that your fan base is building more in Europe."

"The States are a bigger market, though."

"Does that really matter anymore?

"No. I guess not." Lexi looked at the time. "I think I'll call the family in Dallas."

CHAPTER 54

Waterstones Piccadilly practically begged J to hold the launch party for Lexi's book. Their marketing team pitched ideas to J and the publisher, and they were even courting Lexi directly, sending boxes of her favorite writing journals and purple pens to the London House.

They wanted to hold the launch party the day before The Crashers' opening show at Wembley.

"I know that's not their only available day, J."

Lexi was sitting in J's office at Nigel's production company. J and Nigel found their clients' lives overlapped so much that it was just easier to plan together. Plus, J had become Nigel's unofficial sponsor in his sobriety journey. A journey Nigel was failing most days, but he was drinking less and had quit drugs. He still smoked almost non-stop, even with several nicotine patches lined up and down his right arm.

"They clearly want to take advantage of all the press around the live BBC show with The Crashers. The buzz is enormous. People from all over the world are flying in. The Biggin Hill airport is already booked solid for all the jets."

"So, am I just the girlfriend now?"

J took in a deep breath and exhaled long and slow.

"Good question. I don't think so. I think you're now one part of a two-part super couple."

"Ironic, isn't it? The most personal book I've written is coming out when I'm the most public I've ever been."

"No niche author now."

"Ugh. Wait, niche author? You think that's what I've been?"

"No. No." J knew he'd hit a raw nerve.

"Well, then what? You said it pretty fast."

Jarius put his hand on Lexi's arm. "Lexi, you are a multi-faceted, complicated—in a good way—woman. Steve always said you were the most interesting person he'd ever met in his life. And you are. You're the most interesting person I've ever met. But you've not put that fullness of your being into your writing. Until now." J patted the galleys of her book.

Lexi shook her head. "I'm not sure about this."

"It's your call. Nigel and I have talked, and we can schedule it such that Paddy and the band can stop by and show their support."

"You've really become the promoter now, huh?"

"What's the balance, Lexi? That's what we've—you've—got to decide. Your books have always been popular. The *Cally* series on the BBC has been renewed. Now *you*—not just the books, but *you*—you are the point of interest. People are fascinated by you and Paddy. There's such affection for you two and your children. Word's out that Paddy is sober. The band is sober. Everyone credits you for that. People have it figured that you saved Eric. It's all a feel-good story. And you and Paddy both seem to be at your creative high point. I know you've heard the new music."

"It's nothing short of stunning."

"Stunning barely describes it. And it's a risk for them too. Like your book. This music is very different for them."

"You and Nigel have clients who are each about to launch new products, so to speak."

"That sounds harsh. And Nigel is technically part of The Crashers, you know."

Lexi paused. "I'm sorry, J. We should do that, too."

"Do what?"

"Incorporate, or whatever the legal term is. You're right. Nigel is the fifth Crasher, and you're my second half in a writing life."

"Let's think that through later. Right now, we need to talk Waterstones Piccadilly."

"The largest bookstore in Europe."

"The largest bookstore in Europe."

"Has Nigel talked with Paddy about this joint appearance?"

"Nope. Waiting on your okay first."

Just then Nigel walked by J's office area, his smoker's cough announcing him from the hallway. He looked in on the pair. It was clear he knew Jarius had been talking with her about the joint appearance.

Lexi waved him in. Nigel had learned not to kiss Lexi so soon after smoking because it always kicked off a sneezing spell for her. He stood in the doorway.

"J told me about Waterstones' offer. I need to talk with Paddy first."

"You two are a power couple now."

"So, I've heard."

"It's best just to embrace it. That way you manage it better. It doesn't manage you." Nigel lifted his eyebrows to underscore his advice.

"I'm not so sure about that yet, Nigel."

<h1 style="text-align:center">CHAPTER 55</h1>

The full moon shone in on Paddy and Lexi, who were both stretched out in bed. They had decided to keep their blinds open on nights like this, believing that Samantha Peters wouldn't photograph them again. There had been more negative than positive publicity about the photographer publishing her last photos, although everyone seemed to have copies of the couple nude.

Paddy was thinking how Lexi was so much freer with her body and lovemaking when the kids weren't staying at the house.

"I think I've figured out why you and Steve only had one child."

"How's that?"

Paddy propped up on one elbow, his curls hanging playfully over his face.

"You never had sex again." Paddy chuckled, amused at himself.

"What?"

"Indeed. You are so much more relaxed when we're the only two in the house."

"Well, duh, ya think?"

"I didn't expect you to prance around naked when they're here, but I thought, behind closed doors, you'd still be all sexy and everything."

Lexi realized that Paddy had not lived in his house with both a lover and his children. He never let his girlfriends stay at his home. They were only allowed at the flat he owned for just such "relationships." He was essentially on the road the three years when he was with Sofia, and they had Julien and Evelyn, but he didn't remember that much.

"Well, for the record, Steve and I did have sex more than once."

"I'm sorry, I didn't mean…"

"But it is true that I'm different. It's an old habit from when Jack was young. We joked that every time Steve and I wanted to be romantic, didn't matter time of night or if Jack was supposed to be at a friend's house, he would suddenly appear outside our bedroom door yelling, 'MOM!'"

Paddy laid down and pulled her on top of him.

"You are a great mom to him and Julien and Evelyn."

"I'm not totally sure about Evelyn yet."

"Oh? She told me just last Sunday that we finally have a real family."

The couple had started having Sunday dinners with Paddy's parents, J, Evelyn and Julien either in London or at Thames House. Often, Sofia and her husband would stay too. At some point during dinner, they always called Jack, who was back in New York, sometimes keeping him more than an hour. Indeed, a family.

Lexi looked out the window at the moon. It soothed her. She didn't want to talk administrative matters in bed, but it often was the best place for their truest feelings to emerge.

"Paddy, can we talk work?"

"Is this about Nigel and J wanting your book party the day before opening night?"

"So much for them letting me talk to you first."

"Nigel is impulsive, you know. Can't wait on anything. His

strength and weakness all in one. I think it's your decision. It's your book, your night. I don't want the focus on the band and me."

"At the same time..."

"At the same time, I, we, want to support you."

"We?"

"Of course. The guys and their wives have all already told me they want to attend the event."

Lexi felt a surge of joy.

"How did this happen, Paddy? All this. How did you and I and our families and our friends just slip into being one big family so easily?"

"You, Lexi. You. You're how it happened. You are the glue. You set the tone with me the first day. You just accepted me, loved me, from the first handshake. No judgment. You just adored me. And I knew I wanted to be with you forever that day. And I knew there were things I needed to change to be with you."

"I knew I wanted to be with you forever from that first handshake, too. You know that, right?"

"Now I know."

CHAPTER 56

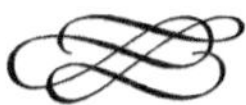

It seemed there was no other news in England other than The Crashers' upcoming shows at Wembley and the live broadcast of opening night on the BBC.

Waterstones Piccadilly had to re-locate Lexi's appearance to the Royal Albert Hall. It sold out the first hour. Lexi's casual book signing was now a major event.

Lexi was still concerned about Paddy's performance anxiety. He still had his beard. In fact, it was longer. His mother had even talked with Lexi about her concerns.

The stage was being built at Wembley. It was massive, with big screens located throughout to give fans good views regardless of where they were standing or sitting. Camera crews from both the BBC and the film production team were everywhere, setting up shots and coordinating locations.

The plan was for the BBC team to take priority opening night for the live broadcast, but letting Nigel's film crew still capture what they needed. Then Nigel's film team would capture all the remaining nights of the seven-night stand and turn it into a film.

"We're rehearsing at Wembley today."

Paddy and Lexi were in the atrium having breakfast.

"How does that feel?"

"That's not the problem. I'll be in producer mode, concerned more about the sound and the flow of our set list. It'll just be the techies and film crews. My focus is the band and the sound."

"Would you like me to come along?"

"You can if you'd like."

She knew he wanted her there.

The stadium was so enormous that it dwarfed football stadiums back in the States. Several hundred fans were lined along the road leading to the service entrance. The band all arrived in different SUVs. All brought their wives, something Lexi didn't expect.

"Do the wives always come to something like this?"

"They did in our early years. Then stopped."

Lexi had been to every Crashers concert in Texas and once in LA, but this was different. She was now walking on the stadium grounds and was, not exactly *part* of the band, but certainly part of the attention the band attracted. Of course, Nigel had both still and film photographers capturing every moment from their arrivals.

Paddy looped his arm around Lexi. He looked casual and in charge, but she felt the tension in his body. He motioned to his technician to hand him his double-neck Gibson guitar as he mounted the stairs to the stage.

"Sound ready?" he asked. Suddenly everyone who seemed to just be loitering about moved into position, and all eyes were waiting for Paddy's signal. He definitely was the leader of this group and this enterprise.

Paddy May ripped into a blistering solo that caused everyone inside and outside the arena to stand still in amazement. After about four minutes, he stopped. Fans let out a huge cheer. The sound hung in the air for several more minutes before dissipating. Lexi had chills and was convinced everyone else did as well.

She noticed, however, that Paddy was facing the drum kit and leaning over his guitar such that his hair almost completely blocked his face. She glanced at Nigel, who was noticing the same thing.

Paddy was trying to hide in plain sight, just as he had in the early years, before he started using booze and drugs to mask his fear. Owen jumped on the drum riser and started a familiar beat of one of their biggest hits. Paul picked up his bass guitar and played as he walked to his side of the stage. He and Paddy always stood on either side of Eric, who preened and danced center stage. Now and then, Paddy would walk to Paul and the two would jam with Owen, oblivious to the crowd.

The musicians played while Eric stood offstage, looking lost.

Lexi wondered if the band could play sober. Then, as if on cue, Woody showed up. He hugged Eric, and they stood away from everyone and talked several minutes. Woody then turned and looked at the rest of the band on the stage. Lexi could tell he was focusing on Paddy. He bit his bottom lip as he watched Paddy's body language shut down.

Then, as only Woody could do, he picked up one of the dozens of Paddy's guitars sitting offstage, asked for a pick from the technician, strummed the guitar to hear its tune, then walked onstage, with Eric following.

Woody started playing rhythm to Paddy's lead. Owen and Paul smiled seeing Woody, but it took Paddy several minutes before he looked up. He was confused, then laughed and turned to Woody to start riffing off one another.

No one had ever played on stage before with The Crashers.

Woody was a master musician himself and was often listed, after Paddy, as one of the best guitarists of all time. Woody engaged Paddy directly and slowly started turning such that Paddy was facing the front of the stage.

Now and then, Woody would lean down to look into Paddy's eyes. After establishing eye contact, Woody would slowly stand straight, causing Paddy to stand straight instead of hunched over.

All the workers in the stadium stopped what they were doing to watch what turned out to be one of the greatest rock sessions of all time. Of course, several in the stadium were recording the impromptu concert on their phones, and it was streaming live to millions within minutes.

Nigel always had a strict rule that anyone recording during set-up or rehearsals would be fired on the spot. But he, too, was so entranced by the spontaneous jam session that he ignored his rule. Plus, he knew the leaked videos only added to the frenzied excitement building for the broadcast and shows.

The band ended up playing with Woody for almost an hour. Eventually the film crew started using the time to adjust lighting and the sound crew made several adjustments.

Paddy relaxed and started dancing with his guitar. It was one of the many things that endeared fans to him. His guitar was part of his body and, at some point in every concert, he started moving with his guitar as if she was his dance partner. His shoulders rolled and his hips twisted and turned as he moved his guitar around his body, over his head and behind his back. Lexi once asked him if he felt like he was making love with his guitar when he did that. He surprised her when he said, "I'm not even aware I'm doing it."

She wondered if he would remember it now since he was sober. Or did it have nothing to do with that? Paddy's mother told Lexi that her son's guitar had been an extension of him since childhood.

Slowly, Woody started walking closer to the edge of the stage, letting the band resume their usual playing. He blew a kiss at the band and handed Paddy's guitar back to the technician.

Woody stood next to Lexi as they watched the band.

"Thank you for doing that, Woody."

"Doing what?"

They shared a knowing look.

Woody continued, "I started worrying when I saw Paddy was growing a beard again. I know what that's all about with him."

"It least he's trimmed it, groomed it this time."

Nigel came over, shaking Woody's hand and patting him on the back.

"You going to be around for our shows?"

Lexi and Woody knew that Nigel was really asking: "Are you going to be here to help should Paddy or Eric falter?"

"I wouldn't miss a Crashers show, Nigel. It's going to be the biggest rock concert, probably ever."

CHAPTER 57

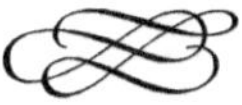

Lexi left Paddy at the stadium to continue their rehearsals so she could meet J and the publicity team at Waterstones. She felt Paddy's world was dominating hers.

"I still keep thinking it's his world or my world, J."

"It's both now, Lexi. It's a merger of two big companies into one."

"But we're different products, to stay with your analogy."

"The merger is your celebrity."

"That word, celebrity, bothers me."

"Don't let it. Keep ignoring it. Let Nigel and me worry about managing that part."

"I am stunned, shocked, at how people are really leaving us alone. It's weird. And nice."

"Nigel is also stunned by it. His theory is that the fans are so happy to see Paddy sober and in love, that they want to protect him. And they adore you."

"Hmmm, they use to adore my *Cally series*, not me. I liked that better."

J stopped what he was doing and turned to his best friend.

"Okay. Let's talk."

Lexi paused a long time. J sat still, waiting. They had always been comfortable being in silence together and both realized now they hadn't been that way in months. It felt renewing to each of them.

Finally, Lexi spoke.

"It feels like I've been on this comfortable sailboat, gently tacking back and forth in my life as writer and mother. Now, suddenly, I'm on one of those big, loud power boats blasting through to, I don't know what."

"Well, that's my fault. I'm sorry I haven't protected you better."

"What? No. That's not your job Jarius."

"Yes. It is now. Nigel fiercely protects Paddy and the band. He has since day one for the Crashers. He is like a bulldog fending off anything that distracts the band from their music. Because of that, they stay in their creative modes. I need to do that for you. You've always protected me, Lexi. Now it's my turn to do that for you."

CHAPTER 58

Lexi had the Thames House all to herself, except for Graham's security scattered throughout the grounds. Fans were back in large numbers due to all the publicity about the new album, the BBC live show and the multiple concert dates at Wembley.

Now, though, there was a noticeable number of fans holding signs with her name and reaching out copies of her books, hoping she'd sign them. Graham's team knew to let Lexi walk outside and talk with the fans and sign books now and then.

Right now, she was as alone as she could be in her new life. No one was in the house. She liked it. She sat out on the deck with her laptop, copies of all her books, and a notepad. The cats, Panda and Vesty, were sleeping, having tired of looking into the Thames for fish. She needed to finish preparing for her "Night at the Albert Hall with Lexi Maxwell."

Her appearance at the Royal Albert Hall reminded her of the first time when she and Paddy had just met. That night felt so long ago. So much had happened. This time, she and Paddy wouldn't need to pretend they weren't already in love. This time, the whole world knew they were. They were the couple the world loved to love. Photos of them were everywhere. Tabloids proclaimed Lexi as "Paddy's savior from years of booze and drugs."

She knew her new book was going to be misinterpreted as her "sexual awakening with Paddy May." Maybe it was. For her though, it was an open expression of the full life she had shared with Steve and the emotional process of that life shifting after his death.

"How much am I going to say to you, dear fans?" She talked out loud as she outlined how she wanted the night at the Albert to flow. The Hall held just over 5,000 compared to 90,000 at Wembley, but somehow the intimacy of a smaller crowd felt more challenging. She was solo, while Paddy had his bandmates.

"Interesting. Am I now competitive with Paddy?"

She shook her head and continued her outline of the evening and identifying what parts of her books she'd read. Her new book was launching that night at the event, and only critics in the press would have read it, or parts of it.

She looked through her computer at different stories and poems that had not been published. She always shared unpublished works with her fans at readings. Her recent poems and haiku had been about her new lifestyle, including many about making love with Paddy.

Lexi laughed out loud at the prospect of reading those poems to her fans. And her family. Unlike the book she was launching, the poems *were* about her sexual life with Paddy. "Oh yeah, the entire family will be there. Shit."

Jack's semester was over for the summer, and he, along with the entire family in Dallas, were coming to London for her appearance and The Crashers' shows. They, along with Paddy's parents and children and even Sofia and her husband, were scheduled to be at her reading and most of The Crashers' performances.

Lexi was restless now. She looked out on the River Thames, noticing for the first time how many boats were floating by, many with fans who weren't hiding the fact that they were taking photos. Graham's security boat kept them toward the far side, but still they were there.

Lexi wanted a long walk. When she was first with Paddy, she could easily take the half-hour walk down the road to the little nearby village. She had gained permission of the landowners in the area to walk through their property. England had a tradition of allowing walkers to roam through property, but that didn't always apply freely. Lexi had taken the time months before to meet all the owners, explain her situation and receive the okay to walk.

Everyone agreed, except one property owner. He hated Paddy May and felt he ruined the peace of the area with his debauchery.

"But have you ever seen him have parties of girls here?" Lexi asked, knowing Paddy's rule of keeping that activity only at his flat in London during his previous party days.

It didn't matter. The owner wasn't going to change. Lexi could make it almost all the way to the village along the banks of the River Thames, only having to step into the narrow lane road at the last part of the walk.

A solo outing still meant she had security. She'd tried leaving the property without telling Graham before, and within minutes, noticed two of his people trailing behind her. They respected her desire to walk alone, but were close enough to be by her side in seconds if anyone approached her.

How much money do we spend on security? she wondered.

Her personal security team was out front. "Let's walk to town," she said to them. The team looked up at the darkening skies.

Lexi followed their gaze. "Let's get our rain gear."

The rain was gentle, not like in Texas.

Walking in her rain gear and Wellies in the fields made Lexi feel like a proper Englishwoman. Just like, at his core, Paddy May was a proper Englishman. He was well-read, had impeccable manners, was groomed, and wore clothes that, while "creative," were styled.

She had coffee at her favorite shoppe in the village. She still couldn't quite become a regular tea drinker. Fans started coming in, leaving her alone, but secretly snapping photos of her such that she cut her visit shorter than she'd wished.

Paddy had called to say he would be a little late for dinner because the rain halted traffic out of Wembley. Lexi was back on the deck, watching the sun set through the remaining clouds. Mostly it was dark, which was fine with her because it meant the boats filled with onlookers left.

She took out her notepad and started writing. She knew how she wanted the night to go at the Albert Hall. She was so absorbed in her writing that she jumped when Paddy leaned over to kiss her.

"Jesus!"

"No, it's just me, Paddy."

Later, in bed, they wanted to continue exploring tantric sex, which they had started weeks before. They had always had enjoyable sex together and wanted to go deeper in their union.

Paddy was the first to suggest it. "Sofia told me about it, but, of course, there was no way I could have that kind of spiritual intimacy the way I used to be."

Lexi was surprised that she felt nervous at the prospect of that level of intimacy, of connection. "You know, I think I give lip service to having full spiritual and sexual union. I'm kind of scared, actually."

"Scared of what?"

"Not sure. Losing myself?"

"Let's just take it at our own pace."

And they did. Little by little, they learned to slow their nightly pace in the bedroom. First by simply standing in front of one another, still clothed and just breathing deeply while looking into one another's eyes.

This was much harder than they thought it would be. Not for Paddy, but for Lexi. Lexi was the one who practiced yoga. Lexi was the one who practiced deep breathing when stressed. Lexi was the one who frequently read about alternative health and Zen and

Buddhism. Still, Lexi was the one who struggled to relax into breathing in rhythm with the man she loved.

Paddy was patient. He was always patient. He was also the one who could lose himself in his music. His guitar was part of him, a partner in expressing himself through music.

Most every week, the couple set aside a night to simply be together in connection. First being comfortable just looking at one another, then syncing their breath, then removing their clothes and carefully studying each other.

They had learned to "slowly roam" each other's bodies, noticing curves, freckles, bumps and skin colors they'd never observed before.

Lexi had become so in tune with the callouses on Paddy's fingers tips that she could tell which finger of his was touching her with her eyes closed.

That night, the couple felt satisfied even before they went to the bedroom. Lexi had her Albert Hall presentation sorted out, and Paddy had started to relax during rehearsals at Wembley.

No moonlight shone through the heavy clouds, but they opened the blinds anyway.

Paddy sat naked in the middle of the bed and helped Lexi sit on top of him. They relaxed. They looked into each other's eyes and saw beyond the surface. Their breathing was aligned.

Paddy slowly moved himself inside her by holding his hands on either side of her bottom as she lowered herself down. Paddy was long and could move deeply inside her. So deep that there was always a moment when he paused when lowering her so that she could relax more inside and let him continue to move in until he was fully inside her and she was resting comfortably on top of him.

Still looking at one another, they leaned in, resting their foreheads against one another. In this position, foreheads touching, and their sexual organs connected deeply, they flowed into meditative breathing and just let happen whatever was going to happen.

The "goal" wasn't orgasm, but an otherworldly connection.

This was the night they reached that otherworldly place.

J had arrived at the River House after Paddy and Lexi had gone to bed. He thought it was a little early for them but knew each were having busy days. J was extremely busy too, but he didn't have to be "on" the way Lexi and Paddy had to. He could stand on the sidelines and watch them.

J woke just before dawn hearing a low-volume hum in the house he'd not heard before. "Damn. Is that the refrigerator?"

No, it wasn't.

He walked the entire house, thinking it had to be something electrical producing such a consistent hum. The house was a long maze of oddly shaped rooms. He teased Paddy once about his creative houses. "Not one of them is just a normal house. They all have twists and turns and unique features."

J walked every room, but the sound led him to Paddy and Lexi's bedroom door. He stood with his ear near the door. He immediately knew what it was. He and Lexi had talked about the kind of sex where two are so united into each other's energy that a hum is produced, much like the hum Buddhist monks generate when sitting in meditation together. He and Lexi wondered if was really possible to create that level of connection.

J wanted to try it during the time he and Lexi allowed themselves to explore sexual love with each other. Lexi just couldn't relax into it.

"Have you and Steve ever tried?" J had asked her then.

"Yes. And no. Every time we started Jack would call from the other room, a cat would start to barf or something else happened. It seemed we were destined to not experience it."

Now, as J stood outside the bedroom door, he knew that Lexi and Paddy had achieved that elusive union. He smiled, happy for Lexi and slightly sad that they had never experienced that. *How would our relationship be different if we had?* he wondered as he walked to the kitchen to make breakfast.

The sun was rising, and J knew Graham would arrive any minute to take Paddy to Wembley. The couple had not emerged from the bedroom, and the hum was still strong.

J worried now that he was going to have to interrupt Lexi and Paddy. He started researching tantric sex, looking for information on whether or not people can become stuck somehow and unable to separate on their own. The internet search led to kinky sites, but he eventually found a site that seemed legit.

J looked at the time and knew he was going to have to knock on their door.

He took a long, deep breath, in and out, and lightly tapped on the door. Nothing changed. The hum was still strong and steady. He knocked loudly. No change. He took several more breaths, then opened the door.

"Lexi? Paddy?"

The room was like a sauna. The air was wet and extremely warm, not hot, but very warm.

There they were. Sitting in the middle of the bed with Lexi on top. Their foreheads touching, arms around each other in a deep spiritual, sexual union.

A sunbeam shone through the open blinds straight onto the couple. The room felt and looked like heaven. Bright light beaming onto a naked couple innocently holding one another in total loving bliss. Tears streamed down J's face.

He heard the crinkling of the gravel driveway outside. Graham had arrived. J closed the bedroom door and walked over to Lexi and Paddy.

"Hey you two. I need to wake you now. I hate to do it, but people are starting to come to the house."

He slowly approached the bed, hoping they would wake on their own. They didn't.

J had to climb onto the large bed. He kept talking as he moved closer. Then he put one hand on Lexi and the other on Paddy, slowly rubbing their backs.

"Hey, you two. It's time to return to this world. It's me, Jarius."

He kept rubbing their backs and slowly they started moving. J was visibly relieved, releasing a big breath and sitting back in the bed, but still next to the couple.

Paddy was the first to open his eyes and lift his head away from Lexi's. It took several minutes before he could see the room and understand that J was next to him. He smiled the most innocent smile. J's eyes teared again at the purity of the love exchanged.

"You two have been humming for a long time. I hate to stop you, but people are coming to the house."

Lexi lifted her head and studied Paddy's face, as if trying to figure out who he was and where she was. She was startled when she realized J was right next to them.

Paddy was more awake now. "J says we've been humming."

"Humming?"

J scooted off the bed. "I'll let you get up now."

The couple stirred, but couldn't move.

Lexi said, "Um, J, I think we need help. I can't move."

Paddy was trying to lift her off him, but he, too, was not moving well.

J crawled back on the bed.

"It's a good thing we are such close friends, huh?"

J put his arms around Lexi, stood in the bed as he lifted her off Paddy, who had laid flat on his back and was using his fingers to separate their bodies. J gently laid Lexi beside her lover. He realized, though, that neither could really move well.

He started rubbing Lexi's legs briskly to wake them. He turned her over on her tummy so he could rub her bottom and legs. He didn't let himself think of how he enjoyed feeling the small of her back become wet when they made love.

Lexi started stretching her legs, but Paddy was still not moving well. J wasn't trying to, but he had noticed how long Paddy was. He pulled a sheet across Paddy and started rubbing his legs to bring them back to life.

Lexi sat up and watched J rub Paddy. Finally, Paddy could move his legs.

J stood up.

The three paused and looked at one another. No one wanted to speak and break the intimacy. Slowly, J turned away from them and walked around the room, closing the blinds to give them privacy against the security teams who were walking the grounds. Then he left, closing the door behind him.

CHAPTER 59

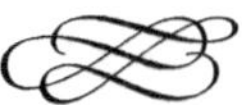

The next day, family started arriving and all the quiet intimacy at the Thames House evaporated. Paddy and Lexi each kissed and held J an extra moment when they saw him later in the morning after he had helped them separate in bed. Though close friends before, the three felt deeply bonded now.

Lexi and J both noticed Paddy shaved his beard that morning. A good sign.

Family was everywhere, going from the London House, to the Thames House, to the B&B Lexi and J had first rented when they came to London. Steve's parents were staying with Paddy's parents. Some of Steve's family had never been to London, and Amanda, Jack and Paddy's children became tour guides.

The rest of the band was also experiencing the same invasion of family and friends. The atmosphere was joyous.

It was two days before Lexi's Albert Hall appearance and three before The Crashers' opening night and BBC live concert.

Nigel decided to invite all the family and extended network of friends to The Crashers' last full rehearsal. There was almost three hundred people sitting in the audience. Another two hundred if you counted the film crew, the band's technicians and roadies, and stadium personnel.

Although nowhere near the 90,000 that Wembley held, it was still more than Paddy had ever performed before sober.

Paddy spent much of the three-hour set facing Owen, the drummer. Eric would occasionally put an arm around Paddy while singing and walk Paddy around to face the audience. It would last a few minutes, all of it with Paddy's face obscured by his long curls. Gone was Paddy's famous dancing with his guitar across the stage that thrilled fans endlessly.

Nigel looked at Lexi halfway through the rehearsal and shrugged. He was chain-smoking and pacing.

Afterwards Paddy sat offstage, alone. Lexi knew he was embarrassed. She sat down beside him, not saying a word.

"I tried."

"I know."

"This is going to be bad."

The family and friends began drifting away. No one came over to Paddy, not because they didn't want to, but because they knew he needed space. Nigel and the directors for both the BBC show and the concert film were sitting in the center of the stadium floor. They were clearly upset.

Paddy looked out over all the empty seats at them.

"You know, Paddy, at home, you're always playing for me. You lose yourself in your music and start dancing and prancing. Would it help if I sat just offstage where you could see me?"

"A performance for one person, with ninety-thousand watching?"

"Yeah. Something like that."

Paddy leaned over, put an arm around Lexi's shoulders, pulling her close to kiss her.

"We can try."

CHAPTER 60

J needed Lexi to focus more on herself—something she did poorly. She had less than twenty-four hours before her appearance at the Royal Albert Hall. It was already a media frenzy. While the book hadn't been officially released, there were enough excerpts released that it was clear that this book was nothing like anything Lexi Maxwell had ever published before.

Of course, it was clear to anyone paying attention that Paddy May and the entire Crashers were clean and sober and surrounded by family. Hardly a bad boy lifestyle, but some rumors were swirling as to how good would The Crashers be "now that they were sober."

Negativity sells, and some of it lingered around Lexi as she prepped for her opening night.

"This is going to be very weird, J. Everyone close to me is coming. I've never had this much family at one of my events."

"You know all of Paddy's relatives are coming too, right? Most we've never met."

"Yes."

"And all The Crashers, their wives, kids, Amanda, Nigel's production team."

"And Cissy?"

Lexi hadn't seen J's girlfriend as much as usual, and was concerned maybe they weren't together.

"Yes. She's coming with Amanda."

"You still together?"

"Yes, but more relaxed since she still has her studies at Oxford."

"You still sure you want to be my manager?"

"Very much. Besides, you really need me." J nudged Lexi playfully.

The two were at the London House getting ready to leave for the Albert Hall. There wasn't a pre-event VIP reception like the last big event. Instead, Lexi had spent most evenings after dinner for nearly three weeks signing books that were going on sale the night before her appearance.

J and Lexi were in the third-floor master bedroom going over what she was going to wear.

They could hear Paddy and Jack on the ground floor playing guitars. Jack knew how to play basic guitar before, but Paddy was showing him things he never imagined could be done.

Lexi finally settled on wide-legged chiffon evening pants and a poet's blouse with an open collar showing her neckline. Her red hair flowed over her shoulders, and she had just a touch of makeup on her eyes and lips. Of course, she was wearing her trademark black "evening" trainers.

She had decided against walking to the Hall tonight. She didn't know why she changed her pattern, and it surprised everyone. Graham was waiting with the cars when she came downstairs.

Paddy literally gasped when he saw her. Their tantric union had moved them into a place where they felt they were the only two in a room, even though it was full of people. They had to work to remind themselves to interact with others.

"Looking good, Mom."

"Jack, you and I'll ride in one car, okay?" J looked at Lexi for approval too. She nodded.

She and Paddy sat in the back of their SUV, holding hands. They drove past the restaurant with the outdoor patio where she and J saw Paddy and his date Penny and Woody and his wife after Lexi's last big book appearance at the Royal Albert Hall.

"Let's go there after my appearance tonight." Paddy smiled at Lexi and asked Graham if he could reserve a table for them on the patio.

Traffic was completely stopped on Kensington Road leading to the Hall. Lexi let out a big sigh, and Graham knew what was coming. He quickly radioed members of his team who were waiting at the Hall that Lexi, Paddy, Jack, and J were going to start walking. They were two to three blocks away.

Graham and a guard from the other car jumped out, leaving the drivers of the cars behind. "Let's move quickly. I think we can manage if we just keep moving quickly. People won't expect you. Well, maybe."

Graham did not like this. Fortunately, he saw his other team members walking quickly toward them.

Of course, people recognized Paddy and Lexi. Paddy was tall, his signature curly hair bouncing in the breeze. He was dashing in an evening jacket with shimmering threads. Lexi's red head was blowing in the light wind. The two together were going to be noticed even if they weren't famous. J and Jack became part of the protection standing on either side, with Graham and his guards surrounding the front and back sides.

Fans and by-passers screamed and shouted as the entourage passed.

"We love you, Lexi!"

"We love you, Paddy!"

There was even a "We love you, Jarius."

J laughed.

Jack joked, "What about me?"

The line into the Hall was long, but the weather was perfect, and people were in a good mood knowing they were at the center of what had become a world-wide event. Lexi knew her relationship with Paddy made the event more globally known than it would be otherwise. It didn't bother her, much.

Graham hustled the group around to the side entrance. His team had all been alerted and quickly escorted everyone inside. Lexi was greeted by the Waterstones team and was led to a private room to relax. J, Jack and Paddy stayed with her.

She was told they might start a little late to allow for the long line to buy her books. Many were buying every book she'd published. The audience was invited to submit questions on cards scattered throughout the lobby. J organized the cards the Waterstones' staff had already gathered.

"Anything interesting?" Lexi asked.

She sat at a table with Paddy. She was calm. Jack said he was going to go sit with the family out in the hall.

J was sorting the cards by types of questions. He held out a large stack and said, "Well, these all are some variation of, 'Did you need to write this book so you could complete your relationship with Steve and be with Paddy?'"

"That's a fair question. Is anyone asking anything that doesn't have to do with Paddy or The Crashers?"

"Yeah." J held up a smaller, but still thick stack of questions.

Finally, it was time for the show to begin.

J was going to stay backstage to be near Lexi and to continue to sort the question cards. Paddy kissed Lexi and held her. "It just gets better and better with you." He leaned back to look at her. "Thank you."

Lexi and J heard the crowd roar when Paddy walked out to his front-row seat. He sat between Jack and his daughter, Evelyn. His band mates were also in the front row with him.

Lights dimmed and the announcer simply said, "Ladies and gentlemen, Lexi Maxwell."

The audience was effusive in their approval of the writer. She stood for several long minutes bowing and nodding her appreciation. J knew how she said she was going to start the program, but he doubted she would really do it.

She did.

She didn't even introduce that it was from her new book. She paused, looked out into the audience—the lighting was such that she could see many faces. She glanced at her family who were all looking at her with smiles and cheering eyes. She looked at Jack. She'd made him read the book, and they discussed it. "Mom, go for it," was all he had said.

Standing at the podium in the opulent, historic Royal Albert Hall, she looked at Paddy, lifted her eyebrows, smiled, and took a deep breath as if to say, "Here we go."

I knew in my sleep that Steve's spirit had returned for this one last time. Our last time to be together in love. He was inside me, lost in the scent of my hair and holding my bottom at just that certain angle that he liked so well when on top of me. It curved me toward him in a way that helped him go deeper.

This wasn't a position I enjoyed most and staying connected, we rolled on our sides. Now this I liked. I moved my hands through his hair and knew he was waiting for me.

The orgasm came in waves. Rolling waves of pleasure that moved deeper and deeper inside. I was looking at him, but his face became blurry. Though I was still dreaming, I knew I was physically having an orgasm, and it was with Steve, but he started to evaporate into a ghost at first, and then the more my orgasms rolled inside, it seemed the more he rolled away into pure spirit.

He smiled at me, looked to his side and another face began to appear. Steve was morphing into another man whose spirit was inside me. Steve was saying goodbye and giving me to this man.

I woke with a gasp. My body still throbbing and wet and warm. I wasn't alone. I laid very still in bed for a very long time, not sure what to do.

Finally, I rolled over in bed and looked at the man Steve brought to love me.

Lexi stopped reading. There was silence. Then the audience stood and applauded for a very long time. Jack said something to Paddy, who put his arm around her son, kissed him on the cheek and hugged him.

Lexi only read a few more passages from the new book. She then alternated between reading from her books, essays and unpublished poems. The audience laughed, gasped, cried, and all were enchanted by her. She was vulnerable in a way she had never been, and they loved it.

She acknowledged she was with Paddy and thanked the London fans for being so protective of them, allowing them to walk and live without too much disturbance.

"You have even become our protectors against overly exuberant photographers. Thank you."

She brought J out so everyone could thank him. It was also the moment when they decided together what song they would play when her appearance was over.

By now, everyone knew of their tradition to play a song that represented someone in the audience. People would listen and guess, but Lexi never revealed.

That night she played one of The Crashers' new acoustical songs from the album that was going to be released the next day.

She'd had permission from the band and thought it was a nice way to transition from her special night to theirs.

She noticed Paddy had tears streaming down his face while he stood and applauded with all the other patrons. He recently told Lexi, "You know, I've cried more since I've been with you that my entire life combined."

"Good tears, though, right?"

"The best tears."

She greeted family and friends backstage for nearly an hour until Graham reminded her that she and Paddy had reservations. Jack said he was spending the night with Paddy's parents along with Steve's parents. Jack had seamlessly added Cara and Edward May as another set of grandparents.

Lexi and Paddy decided to walk.

"The traffic's jammed anyway, Graham."

Graham wanted to give the couple the semblance of being on a simple date, but the thousands of fans outside meant he needed to add more of his team to protect them.

They managed. Once again, the fans were thrilled at seeing the couple, and yet very few reached out to touch them or ask for pictures or an autograph. Graham had never seen anything like it in all his years with The Crashers. His challenge was to keep his team and himself alert and not drop their guard just because everyone seemed respectful.

It was either lucky coincidence, or someone at the restaurant had remembered the exact table on the patio where Paddy had sat all those long months ago. The patrons applauded as the couple walked through the tables.

Before their salads were served, Lexi said, "You know Samantha Peters is across the street taking photos of us?"

Paddy bit his bottom lip and looked for Graham, who immediately came to their table.

"Samantha's here."

Graham stiffened into defense mode.

"Wait a second, Graham," Lexi said. "Sit. Let's talk about this." Lexi felt it was time to end the charade with Samantha Peters.

Graham apologized to Paddy, explaining how he had new people on detail and obviously didn't know how good Samantha was at stalking.

Lexi turned and looked at Samantha, who was nestled in the bushes across the street. She smiled at the photographer.

Graham said, "Lexi, we have laws here that protect people like you and Paddy from this. Somewhat."

"Here's what I think. Let's stop this negativity now. This has been going on too many years. It's clear to me, Paddy, that she's never gotten over you. Yeah, she was wrong to publish that picture of you passed out on the train. You were still a teen. She wasn't much older. You were both thrown in the wild world of rock and roll. And yeah, she was wrong to publish the nude photos of us. Let's let it go. Let's just let-it-go."

Paddy anticipated what Lexi was about to say. "So, you think I should just invite her over?"

"Let's be the bigger people, Paddy. Look what you and I have created over the last year and a half now. Look at our families, our friends, ourselves. It's stunning. It's love. Let's not have her be a negative for us. Let's turn her into a positive. She is, after all, an amazing photographer."

"Just forgive her?'

"Just forgive her."

Paddy took a deep breath, then stood. "I'll be right back."

Graham followed Paddy out the restaurant and across the street. Samantha grabbed her gear and started to jog away, but Paddy said, "Please stop."

Paddy stood talking to his nemesis while Graham and two other security guards stood nearby. It was clear to Lexi that Samantha was at first defensive, then stunned and then deeply moved by whatever Paddy was saying to her. She started crying. Sobbing. Paddy reached out and hugged her. Graham glanced back at Lexi, who smiled.

After several more minutes Paddy walked back to the restaurant with Samantha. He had invited her to have dinner with them. Samantha approached Lexi hesitantly, much like a child who knows she's done wrong and disappointed her mother.

"I don't really know what's going on right now," said Samantha.

"I told her she can have full credentials as a photographer for our shows."

"Great idea." Lexi turned to Samantha. "You are an extraordinary photographer. I've never told Paddy this, but I had that picture you took of him on the train over my bed for years. I became a woman looking at that photo of Paddy and pleasuring myself."

Paddy and Lexi laughed. Samantha was uncomfortable, but smiled and started to relax, realizing the couple were really sincere in forgiving her.

Graham sat at the next table, texting Nigel and Jarius. *You're not going to believe this...*

CHAPTER 61

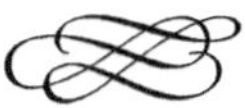

"Oh, I wish we could just stay in bed and make love all day."

"Agreed."

Lexi and Paddy made love off and on all night. They felt good about what they'd done with Samantha the night before. J had texted Lexi before they'd left the restaurant that the press was "absolutely nuts about you, Lex."

Now it was time for The Crashers' live show on the BBC and the first night of multi-nights at Wembley Stadium.

They heard Graham's cars arrive.

"And so, it begins." Paddy's mood shifted into work.

"You okay?"

"We'll find out tonight."

Lexi studied him.

"Lexi, I am tense. A little scared, but, even with all that, I haven't wanted to drink, and I have all my nicotine patches." He pushed up the sleeve on his t-shirt showing the strips on his upper arm. "I'll be glad when that craving is over, but I'm not taking them off today."

"We haven't talked about when you want me to come to the stadium."

"I want you to be with me all day, Lexi. Please."

"Of course. I was just checking."

"Can't get rid of me, lady." He pulled her back into bed for one more moment of union. She noticed there was more intensity in his love-making this time. It was as if he was trying to capture something from her. He was needing her confidence.

The band arrived at the massive stadium in the early afternoon, although the broadcast didn't start until seven. There were so many fans camping outside. It was one big party with tables of food, frisbees flying, music playing and dancing.

The atmosphere inside was like a choreographed dance with everyone moving as if rehearsed. Nigel was almost invisible in his cloud of cigarette smoke. Lexi waved at him from a distance.

The area for the band was set up like a living room with couches, chairs, and even a kitchen area with a refrigerator filled with juices, water and sodas. No longer did the band require a "booze table."

"I'm going to sit out in the seats and write, Paddy. Holler if you want me."

"I'm hollering now." He kissed her, held her tight, turned, and became the band leader he was.

The band rehearsed a few numbers for sound and mostly for the camera crews. Lexi was so absorbed writing her short story that she was startled when Samantha sat down beside her.

"Thank you," was all Samantha said.

The two women sat side by side in comfortable silence for a long time. Finally, the photographer stood and turned to leave. She paused and asked, "Is it okay if I take your pictures also, Lexi?"

"Of course."

"Don't pose. Just be you. You're radiant and I think, maybe some kind of angel, too."

Lexi smiled just as Samantha snapped a pic.

The low hum of activity inside the stadium slowly built into a thrilling buzz as more family and friends started arriving for the show. Paddy greeted everyone politely, but was very focused on being sure the sound was perfect for the night. He kept checking his instruments with his technician.

The crowd was happy, people laughing, joking. It was a party.

J whispered to Lexi before taking his seat, "Have you seen how many people are carrying your new book? I think they are hoping for an autograph."

The band was left alone in their dressing area an hour before the show. Lexi was working out where to sit just offstage so Paddy could see her. Paddy had told Nigel he wanted Lexi "where I can see her all night."

Nigel understood without it being explained. He'd even found a comfortable club chair for Lexi.

The day seemed to move in a long, controlled pace, but then Nigel announced loudly, "It's showtime, folks. Family, friends, time to take your seats." He motioned to the tour manager and the BBC director. Suddenly, everyone around her was wearing headsets and moving into position.

A roar soared from the crowd. They knew.

Lexi found the restroom, knowing she'd not be able to go for almost three hours. Paddy was standing just outside the door when she emerged. He reached out and held her. He was already warm with perspiration.

The rest of the band was standing nearby, acting like they weren't closely watching their band mate. Eric's sobriety made him the playful, happy extrovert he'd always been, and he was thrilled that he was about to sing and perform all night with his best mates and devoted fans.

Paddy's sobriety made him the shy introvert who just wanted to play guitar. Being with his lifelong mates was about the only reason he could consider standing on a stage before ninety people, much less 90,000.

Lexi squeezed his hands. "Just play for *me* tonight, Paddy. Dance and prance for me. Lose yourself in the music. The music you create, Paddy."

They kissed and turned to walk toward the stage, Paddy's arm around her shoulders. Lexi kissed Paddy and walked up to her club chair sitting just off to the side.

The lights went down, and the roar went up. The band walked to their positions on the stage. They looked at Nigel for their cue to start. The plan was to start the BBC show with one of their most popular, high-energy songs that was known as the best rock and roll song ever.

Paddy was facing the audience. At first. Within seconds, though, he turned toward Owen. The audience was used to Paddy turning toward his drummer to fist-pump the count with him, but Lexi knew this was different. Nigel knew it, too, and looked at her.

Owen smiled at Paddy, his eyes trying to infuse safety to his childhood mate.

The band rolled right into another hit, and Paddy wandered the stage, still not looking at the audience. The camera woman assigned to Paddy was trying to capture his face, but he was clearly hiding under his hair now.

Lexi leaned forward in her chair, making sure he could see her.

He did.

Suddenly, Paddy turned around, looked straight at Lexi, and ripped into his guitar, sliding his hand down the neck in a blistering solo. He grinned at the woman he loved, then turned and pranced across the stage while the entire stadium audience stood and screamed.

He was happy. On the far side of the stage, Samantha Peters snapped a photo. It was Paddy May and The Crashers. In the corner of the photograph was a smiling and cheering Lexi Maxwell, a copy of her already best-selling new book at her feet.

It became the photograph published worldwide. The new iconic shot of rock and roll and love with the full moon shining above.

AFTERWORD

Dear Reader:

I first met Lexi and Paddy when they started "talking" to me while I was in a coach being driven around the chilly, wet, wind-swept green hills of Ireland. It must have been the very romantic setting that awakened their story because I hadn't read many romance novels or love stories before that day. (I certainly have since).

As I looked through the rain drops on the glass window that fall day, I could see and hear Lexi and Paddy as they met at the bookstore and started their walk around London. I fell in love with them and started writing their story that night in my cottage. They talked to me night and day and I carried a journal to capture what they were sharing. Back home, I would wake before dawn, ride my bike to the nearby café and write for hours every day. I had no idea where they were taking me, or how much they wanted to share, but I felt their vulnerability, tenderness, and deep sensual passion to connect on levels deeper than most people can go.

A few weeks after I finished a first draft of Lexi and Paddy's love story, I read an article about "disability romance" stories and wondered, "What if Lexi had one hand like me?"

I needed to ask Lexi what she thought. It took a few days, but then she started telling me about little ways in which she delighted at how Paddy would "shake left," hold her arm and watch her. Lexi "told" me about the night Paddy asked her to sit on his lap so he could be her right hand and she his left hand while they played his guitar together. The tenderness—and intimacy—of that night touched me unexpectedly. Lexi had given me permission to share her story as a full-grown, complex, passionate woman who also happened to have one hand.

I hope you fell in love with Lexi and Paddy as much as I did. Let me know what you think.

Keep in touch through bethenylynnreid.com. I'm also on Instagram, Threads and other social media @bethenylreid.

If you liked *Under The Autumn Moon*, I'd appreciate it if you would tell others about my book.

ACKNOWLEDGMENTS

First, I want to thank you, the Reader. Without you, the stories of the people I write about would not be heard, and that is what they want most. My characters talk to me, saying, "Please tell my story." While they are fictional, they don't feel that way to me, and so I write. They want to be heard and, on behalf of Lexi and Paddy and others in this story, "thank you for reading and listening to the story of their love."

Unconditional love is when you just love someone for everything they are and aren't. You just accept, support and believe in them. Being loved that way every day strengthens the loved one's ability to become their full self. I am loved that way by four important people in my life. Cally Simpson and I met as teenagers and she has been my "rock" through dating, college, jobs, marriage, pregnancies, miscarriages, family dramas and death, and adventures. My husband, Rick Loessberg, is the one who taught me about unconditional love. He just "gets me" and loves me. We have been together almost half of our lives now and I still feel so fortunate to have such a partner. Our son, Jack Loessberg, continually amazes me with his insight, resilience and love. He walks ahead of me at book fairs telling every publishing vendor that his "mom the author" is right behind him and they should talk to her. Jack has brought his beloved, Tori Karker, into our family and we could not have a more perfect addition. Smart, talented and loving, Tori regularly encourages me to write all the stories swirling in my head.

Cindy King took the time to read an early draft providing me with page-by-page feedback. Her approval and encouragement were the confidence booster I needed. Kate Hunter spent the better part of a summer holiday reading to check that I'd captured London and the British accurately. Heather Piedrahita added some steamy music to the playlist. CH gave me critical insights but, as always, she is modest about being credited.

Author Lori Ann Stephens was the first reader of *Under The Autumn Moon*. We meet weekly to each write on our stories. She is an accomplished and award-winning writer, and her feedback was critical. Author Alex Temblador champions my writing and is always willing to "have a cup of coffee and talk about writing." Author Kathleen Ayers provided information about resources that have contributed to her success as a leading romance author. Author Jalynn Venis has told me for years, "Just keep writing."

An extra thanks to Author Leslie McElroy who introduced me to Dallas Woodburn and the team at Breakthrough Books. I met Leslie at one of her bookstore appearances and her extraordinary generosity in sharing her publishing process was exactly what I needed. Leslie calls Dallas her "book doula" and I can't think of a better term. Dallas is not just an editor, but she is the guide taking the story from manuscript to publication, from dream to reality.

Writing is a solitary process, but everything after the first draft involves an entire community of family, friends and a support team. I am grateful for them all.

PLAYLIST

I Only Have Eyes for You, The Flamingos
So You Want to be a Rock and Roll Star, The Byrds
Love Is a Stranger, Eurythmics
Remember Me, Miguel
Tu Eres Para Mi, Elvis Costello & The Attractions (Spanish Model)
Mandolin Wind, Rod Stewart
invisible string, Taylor Swift
If You Can't Rock Me, Rolling Stones
Leaving India, Mychael Danna
Tunnel of Love, Bruce Springsteen
Give Up The Ghost, Radiohead
Let's Go Back, Jungle
What a Day That Was, Talking Heads
Embryonic Journey, Jefferson Airplane
Well All Right, Lyle Lovett
Into the Mystic, Van Morrison
Space, French Fuse
Wait For The Morning, Marty Stuart & His Fabulous Superlatives
Harvest Moon, Neil Young

If I Needed Someone, The Beatles
Ramble On, Led Zeppelin
Wanna Be Startin' Something, Michael Jackson
Lover, Taylor Swift
Get Together, The Youngbloods
Thunder, Imagine Dragons
Thank You, Led Zeppelin (for the last chapter)

The full playlist for *Under The Autumn Moon* can be found on Spotify.

BOOK CLUB DISCUSSION QUESTIONS

BOOK CLUB DISCUSSION QUESTIONS

- Did you ever meet a celebrity crush? If yes, what did you do? Would you have done something differently?
- Why do we have crushes on people we will probably never meet much less start a relationship?
- Would you ever be as candid with someone you liked as quickly as Lexi was on her first walk with Paddy?
- Would Lexi and Paddy have been able to be so at ease with their sexual love for one another if they had married young and had young children at home?
- Would Lexi have been able to be with Paddy if Steve's spirit hadn't visited her and given her permission to love another man?
- What would Lexi have done if Paddy didn't stay sober?
- Is there someone you love but haven't told them? (Maybe today's the day!)

ABOUT THE AUTHOR

Betheny Lynn Reid is an award-winning poet, essayist, and author of short fiction. This is her first novel. She has published in The Sun magazine, The White Rocker and Big Bend Literary Magazine.

Her non-fiction writing has propelled her around the world in communications/marketing, public affairs and higher education executive management.

Not wanting an Emily Dickinson-type obituary where her massive collection of novels, short fiction and poetry is found postmortem, Betheny is now focusing on her true love—listening to and writing the stories her "characters" ask her to share.

She is often found reading her poems during Inner Moonlight at the Wild Detectives Bookstore or sitting at the local coffee shop writing poems, essays, short fiction and novels. She hikes and travels as much of the world as she can possibly reach to meet people. She prefers to ride her bicycle anywhere and everywhere. She lives with her husband and two cats and enjoys frequent visits from her son and his beloved.

She also publishes as B.L. Reid and Betheny L. Reid. You can keep up with her at bethenylynnreid.com and @bethenylreid on Instagram and Threads.